TSELANE

J. LOUW VAN WIJK

TSELANE

HOUGHTON MIFFLIN COMPANY BOSTON
THE RIVERSIDE PRESS CAMBRIDGE

TO
DR. MAURICE WEINBREN

ACKNOWLEDGMENTS

MUCH of the story of *Tselane* is true. During the writing of it, I have gone to the places where such things happened and met the people who lived them. Only to help keep the horrors of the past out of their minds and hearts have I changed their identities and altered the events. But there is something to learn from even the worst deeds men do against each other, and it is for this reason that I have written the story.

This book has already brought me an unexpected reward— friends in America who advised me and encouraged me during the five years that have gone into it. For their perceptive editorial suggestions that contributed greatly to the final draft and for their faith in both *Tselane* and myself over the years, I wish to extend my gratitude and affection to New York friends I hope one day to meet: Evelyn Singer Haber and Sidney Porcelain.

To Glenn D. Kittler I give special thanks for his help in the writing and dramatization of the novel during a period in which I could not work on it.

JACQUELINE VAN WIJK

Johannesburg, South Africa
January 1961

TSELANE

1

TSELANE stirred in her sleep. Khama turned over on his grass
sleeping mats and looked across at her for a long time. He could
only make out her shape dimly in the glow of the last embers on
the fireplace in the middle of the floor. She was lying on her back.
He saw her lifting her hand and clutching the side of her body.
Their unborn son must also be stirring in his sleep. Khama smiled.
How proud he was of her: his wife.

She was the most beautiful woman in their village. Even in the
cities of the white people he had never seen a woman who could
compare with his Tselane. Straight as a young tree, always friendly
and helpful; the fire inside her never cold, her passion sometimes
even greater than his own. Clean and neat; a woman who was not
lazy and who did not spend the money he sent her, when he was
away, on unnecessary things. The cattle she bought with the money
would make him rich by the time his son was big enough to go
to work in the places of the white people. The thoughts of his
son sent a warm glow through his heart.

His son would be different. He would not grub after gold in the bowels of the earth or work like a slave in the factories; he would go to school, he would later go to a university in Durban, perhaps, or Capetown, and become an educated man. In his mind Khama conjured up pictures of the happy times he and Tselane would have together with their son. He would buy him a pony as soon as he was big enough to ride; like his father he must be a good rider. Perhaps he would marry the daughter of a chief, perhaps— Khama yawned and soon after fell asleep.

The embers had died down by the time Tselane woke up for the first time. In the inky darkness of their hut only Khama's deep breathing disturbed the silence. How she would miss him! Soon after the first light of day, he would have to leave with the other men on the first stage of their trek to the cities of the Europeans. If only Khama could have stayed with her until their child was born how happy she would have been. But if they wanted all the good things they had been dreaming of for their son, Khama must go.

Tselane pulled her blanket closer around her and lay with her thoughts of her husband. Nowhere in the mountains—not even in the whole of Basutoland—would she find another like her Khama. Big, strong and clever. A man that could fight with the best and love better than the best. He drank his beer but did not make a pig of himself like other men. He liked things clean and he kept them clean. He loved her even more now that she was big and heavy with their child and did not turn away in disgust like other men to go to cheap women. "Three months," the old woman had said. In three months time she would hold their child in her arms. A thrill as she had seldom before experienced surged through her at the thought.

Quietly, so as not to disturb him, she got up. She took the smallest of her two sleeping mats and placed it next to his. She lifted the side of the blanket and lay close to the warm nakedness of his strong body. For a short while he was unaware of her. She caressed his arms and chest, she kissed the arm he had flung across her in his sleep and whispered his name softly. Suddenly she felt his arm stiffening as he drew her close to him.

"Tselane. Little one. Little white calf of the mountain." Tenderly he held her in his embrace.

"Khama, will you write a letter soon and tell me that you are safe in the place of the white people?"

"Didn't I do it last time?"

"You did, but I am so afraid."

"Afraid of what?"

"I don't know. Something might happen to our child and you will be so far away."

"Nothing will happen to him. I have spoken to my mother and she will take good care of you."

"Your mother is old but I know she will be good to me when I come back with my child. Next month will be my seventh month and then I must go to my mother's kraal."

"MaTselane is a good woman, she will look well after you and our son. You are young and strong. Young and strong cows never die when they have calves, nothing ever goes wrong with them. You must not be afraid."

"I am not afraid because I shall have pain but—"

Khama did not give her time to finish the sentence. He kissed her on her mouth.

"You will have a strong son, Tselane, and we'll call him after my father."

"He will be a year old before you will see him for the first time."

"That is as you say. There is nothing we can do, I must go."

"Yes, you must go." The dull tone of her voice echoed the cry in her heart. So many lonely nights, so many hours of longing for him. So many days of emptiness without the tasks which a man in the hut brings for the woman. Nobody to prepare good mafi for, to make stiff porridge for and watch him eat big white chunks with his fingers. Nobody to shout to when she was still a long way from home after the day's work in the fields. Nobody to wait for when there was a big beer-drink at the Chief's hut and to wonder why he was coming home so late. Nobody to tell her that she was beautiful and to make the fire inside her burn until the scorching flame dazed her and her thoughts were only of his strong body and the strength of his arms. How she would miss him!

"Yes, you must go," she repeated dully.

"I spoke to RaPalla yesterday. He will see that everything is well with our cattle."

"Your cousin RaPalla will also have to go away soon."

"He will be here until after our child is born."

"I am glad; I trust him."

"I have spoken to the Chief about the time that you have to go to your mother's kraal."

Tselane did not answer. Molili, her cousin, married their young Chief but Tselane had no great liking for him. Often in the morning when they went out to work, Molili walked painfully. Once when she asked her about this Molili had answered sadly: "I must have a son. My husband paid very much for me. He does not go gently when he plants his seed." But in spite of his violence his wife had been unable to raise his seed. Tselane felt sorry for Molili and had no love for the Chief.

Khama waited for her reply and when she did not answer he asked: "Do you go to the Chief's hut every day to fetch Molili to go to the lands?"

"Yes, we always go together."

"Is she with child?"

"No, she is very sad. The Chief must have a son."

"The Chief must have a son. It is a pity he married your cousin."

"Why?" Tselane was surprised to hear her husband say a thing like that. She knew he liked Molili, that he was a good friend of their young Chief, so why was it a pity that they had married?

Khama said: "Three times there has been snow on the mountains since they were married and she cannot give him the child he wants."

"It is not her fault."

"Who can say whose fault it is when no child comes to make his father happy? That is why I am so proud of you. We waited a long time but soon now we'll hear him cry."

They lay quietly for a time; Khama stroking her stomach to feel the movements of his child and Tselane too sick at heart over his departure to talk.

Their love-making, usually wild and violent, was tender and controlled. For a long time to come they would both have only their memories to remind them of wonderful nights of love when their young hearts thrilled to their promises of loyalty and trueness.

The crowing of a cock suddenly shattered the stillness of early Basutoland morning just before dawn. A dog yelped short and sharp, as if he had been rudely awakened by a kick. The atmosphere of absolute peace and quiet was broken by voices in the night. Somebody passed their hut leading a horse.

"Hey, Khama, time to get up. The light is coming in the east."

Khama did not answer. He was holding Tselane in their last embrace and the moment for parting had not come yet. The man outside waited, then knocked again. Khama released Tselane just enough to say: "All right, Taba, I am getting up."

Tselane clung to him when he had said this.

"My little white bird, the time has come. We must get up."

"Yes, Khama, the time has come."

Alone with him she could let him see her sadness but soon, when they were with the others, she would have to laugh and talk or they would later say that she was a bad wife, one who let her man go away to the white people with a stone in his heart.

Tselane got up slowly and pinned her blanket into position round her shoulders. She rolled up the sleeping mats and passed Khama his clothes to get dressed. Since the first day that he had come home for his long leave he had worn khaki trousers and a blanket like all the other men. Now she had to pass him his European clothes which he must wear when he went back to Worcester where he worked in the factory of the white people.

In his blanket he was her husband, the man she had loved from the time when they were still very young. When she saw him now in his European clothes, the neat trousers, the shirt and tie and long jacket, she felt shy and embarrassed. There was something strange about those clothes. They fitted Khama well but he was like a stranger; now, he was not the Khama whom she knew and loved.

Khama finished dressing and said: "We will get the airplane at Mashai when you will be making porridge for the evening meal."

"Hau! And you say you will sleep in Maseru tonight?"

"Yes, the big bird flies quickly. From Maseru the train will take a long time but that does not matter."

Khama talked about these things to take her mind off the parting which would come only too soon, and Tselane understood.

"Hau, Khama," she said, "you are so clever. You are not afraid of these things?"

Khama laughed loudly. "Tselane, when you see a thing and you don't know him you are afraid. Once you go to him and look in his face and see what he is, you are no more afraid. It is like this with all these things which the white people have that we do not understand."

"Hau!" Tselane was not convinced that her husband was not afraid because he knew these things. He must be very clever. To the day that she died they would not get her to fly in the big bird. Khama had told her about the train but she did not understand how he could say it was nothing to ride in that thing. Many, many little rooms pulled by one big one in which they made a fire; hau, it was hard to understand.

She opened the door of their hut. The faint light of day was breaking in the east, as Taba had said. Everywhere smoke was rising in long thin spirals from outdoor fireplaces. People were already preparing food for the first meal and porridge for the men who were leaving to take with them in their little pails. The first time when Khama had gone away she had also made a pail full of porridge for him to take for the road. When he came home again he did not bring the pail back and told her that it was unnecessary to take food for the road. She did not understand this but she did not ask him about it. In the time that he had been away among the white people he had learned many new things.

In their outside fireplace she deftly kindled the fire and soon the water was singing in the three-legged pot. Her mother-in-law came from their hut and greeted her.

"Have you slept well, my child?"

"I have slept well, Mother."

"You can go to Khama; I'll make the porridge."

Without a word Tselane handed her mother-in-law the wooden spoon to stir the porridge and went back to her husband. How well her old mother understood her agony. Often in her own life she had suffered the same ordeal and knew the feelings of a mother expecting her first child and seeing her husband leave home not to return for a year or perhaps longer.

"I thought you were making the porridge." Khama looked up surprised to see her.

"Our mother is seeing to that."

"I must go and saddle my horse. Sobeti will bring him back from Mashai."

"Leading or riding?"

"Leading, why?"

"Sobeti is a wild beast on a horse's back."

"He is young and will learn. Sobeti is a strong lad."

"He is old enough to work; why doesn't he?"

"Sobeti's father is rich and he need not work. Why don't you like him?"

Khama was struggling to fasten his suspenders at the back and Tselane helped him without answering his question. There was a time in the first year of their marriage after Khama had gone away when she always found Sobeti in places where she had to work. People whispered strange things about his behavior with women and she was afraid of him. Khama did not wait for an answer but left to saddle his horse.

As the light of day became stronger the activity in the village grew to fever pitch. In the last moment there were still so many things to talk about and so many things to do. People were shouting to each other from hut to hut. Those who had to leave were saddling their horses, and those accompanying them were laughing and talking gaily about their ride to Mashai.

"Dumela, Khama!" The Chief greeted him. He had come to take leave of his people. In odd little groups the people were saying their farewells.

"Remember what we told you of the big city of the white people. Listen to what they say and do what is right," an old mother was saying to her young son who was leaving the village for the first time to work in the mines. He was wearing his patched pants and bright Basuto blanket, his straw hat which his father had woven for him and in his mind he was just fine for the big city his mother was talking of. He was wearing his best clothes. His father had even bought a pair of shoes for him from the white trader but that he would only put on when they came to the place of the white people.

Last-minute bickering from wives, who suspected their husbands of infidelity while away, filled the air. It sounded lighthearted and gay but people who knew and had heard what kind of lives many of these men led in the cities shuddered for their sons who were leaving too. Many of the younger men were going away with only one aim: to earn money as quickly as possible to be able to pay the price for their brides. They were eager to be off and impatient because it was taking such a long time. The whole village had turned out to speed the travelers on their way. In the crisp morning air, naked little children clung wide-eyed to their mother's skirts and blankets. They did not understand what was going on but sensed something must be happening. The big people were all too busy to notice them and with the numerous dogs and hens they swelled the audience at a farewell which for some was sweet and for others bitter.

Tselane and her mother-in-law were standing a little apart from the rest. Khama was speaking to the Chief. His father was listening to their conversation and confirmed everything his son said with a nod of the head or a few affirming clicks.

"Let things be well with you, Khama. I shall look forward to seeing you before the snow is on the mountain again."

Khama laughed. He had no hope of getting another leave to visit his country so soon, but things sometimes happened swiftly with the whites. On Monday you may not know it but on Tuesday they may come and tell you that something has happened and now you need not come to work again. It happened the year before when the crops were so bad. All the men who had not been working well in the canning factory where he was employed were one day given their money and told that they could go back to their homes. Fortunately that could never happen to him. For two years now he had been wearing his bronze badge which was given to him for his honesty and loyalty. He would have to work the full time before he could come home again. Nevertheless, the Chief did not know about these things so Khama answered politely: "Thank you, Morena, but the snow will long have been melted before I can come this way again."

They talked of this and that and when everybody was ready for the final farewells to be said, Khama took Tselane's hand but would not kiss her in public. They were both sad but felt that before them stretched a future which could only bring happiness and prosperity. He was strong and could work for the white people to earn money; she was young and beautiful and could bear him many strong and healthy children.

With shouts and laughter the men mounted their horses and started in single file down the footpath which would bring them to the road to Mashai. Some were dressed in their European clothes. Others sat erect under their straw hats, their brightly colored blankets draped over their shoulders. They were the excited ones. The ones who had never been away from the mountains, the ones for whom a great and wonderful world waited in the places far from their homes.

For Khama and those who had been on leave and were returning to circumstances they knew only too well, there was no such excitement. They knew the world of the white people. Hard work and hard times, the longing for their homes and the frustration, the constant anxiety for those they had left behind—these were waiting, and not the wildly wonderful world the youths were dreaming of.

Sobeti started a song and soon the valleys echoed with the powerful rhythm of twenty strong young voices. With his high tenor Sobeti sang the solo parts and in a deep rumble of perfect harmony his comrades answered. At the bend in the footpath they took their last look at the village and waved to the people still looking after them. When the last man had rounded the bend only their song and the wild shouting now and again of a youth hung on the air.

"Come, my child, we must go home." Tselane did not answer her mother-in-law immediately. The great emptiness and the loneliness which she had feared when she was still lying in Khama's embrace that morning was already taking hold of her.

"Tselane."

She turned to answer then.

"Yes, Mother, I am coming."

Together they returned to their huts where work was the only antidote to the nagging feeling of loneliness and longing. Tselane was looking forward to her walk to the fields with Molili and to their work in the warm sun.

2

JUST AFTER sunrise Tselane went for Molili. On the way to the Chief's hut she had to pass through a deep donga. Every time she went through this donga she thought of the change that had come over her since she had been expecting her child. The year before, she could run down the one side and up the other without stopping once but now she could not be careful enough. She did not fear for herself but nothing must happen to their child. If something should happen because of her foolishness, Khama would kill her.

Molili was waiting for her when she arrived.

"Héla, Molili, did you sleep well, my cousin?"

"I slept well."

"Khama has left."

"I heard them going. I am sorry, my cousin, you will be lonely in your last months."

"Yes, I shall be lonely but there is so much to do now that the time will rush like a thunderstorm."

"When are we smearing our huts?"

"Next week. I have heard of the best clay that we could hope to find but it is a long way from here. It will take time to fetch."

"This time I am going to change the pattern. We always make lines up and down, I am going to change that."

Tselane laughed. "My cousin, changes are not always good. How do you know this new pattern will look well on your walls?"

"I tried it on the ground and I liked it."

Tselane did not answer. She shouldered her hoe and waited for Molili to do the same and take her pail of mafi. There was a sad line round Molili's mouth and Tselane was quick to notice this. She could not become used to seeing Molili so sad. Shortly after they were both married they had been so very happy. They always talked of the children they were going to have. After the first year Molili talked less, and now in the third year of her marriage she never spoke of her children. Tselane understood her disappointment only too well and never mentioned the child she was expecting although she often burned to speak of him.

When they were still young girls and making the scarves which they had to give to the men of their choice, they had often laughed and vowed that they would only give their scarves to men who were really worthy of being the father of their children.

"I want only strong sons, six or maybe seven," Molili used to say.

"I would like to have three daughters and three sons."

"I shall only choose a man who is big and strong because I like big strong sons."

"Sometimes small fathers have big sons."

"No, I am small, so if I marry a small man, my children may be small too."

Molili married a big strong man, a chief, but her dreams remained only dreams. Tselane married Khama who was even bigger and stronger than the Chief, and soon she would see the fulfillment of her dreams.

Often in her moments of despair, Molili's thoughts turned to the one source of help which might still be of use: the witch doctor and his medicine. But always she put the thought out of her mind. As a child in her father's home, she had often heard him speak against the evil of the witch doctor's medicine and the futility of the people's belief in the power it was supposed to have. She knew that Tselane believed in it, like the rest of the people, but her pride prevented her from discussing the delicate subject of her failure even with Tselane who had been her confidante since they were small girls.

On the way to MaPhépa's hut, Molili was exceptionally quiet. Tselane tried to make conversation but it was obvious that Molili was in no mood for idle talk. Tselane thought of the talk she had had with her husband during the night and in a sudden rush of sympathy for her cousin she said: "Majara must get medicine from his father to have you doctored."

Molili, who was walking in front, turned her head slightly but did not answer. From far down in the valley somebody called out to them and Tselane shouted back, answering the questions about where they were going and in whose lands they were going to work that day. Molili did not take part in or listen to the conversation. Her thoughts were frantically lost in the turmoil of her feelings. Maybe her father had been wrong. If Tselane believed that the medicine of the witch doctor could help her, she was perhaps right. But her father had taught her—

Tselane interrupted her thoughts. "Why don't you answer me about the medicine?"

"My father does not believe in the power of the witch doctor."

"The missionary taught your father not to believe," Tselane scoffed. "The other white people also do not believe but they do not know the things our doctors know. Can they give us anything that will keep the evil spirits away, that will make rain when it is dry, that will open the eyes of our children when they are born? What can they give us that will guard our men and keep sickness away from them while they are working for the white people? Tell me, Molili, have they told you of anything that is as powerful as the medicine of our chiefs?"

"Yes, the Moruti taught us of Jesus."

Before she could say anything more, Tselane laughed loudly. "Don't talk like that, Molili. That is a man we have never seen. We know our Chief and we know old Metlae, our witch doctor. Didn't he cure RaPethe's son, didn't he chase the plague away from our village when hundreds of people died in other villages where people believe in Jesus? You have listened too much to the white people. You must believe in the doctor and let your husband get medicine from his father. You will still have many children."

Molili was quiet. She saw before her the earnest face of the young missionary who had often come to their house to talk to her father about the things he taught them. Then she saw old Metlae in her mind's eye: his dirty bag full of bones and little pieces of rag, little stones and animal claws and tails. How could these things help her? She heard his mumblings and the nonsense he sang in his practice as a witch doctor. But yet could all her people have been wrong for so many years? Did the witch doctor possess powers that she could not understand? Perhaps her father and the missionary had been wrong.

"Why don't you say something, Molili? Don't you want to have children?"

A look of pain crossed Molili's face. "You talk like a small child, Tselane. You know how much I want children. Perhaps I shall speak to my husband tonight."

"Hau, Molili, you must. You must not be afraid. Speak to him."

"I shall speak to him." A smile suddenly filled her eyes. Tselane had helped her to make a decision with which she had been struggling for months. The very thought of the possibility that she might have a child brought her happiness and by the time that they reached MaPhépa's hut, she was laughing and talking gaily.

"Dumela, Molili; dumela, Tselane," they were greeted from all sides by the women already gathered there.

"Is your heart heavy, my child?" an old gray-haired woman asked Tselane.

"Yes, Mother. Khama will not come back for a long time."

"While he is away you will at least be sure that he will not go with other women like some of the men we know of." With a spiteful glare she looked in the direction of Katila who was resting on a hoe. It was common knowledge that Katila's husband kept another woman in the place of the white people but that was no more than Katila deserved. She was a loose woman who slept with every stranger who came to their village. Katila spat on the ground and turned the other way.

Soon all the women were there. With their hoes over their

shoulders, the pails with sour milk and porridge balanced on their heads, and the babies tied on their backs they started in single file down the footpath which led to the lands in the valley below.

In front of their huts the men lounged, smoking their pipes and drinking beer.

"Our mothers take too much time to get to the lands."

This was meant as chaffing and quickly one of the older women answered. "Time seems to have been made for women only. Men have no time. They sit and talk and drink and smoke."

"That was what men were made for."

"And women?"

"To bring us the good things."

The women all started laughing. The man who had spoken was known to beat his wife when the slightest thing was not to his satisfaction.

At every hut the women paused and chatted and eventually they reached the tree which stood in the middle of MaPhépa's land. There they left their pails with food, their babies and their blankets. They took their positions in the line and when MaPhépa's shrill voice started the song of hoeing they all took it up and soon the valley re-echoed with their song. Molili's and Tselane's clear young voices rang high above the deeper tones of the older women. Shifting and lifting to the rhythm of their song, the line progressed down the land.

"Hau, Tselane, go slowly my child, go slowly." MaPhépa was working next to her and wondered at the strength with which Tselane swung her hoe.

"Why, Mother? You all work to the last hour; I still have a long time to go. Why must I go slowly? There are still so many things that I must learn before my child comes."

"That is strange to hear you say a thing like that, Tselane. Most of you young people today believe in the things the white people teach you. You want to do the things the way they do them. You have forgotten the customs of your parents."

"It is not that we do not want to follow the customs but we do not know them."

The older women laughed loud and long. One said: "If the little cowherder wants to have his cows' stomachs full, he looks the other way when they break into a neighbor's mealielands."

"He'll get a hiding for that," said another.

"And if you young people look the other way from the old customs, who is going to give you a hiding?"

Tselane laughed. "Nobody could point at me and say that I have not observed the old customs. Every time when I go through the river I smear some of the clay on my forehead and swill my mouth with water. All pregnant women must do that and I have always done it."

"And," MaPhépa asked, "will you go to your mother's hut in the seventh month and have your eyebrows shaved, your face smeared with clay and butter? Will you wear the smeared sheepskin tied round your breast to keep your unborn child warm? Will you wear the gall-bladder of the sheep they kill for your homecoming and the ostrich egg-shell beads round your neck? Will you wear the pumpkin pip necklace, the claw and tail of the wildcat? Will you, Tselane? We don't believe that."

"You are right, MaPhépa," an old woman said, "the young people today want to be pretty; they want to wear fancy blankets and not a skin smeared with butter and clay. They want to wear beautiful beads from the shop, not egg-shell and pumpkin pips."

The mournful voice of Kosa interrupted Tselane's thoughts. She could not imagine what she would look like with her face smeared like that and those awful smelly things round her neck. Before she could think of a suitable answer, someone else said: "And where will we find Khama to beat him with a stick if the child is a boy and to drench him with water if it is a girl?"

Tselane laughed again. It was a funny thing that the old women could think of treating Khama like that to announce to him the sex of his child after its birth.

Another said: "And will Khama be here to cut the nails of his son for the first time so that the child does not grow up to be a coward?"

Tselane only smiled, and under loud laughter MaPhépa said: "The little cowherder is going to get such a beating!"

Everybody joined in the laughter because it was only too clear that she meant that Tselane was not going to follow the old customs after all. Tselane looked at Molili and saw that she was not laughing. Was she thinking of her failure or of the time when she would have to observe these customs?

Under the tree when the sun was at its highest, they ate their porridge and mafi. Molili saw how the other women were feeding their children. Thoughts of her conversation with Tselane made her eager to finish the work and get home to her husband.

"We have done a lot this morning. If we go on like this the work will soon be done," Kosa said.

"MaPhépa, when do we go home this afternoon?"

"When the shadows are halfway down the mountain and not before. Are you lazy, Sikata?"

"No, MaPhépa, I am not lazy. I just asked."

"Taba will not be home before dark, so why do you want to finish so early?"

Sikata smiled. She was promised to Taba and soon she would be working in their own lands and not always on the lands of others.

Tselane thought of Khama and the other men. He had said that they would leave in the big bird by the time that she was making the porridge for the evening meal. They must be near Mashai now. Just for a moment her heart contracted with longing for her husband. MaPhépa, who had been watching Tselane's face, got up.

"Come, children, time for work." She took her hoe and when they were working steadily in their row again she said softly to Tselane: "Molili smiles often today. Is there something?"

"No, Mother, but perhaps she has hopes."

With laughter and song, the time passed quickly and when the shadows were halfway down the mountain they prepared to go back to their huts to cook the evening meal for their husbands. They called their children, fastened the babies on their backs, balanced the pails on their heads and with the hoes over their shoulders started the procession back to the village. When the huts came in view, Molili's heart started beating faster. How would she start the conversation with her husband? How would she tell him that she had now changed her mind and that she thought that medicine would perhaps help? Nearing their hut she saw her husband sitting in front of their door. His skin gleamed in the soft light of the setting sun. Pride filled her at the sight of his strong young body. He smiled when he saw her.

"It was time you came home."

"Have you waited for me?"

"I waited all day."

Molili entered the hut. Majara followed her. While he was lazing in the sun all day, drinking beer and talking to his friends, his wife had hardly ever been out of his thoughts. His preoccupation with a plan that had come to him made her body more desirable than ever before. When he first got hope of bringing their love to perfection his urgency to taste fulfillment had made him eager for her return. Molili put her hoe in its place. Without asking her consent, Majara pulled her down with him onto the sleeping mats where he had been dozing during the afternoon.

He gave full rein to his wild passion and nearly crushed the life out of her. Molili was unprepared for this and just for a fleeting second the urge to push him away took possession of her. She loved him when he was gentle. Sometimes his love-making filled her with an ecstasy that was beyond words, but this brutal show of power always reminded her of the price he had paid for her in marriage. Never before had such a bohadi been paid for a chief's daughter. Two hundred head of cattle, twelve sheep, a horse and twenty pounds in money. With that she became his goods and chattel, his property to use in whichever way it pleased him. Her body, her very thoughts, belonged to him. She had no say, no right to push him away from her when he had been dreaming the whole day of satisfying his wild urges for the cool and perfect body of his wife. In spite of being tired from working in the mealieland all day, she had to answer his passion or later suffer the taunt that being unable to bear a child, she was incapable of making love properly.

He was reluctant to let her go even after his passion was completely spent.

"I must boil the water for the porridge."

"The night is young, we have plenty of time to eat."

"You must be hungry."

"The mafi and the stiff porridge you left for me was enough."

Molili lay next to him wondering at his strange behavior. Was this perhaps the correct time to speak to him about medicine?

Should she tell him of the conversation she had with Tselane that morning? Would he also think that his father's medicine was strong enough to help her? Suddenly she smiled. Majara pressed her closer to him and then released her.

"You can cook the food now."

Molili got up and started the fire. Majara wrapped his blanket round him and sat at the doorpost watching her. How perfect she was. Her small hands were strong and sure. He had been right on that day when he told his father that she was the most perfect woman he had ever seen. How well he remembered that day. His father had raged and stormed when he first told him that he wanted to marry the daughter of Chief Thotofeane.

"Thotofeane believes in the things the missionaries teach. How can you marry his daughter? He hasn't even got a doctor or a lenaka."

"I won't need his lenaka," Majara had replied.

"If you marry his daughter you will have only one wife. A chief who believes in the many words of the white people has only one wife."

Majara thought a long time about these words of his father. According to their custom his first wife must be chosen by his father for political or material reasons. His second wife he could marry for love and those coming after her for various reasons or whims. But Molili would be his first, second and last wife; he wanted no other besides her.

When his mother had heard of his wish she had commented: "Like her mother before her she will give you no son. Her mother had only one child and that child was a daughter. Think well, my son, before you do this terrible thing."

He had laughed at these words. His mother was like every other old woman, full of stories of things that could happen. It was too ridiculous even to think that Molili would bear him no children. Certainly she would have strong sons to accompany him on horseback, who would be worthy of their beautiful mother and follow in his footsteps as a good chief to his people.

Now in the third year when there was still no child to make him happy, his thoughts were turning to medicine. His father had strong medicine. When he had persisted and had married Molili his father had said in his anger: "My medicine is the strongest there is in this land; marry her and you will see what will happen."

His father had been beside himself with fury. Often in the night when Majara listened to the heartbreaking sobs of his young wife because she had failed him, he thought of his father's medicine.

Where did the witch doctor of his father find the diretlo that was strong enough to charm a chief? In the kraals on the other side of the mountain he had heard people whisper of another chief who had disappeared. At the foot of the cliff they had found his body. There was a hole in the skull through which brains had been taken and his right eye, left ear, the soles of his feet, his genital organs, the fingers of his right hand and his navel were missing. The story was spread that he had lost his way from a drinking party and had fallen down the cliff in the dark. Wild animals were held responsible for the missing parts, but always in connection with this story people whispered of the strength which the medicine horn of his father was supposed to have.

His father was one of the richest chiefs in all Basutoland. Majara was present when some of the medicine was spread on small black stones and put on the bridle path which led to his father's kraal. When the site for Majara's own village was chosen his father had taken part in the ritual of burying the little black stones to keep the evil powers away and give prosperity to him and his village.

Where did his father get such strong medicine? Only diretlo taken from another chief could be so strong. If Majara could make medicine that was stronger than his father's he would be able to have his wife doctored so that she could bear him children. Like a sudden whirlwind, the thought of this brought excitement to his mind. Molili was a Christian and did not believe in the power of medicine, but he would have her doctored all the same.

Molili looked up and saw her husband looking at her intently with a queer smile on his lips. She wondered what he was thinking. The porridge was ready so she dished out a plateful and brought it to him. For herself she took very little. She had no appetite. Excitement as she had never experienced now took possession of her. That night she would have to speak to her husband, and in doing so she would have to admit failure and renounce her Christian upbringing. How disappointed her father and the missionary would be when they heard of it, but they did not understand. They would never understand. She must either bear her husband children or allow him to take another wife to do so. Whichever way she turned she had to break with her Christian beliefs. It was not as if new medicine had to be made. No victim would be killed to get diretlo. His father had the medicine already; they must only get it from him.

They were hardly in bed that night when she turned to Majara. "Your father has very strong medicine."

"Yes, the medicine of my father is strong."

"Will he give you some of it?"

"For what shall I use the medicine of my father?"

Molili lay still for a while. She searched for the right words in which to admit her failure. At last she answered softly: "Tselane thinks that the medicine of your father will help me."

Majara's body contracted sharply. Her words shocked him. For days he had been thinking about medicine and now she proposed using it. He started breathing quickly. She felt how his nails were cutting into her flesh where his hands were on her back. Completely surprised by his violent reaction to her words, she hastened to ask him whether he did not believe that medicine would help her.

"Tselane is a clever woman. Perhaps medicine will help in your case," Majara said.

"When will you go to your father to get it?"

"In two months' time."

"But that is a long time. Why must you wait so long? Tselane will already hold her child in her arms before I start mine."

"It is not easy to get the medicine."

"But your father's medicine is already made."

"My father—" He did not finish what he wanted to say. How could he tell her that his mind had been busy for days thinking of his own medicine? Medicine that would be stronger than that of his father. He could not use medicine that was not specially prepared to help a woman to have children. Nobody must know that he was on the lookout for a victim, that he was going to find his own diretlo and fill his own horn.

"What did you want to say about your father?"

"My father needs a long time to think about it."

"But will you get the medicine?"

"Yes, Molili, I shall get medicine."

Satisfied with this answer Molili put her arms around his neck to show her acceptance of his greater knowledge of such affairs. Soon she was sleeping peacefully, happy with the thought that there was now hope for her.

3

I T W A S pitch-dark in their hut. Molili's breathing was soft and
even; it irritated Majara to listen to her. He tossed and turned but
could find no peace. Like a wasp in his empty porridge pail on a
hot afternoon the one word *diretlo* kept buzzing in his mind. What
had only been a vague plan and dream was suddenly stark reality.
Never in his wildest dreams would he have thought it possible that
Molili would be the one to suggest medicine. There was little time
to waste. Soon, as soon as possible, a suitable victim must be
found: his horn must be filled.

The atmosphere in the hut was suffocating. Majara took his blanket and got up quietly. He must go out into the open where he
could think.

He walked round the hut and looked far down into the valley
where the silver thread of the little stream gleamed white in the
moonlight. There was peace and quiet in the village but inside him
there was a wild torrent of cascading thoughts. As soon as one was
half formed, it was ousted by another. He must have human flesh

and blood, and soon. Frantically his mind rushed from one possibility to another. He sat down on the big stone behind his hut and pulled his blanket closer. A chilly little wind had sprung up. Suddenly a dog howled. Listening to the eerie sound in the mountain stillness, Majara smiled. A cruel light burned in his bloodshot eyes.

Murder was inevitable and the victim of no consequence. He would be careful. Discovery meant death because the stupid white people did not understand their customs. But a chief must have a lenaka, a horn full of medicine. He must have a son to be chief after him; it was his duty.

In some cases it was easy to get diretlo. Once the victim was decided on, it only remained to get him to a lonely place. Majara thought of the caves he had seen the last time he went hunting. A cave was the best place to hide a body after taking the pieces for the medicine. The men chosen for the deed could then one night go and push the body over a cliff. Wild animals would remove all traces of the wounds and after that, people would whisper and mention diretlo but never in connection with his horn.

Figures and faces flashed before him. He'd go against tradition: he'd choose somebody from his own kraal; nobody would suspect him. When the body was found it would be said it was brought there from far so that the people of his village could bury their own dead.

There was 'Mamohapi Mofo, the old blind woman. Perhaps it would be a very good thing to take diretlo from a blind person. If the police should find out about the murder, the diretlo would make the judge blind, too. But what if his child was born sightless because of that? No, a blind person would not do.

Motsuelinyana Mafa, the three-year-old son of his friends, was a perfect child, healthy and clever. If his son would be like that he could ask for nothing better. Suddenly he remembered the last time he had seen the child. His mother's face had lit up and pride had shone in his father's eyes when he had picked him up. A feeling of revulsion came over Majara. He could not think of murdering the child, not even for his purpose.

There was Sefate Rasoeu; he was an old man, a Taung, who wandered from kraal to kraal living from the bounty of those who took pity enough to give him food and shelter. If he should be killed on one of his wanderings, nobody would be the wiser. Nobody would miss him. But Sefate was old and sickly. Diretlo from a sickly person was not good enough for Molili. No, the victim must be young and beautiful, strong and healthy like his wife. Most important of all, she must be pregnant. Of her unborn child such strong medicine could be made that nobody would ever challenge his power again.

Majara had no clear picture in his mind of who the victim would be, but a certain measure of peace came to him because he knew now what it was he wanted. It only remained to choose the person and then to prepare for the great day.

He was weary. The stone was becoming colder and colder under him. Wrapping his blanket tightly round him he got up and turned in. Molili was still sleeping peacefully. Carefully he stretched out on the sleeping mats and was soon fast asleep.

The first sounds of the new day were already in the air when Molili woke up. She was strangely aware of a feeling of happiness which she could not understand. Then she smiled. She was going to have a baby. At least she would be doctored and then she would have her child. She looked across at her husband. He was still deep in sleep. She wished that he would wake up too. Every morning when it was still too early to get up and too late to go to sleep again, they had their moments of greatest love and this morning she felt tender towards him. Majara turned over in his sleep. Molili stretched out her hand and touched his face. He must have been near waking because he got up immediately and came over to her sleeping mats.

"Dumela, did you sleep well?" he asked.

"My sleep was sweet because my happiness is great."

He did not answer to this but took her in his embrace. Soon a passion with a new quality surged between them. Where Molili would have found his love-making brutal before, she now reveled in his violent strength. She answered his violence with a passion that left them both breathless and gasping. Satisfied and weak, their passion spent, they lay talking in whispers about the future.

At last Molili stretched and yawned. "I must get up. Tselane is coming for me just after sunrise."

Majara stiffened. Like a white-hot bolt of heat searing his mind the name fell on his consciousness.

"Tselane!" He repeated the name. A joy bordering on exhilaration filled him. Suddenly he started laughing wildly. Molili put her hands on his chest.

"Why are you laughing like that?" She was frightened.

Majara caught her to him. "Who will tell a woman why her husband laughs?" He was trembling. His feelings were a jumbled mass of ecstasy and excitement. The moment passed and roughly he pushed Molili from him. There was an urgency in his manner and a look which baffled her. He looked cruel and yet a moment ago he had held her tenderly in his arms.

"What is the matter, Majara? Why do you look like that?"

"Like what? Don't ask silly questions. Give me my clothes."

There was no tenderness now. Molili gave him his clothes and wondered at his strange behavior. The laughter faded from her eyes, and sick at heart she went out to start the fire.

Tselane came just after sunrise and when Molili saw her, joy returned to her because of the good news she had to tell her cousin. Tselane noticed the joyful smile and the cheerful greeting. "Hau, Molili. It seems to me you have slept well, my cousin."

"Very well indeed. I shall tell you about it on our way to the lands."

Molili went into the hut to fetch her hoe and when she returned, Tselane was eagerly waiting for the great news.

4

FROM behind the hut where they could not see him, Majara watched Molili and Tselane leave for the fields. His excitement of the night before rushed like a mountain stream through his mind. He felt lightheaded and dazed.

"Kera! Kera!" he called to a youth in the hut next to his.

Kera came running. "Dumela, Morena."

"Dumela, Kera. I want Metlae; call him."

Kera sped away, jumping over dogs and shouting to little children who wandered around to get out of his way. At Metlae's hut he found the old man sitting in the sun, his eyes half closed and his hand resting on his bag of bones.

"The medicine man must not sleep when his Chief wants him," Kera shouted to the witch doctor.

Metlae sat bolt upright. Cold premonition gnawed at him. This was the first time that the Chief had asked for him in all the time he had been in his kraal. People whispered that the Chief's Christian wife had influenced him and that he had no need of a medicine man. They said that the day would still come when he could be sent away from the kraal, a lonely outcast. Had this day come, was this the moment?

"What does the Chief want?"

"Does the Chief tell a messenger why he wants his medicine man?"

"Did you see his face?"

"The great Metlae has fear, it seems to me."

Metlae grabbed his knobkerrie and flung it at Kera who disappeared as suddenly as he had arrived.

Carefully Metlae draped himself in his ceremonial outfit. He stuck the feathers and porcupine quills in his hair, hung his monkey-tail necklace round his neck, fastened the skins round his waist, tied the string with bladders around his right arm and then took his bag of bones and the oxtail. Dressed like this he considered himself worthy of the occasion.

Slowly and with dignity he went to the Chief. If this meant dismissal he must be prepared. A curse at the right moment might influence the Chief to change his plans. In his wily mind he cast around for possible reasons why the Chief had called for him.

Majara watched the old man as he came walking towards him. Not by a sign did either of them show what was going on in his mind.

"Dumela, Morena, I greet you."

"Did you rise well, Metlae?" Majara answered the salute.

They talked about the weather, the cattle and the village. Majara offered the old man beer but he refused. Beer made the thoughts lazy and he must have his wits about him. He squatted on the ground in front of Majara and tried by every means to find out why he had been sent for. In spite of his impatience and the urgency of the matter, Majara was taking his time. Like two fighters, they feinted and stalled. At last Metlae's curiosity got the better of him.

"There is something you want to know?"

"Yes, there is something I want to know."

"Do you want me to ask the bones?"

"Let us hear what they have to say."

Metlae relaxed. The Chief was not going to send him away—

or was this just a test? Immediately he was on his guard again. Was the Chief trying to prove that he had no power?

With great theatricals and mumblings to impress Majara, Metlae grabbed his bones and strewed them on the ground in front of him. He looked at the lie of each little bone for a long time. "Your rest is not sweet."

"No, my rest is not sweet."

"It is a woman. It's a woman that is worrying you." Metlae took the shot in the dark. A man with the body of the Chief could easily have woman trouble when his wife could not produce a son for him.

"That is true; it is a woman."

A glow of warmth spread through the withered old spider. It was a true shot. "The woman is growing big with child."

The Chief smiled. Made bold by his success, Metlae continued: "She makes great trouble but you have a plan."

"I have a plan."

Metlae was at a loss. The story must develop but in which direction? Hopefully he looked at the Chief to give him some indication.

After a silence the Chief asked: "Is the plan which I have a good one?"

"The plan is a good one and must be fulfilled before it is too late."

Metlae tried to think of plans which the young Chief could have with a woman who was becoming troublesome after her indiscretion in allowing a man, hungry for a child, to make love to her. What was it he wanted to do? Was he going to ask help to get rid of her or of the child? He started when the Chief suddenly asked: "When?"

"Before the harvest has been brought in."

Metlae calculated quickly and so did the Chief. That meant that he had three months in which to get the diretlo for the medicine. Three months in which he could see the fulfillment of all his dreams—a lenaka stronger than that of his father, stronger than that of any chief. Metlae was thinking that three months would give him time enough to find out exactly what the Chief had in mind so that he could throw his bones the right way. Majara was quiet for so long that Metlae became uneasy.

"What is this plan?" he asked.

Majara looked up. The moment was there. The cruel light of triumph which shone in his eyes when he looked at Metlae made the medicine man wince. The Chief leaned forward.

"Diretlo," he whispered.

As if stung by a scorpion, the old man jumped upright and uttered a loud "Hau!" Never in his most drunken dreams had he ever thought to have such good luck. Once he had secured diretlo for the horn of the Chief his power was established for all time. Never again could the Chief send him away. Mentally, he started counting the cattle he would get for this. He spoke, mumbling until froth stood at the corners of his mouth: "The Chief's wife, no children. Pregnant woman, diretlo. The bones said before harvest time—yes, yes, before the harvest is brought in."

Majara watched the old man with disgust. He was impatient and eager to discuss the procedure, the men who must be chosen for the deed, the time and all the details. Metlae took his time. With a wild gesture he suddenly flung the bones out in front of him. Majara was taken by surprise. Intently he watched every movement of the old man. What was he trying to find out?

"Six," Metlae said, "six men must be chosen."

Majara realized that the wily old spider was already working out the details.

"Do the chiefs always use six men?"

"Six strong men, six strong young men must help us."

"Could you name them?"

"The Chief must not be in a hurry. We must think carefully."

"I want RaPalla."

"Why?"

"RaPalla is a good man, a man who keeps to himself. He will not talk."

"That is as you say, Morena. Then there is Sobeti. He is strong and wild. His father is rich. Sobeti will not talk."

"Taba."

"No!" Old Metlae shouted.

Majara glared at him. "You speak your mind with a shout."

"Taba is young. He waits for the time of his marriage. Let him not see blood before his first child is born."

Majara wondered at the witch doctor's concern for Taba. "Seiso, Molapo, Mofokeng, Sello." Quickly Majara named these men.

"My Chief thought of these men before."

"I have thought of them."

"Molapo is a wind that will blow the truth in the ears of other people. Sello will barter the truth for an ox. No, these cannot be trusted."

"What of Pitso and Mokwena?"

Metlae did not answer. He grabbed the bones together, separated them into two lots and threw one lot down first and then the second lot on top of that. He contemplated the lie of the bones for a long time. "They say that the Chief has chosen well. RaPalla, Sobeti, Seiso, Mofokeng, Pitso and Mokwena."

"Get the men together and bring them here. They must be instructed."

"The Chief walks with the wind."

"Time is short and we must not delay."

"Time is short."

Metlae thought of his payment: the fattest and the sleekest cattle from the Chief's kraal. Hurriedly he scooped the bones together and scraped them into his bag.

"I greet you, Morena."

Majara returned the salute. He watched the old man walk back to his hut. There was a new lightness in his step. He was carrying himself erect; he was important again; he was established.

In his hut Metlae added a few extra bits to his outfit. He still had a tortoise shell full of herbal medicine which he did not put on when he went to the Chief. Now he felt the need for it. The young men he had chosen must accept and not ask questions. They must obey and become drunk with the power they would have after the diretlo had been taken.

Only once before had Metlae taken part in a ritual murder. He remembered the madness that had taken hold of him when the first screams of the victim echoed in the night. He had been chosen with five others to follow the victim from a beer-drink. They had bound him and when the razor-sharp knife had cut off the first piece pointed out by the witch doctor the inhuman sounds uttered by the man had made them insane with brutal passion. They had cut off all the pieces the doctor wanted and had then burnt the wounds with red-hot stones to stop the flow of blood.

This time it was going to be a woman. Old and withered as he was, the vision of the sexual act that must precede the deed whipped up a passion in him which dimmed all thought of the murder and the men he had to instruct.

He did not discuss the woman with the Chief but she would be strong and young. In her agony she would hold him; he would again feel the joy of a woman's arms and the smoothness of her body; the warmth of her breath on his face and the rejuvenation of his tired flesh. A cruel lecherous smile flitted across his wrinkled face. Soon—it must happen soon! He was eager to taste power, passion and the glory that would be his.

Separately Metlae instructed the six men to go to the Chief's hut when they had had their midday meal.

"The Chief has important work for you."

That was all he told them. Each one wondered what the work could be but no one said a word because Metlae warned them not to speak. With impatience they waited for the sun to climb the sky and when the shadows were short, they hurried to the Chief's hut. Metlae was there before them and brought each one into the hut as he arrived.

"Dumela, Morena."

Majara lifted his hand in salute as each one greeted him and told him to sit down. Suspiciously they watched each newcomer. RaPalla was the last to come.

From the moment that Metlae had told RaPalla to go to the Chief's hut in that solemn and important tone, RaPalla had been uneasy. What was it they wanted of him? He had been to the places of the white people, he could read and write; they knew that he did not believe in the witch doctor. Why had the Chief thought it well to send the witch doctor to summon him?

RaPalla took his seat at the end of the row and watched the Chief's face for some sign but Majara stared straight in front of him, waiting for Metlae to begin.

Metlae threw his bones. The sinister atmosphere, his mumbling and chanting filled his audience with dread. For what purpose had the Chief assembled them there?

Metlae said: "Hau, the bones do not lie! They say that there is a man here who is not willing."

Each one of the men hurried to assure the Chief that he was there to obey whatever orders the Chief wished to give.

"That is good," Metlae answered for the Chief. "The bones say that the one who does not agree will lose his way on the mountains."

RaPalla's heart beat fast. What was this leading to? Why were six men chosen to do one job? What had Metlae and his bones got to do with it?

Metlae continued: "You are all brave and strong. You are men who do not speak like the wind. You do not whisper to women. That is why the Chief had seen fit to choose you."

Uncomfortably the six men looked at one another. They felt that this was no light matter. For what had they pledged themselves when they assured the Chief of their obedience? Metlae waited for his words to strike home.

"Lenaka!" he whispered dramatically. "Our Chief needs a horn full of strong medicine."

The impact of this announcement left them speechless. It could mean only one thing. They had been chosen for a ritual murder.

Sobeti smiled. Seiso, who had been resting on his haunches, suddenly sat flat on the cold dung-smeared floor. Mofokeng, Pitso and Mokwena stiffened. Their young faces wore the signs of their conflicting thoughts.

RaPalla's mind was in turmoil. The police. How did they think they would get away with ritual murder when the white people would sooner or later catch them and hang them for it? He had read in the papers of these things and he knew that the white people did not rest until they had found the people responsible for the murder. But these thoughts must die within him. Metlae had said that the one who was unwilling would lose his way on the mountains.

As if Metlae could divine these thoughts he said: "Nobody will ever find out. I have strong medicine that will protect each one of you. I shall tell each one later what he has to do. You will all come to my hut again tomorrow night."

He looked at each of the six men in turn. Fear struck them with silence. He said: "It would be better if the dogs ate the tongue of the man who spoke about this. That is all."

They knew that they were dismissed with these words. They had to leave the presence of their Chief. Slowly they got up to go. In all this time Majara had not said a single word. He saluted the men when they left but did not get up. Metlae followed them out but soon returned, saying: "We have chosen well. Before they come to my hut tomorrow night, they will be drunk with the thought of their importance."

Majara's lip curled with derision. He knew that Metlae was also not only drunk with his importance but mad with the hope of the power that he would have over the Chief and the six men when everything was done. But that could not be helped. Diretlo must be found and his horn filled. His wife must be doctored. She must bear him a son.

Majara prepared himself for the struggle that must come. He must match his wit with that of the wily witch doctor. Metlae must name the victim that he, the Chief, had chosen. It was the witch doctor's prerogative to choose the victim but no other would do. He had chosen her and only diretlo from her would be good enough for his wife. His seeming indifference left him. Shrewdly he watched Metlae taking his place opposite him, then said: "We must go against tradition."

Metlae looked up quickly at these words of the Chief.

"The old chiefs looked for a victim in the kraals far away from their own. We must take a person from our own kraal; the police will not suspect," Majara said.

Metlae thought about the wisdom of such a step for a long time. His quick mind had darted to one logical conclusion. The Chief had chosen the six men long before he had spoken to him; the Chief had chosen his victim too, and would now force him to consent. The Chief was a strong young bull but not clever enough for him, Metlae.

The Chief said: "She must be young and strong and with child."

"I have said that she must be big already with the child that she carries."

"She must be related to my wife. That will make the medicine stronger."

Metlae did not answer. He was frantically thinking of all the young women in the village who were pregnant. Which of them was related to the Chief's wife?

Quietly he took the larger bones out of his bag, together with the stones and a few pieces of rag. He took one of the bigger bones, wrapped it in a piece of rag to represent a woman, placed her in the center of a circle which he drew with a small black stone and then chanted a monotonous song very much like a lullaby. He strewed the rest of the bones round the one representing the woman, chanting all the time. With closed eyes he spread his hands a few times over the bones and then contemplated them.

Majara's impatience tensed to breaking point. What good could mumbling and the bones of the witch doctor do when he had long ago decided who the victim was to be? He waited for Metlae to speak but when Metlae only sat there staring at his bones Majara's temper mounted. He grabbed Metlae by his withered shoulders and roughly shook him.

"Speak, Metlae, let the bones be."

Metlae jerked himself free. A new dignity came over him. "The bones will not speak when the Chief shows the madness of the bee who stings and knows not what he does."

"His stinging brings pain; do not forget that, Metlae!"

"I shall not forget."

For a fleeting second murderous resentment shone in the veiled eyes of the witch doctor. On the first day that Majara's father had asked him to go to his son's village, Metlae had said that the days of the year which were still lying under the mountain of the future would bring sorrow to this young man who relied on his strength and flashed his anger like lightning in a thunderstorm.

"Think, Metlae, who in my village is young and beautiful—my wife's cousin and big with the child that she carries?"

The thought flashed through Metlae's mind: Fool, you know her name but want me to say it. For this you will pay more than you would have done if I had chosen her. I know whom you mean but the time has not come to say her name.

He said: "My Chief knows that these things must be said by

the bones. The spirits of our ancestors must guide us. This matter cannot be decided lightly."

Majara was exasperated. Why beat about the bush, why wait for him? But the onus must be on Metlae; he must say her name first.

"All right, ask your bones again."

"Morena does not believe in the bones, it seems to me."

Majara glared at the witch doctor. He had to keep a tight hold on himself not to take the wily old spider and throw him out of his hut.

"I want diretlo, that is all."

"The Chief will have diretlo."

"Then name the victim."

Metlae pointed to a big bone lying a little apart away from the one which represented the woman.

"Her husband is not here. She is a good woman."

Excitement took hold of Majara. At last the old fox had decided to speak. "What else do they say?"

"That the Chief must be careful. This woman is strong and loved by the people in the village."

"I know. Name her! Name her!"

Metlae looked at the young Chief for a long time. He scraped his bones into his bag, got up and pulled himself to his full height. Majara got up too. They faced each other. In their minds one name kept repeating itself. At last Metlae spoke.

"Tselane."

Majara sighed; he had won. He was too clever for Metlae. He had not named her, the witch doctor had. This was as it should be.

"You have chosen well, Metlae. Tselane and nobody else."

Metlae left. Majara took the beer pot and drank long and deep. He threw himself on the sleeping mats. He felt exhausted.

5

ON THE WAY to the lands Molili talked and laughed. It was like old times again. Tselane was happy for her cousin.

"Have you spoken to your husband? What did he say?"

"He will get the medicine from his father."

"When is he going to get it?"

"In two months' time."

"Two months is a long time. Why does he want to wait so long?"

"His father must have time to think about it."

"Did he say that?"

"Yes, but why do you look like that? Don't you believe me?"

"When is he going to tell his father about it so that his father can start thinking about it?"

Molili frowned. Majara had not spoken about a time that he would go to his father. Perhaps he was going to send a messenger. She decided to ask him that night.

All day Molili was in such a good mood that the other women started whispering.

"Perhaps she is at last sure that she is going to have a child. How happy the Chief will be."

"I am glad; she is a good woman."

Tselane listened to this talk but made no comment. It must not become known that her cousin, who was a Christian, would make use of medicine. Nobody must know that the Chief was going to have his wife doctored. Molili must ask her husband to go to his father soon.

On their way home in the late afternoon, Tselane again urged Molili not to wait but to ask her husband as soon as she got home, and Molili said: "I shall ask him. I am sure he will not wait."

When Molili reached home, Majara was not there. She wondered at this because he usually waited for her. She prepared the evening meal. Long after the beans and the maize had been cooked there was still no sign of her husband. Molili became uneasy. It was the first time since they had been married that he was so late. There was no beer-drink in the village because everything was quiet. There were only the usual sounds of children being called to eat, women singing softly while preparing the evening meal, and the high laughter and giggling of the young people reluctant to part company and return to the huts of their parents.

Molili went into her hut to roll out the sleeping mats ready for the night. She put a few sticks on the small fire in the middle of the floor and cleared away the ashes. She fetched the three-legged iron pot with their food and placed it near the fire to keep warm. She put their plates and spoons ready and then went out to see whether Majara was coming. There was still no sign of him. Molili called Kera who was just then passing their hut.

"Have you seen Morena, Kera?"

"Morena went to Metlae when the sun was still high. Perhaps he is still with the witch doctor."

Molili thanked the boy and went into their hut to wait. Majara returned soon afterwards. He was quiet and did not speak. Molili knew that the time to ask questions had not come and that she had to wait until they were in bed that night or until early the next morning.

Majara was deep in thought and hardly took any notice of Molili. She wondered what he was thinking and what he had been doing at the witch doctor's hut. He never called the doctor and always spoke jokingly of the power that witch doctors were supposed to possess. What had changed his mind? Was he speaking to the doctor about the medicine and how it must be used once they had it?

As soon as the meal was over, Majara loosened his blanket and lay down on the sleeping mats. Molili washed the plates and their spoons and then turned in too. She was anxious to talk about the medicine but did not know how to start the conversation. Majara lay looking into the heart of the fire and hardly answered when she addressed him. At last she scraped up enough courage to ask: "Will you be going to your father's kraal to speak about the medicine?"

She saw how he stiffened. He scowled darkly. "I forbid you to speak about medicine. I do not want to hear that word again."

Molili was taken aback. She could not understand his attitude. "But you must go to your father otherwise he will not know that we want the medicine."

A cruel light came into his eyes which frightened her. The red glow of the fire made his eyes look even redder and more bloodshot and his black skin glistened in the flickering light.

"And why should I go to my father?"

"But you said that it would take him two months to decide to give the medicine. If you do not go immediately, it will be such a long time before we know whether the medicine helped."

Majara smiled. More than his frown a moment ago, his smile frightened her and she shrank away from him.

"Don't worry about the affairs of a man," he said. "When the time is ripe, the medicine will be made and you will be doctored. All will be well."

In sudden fear Molili's heart contracted. Why was her husband talking like that? At first he forbade her to speak of medicine, then he was angry and then he smiled in that peculiar way. Dark suspicion entered her mind and left her weak. Was he going to fill his own horn? His father's medicine was mixed to bring prosperity to his kraal, to make his harvest big and the village strong; did he think that this medicine would not help her to have a child? Where was he going to get diretlo?

It was impossible to believe. Her husband, the man she loved, could not think of doing such a thing. How often she had heard her father telling people that no matter how hard they tried to conceal the crime, they would be found out. The penalty was death but what awaited them after death was even more horrible than what they had to suffer while waiting for the time when the rope was put round their necks and they breathed their last.

For days afterwards these thoughts tortured her. She winced whenever her husband touched her. All the tenderness which they had experienced after they had first spoken of medicine was lost. He became brutal in his love-making and stayed away from home more often.

Molili suffered but did not speak of this to Tselane. All hope, all the pleasure she had found in thinking that medicine might help her, all the dreams of her child, vanished. On her face the sad expression could be seen again. In the fields the old women soon started whispering again.

"It was a false alarm. She is barren, she will have no children."

"She is a failure. The Chief will have to take another wife."

"And she hasn't got a younger sister to give him. Her father will have to pay the bohadi back."

"Hau!" They were not thinking of Molili's feeling but of the disaster when a father has to pay back the price which he received for his daughter.

Tselane listened to the talk and it pained her. It was even more painful for her to see Molili so quiet and often with that sad and anxious expression on her face. Once when they were working in the fields and Molili was particularly quiet, Tselane laughed and said: "Oh, my cousin, the medicine is not even here yet and you are already like a woman who is with child."

Molili did not answer at once but later replied: "No, Tselane, you are mistaken."

"Well, what is wrong with you?"

"It is the medicine. Majara is not going to his father."

"Where is he going to get it?"

"I don't know."

"Is he going to make his own?"

Tselane did not realize the portent of the words she had said and looked searchingly at her cousin, waiting for the answer. Molili was quiet. How could she tell her of the fearful thoughts that came to her in the night? To get the best diretlo to make her pregnant her husband would have to get a woman who was with child. In her imagination she saw the poor unfortunate soul shrieking in her agony, with nobody to help her, only the darkness and the night winds on the mountains to bear testimony of a cruelty beyond words. How could she ever be happy with a child whose very beginning brought suffering and death to another woman and her child?

Tselane looked at Molili and suddenly her legs refused to hold her upright. She put down her hoe and squatted on the ground. She could not explain the fear which had taken hold of her.

"Hau, Molili," were the only words she found to say. Molili kept on hoeing and did not look at her.

"Hau," Tselane said again and looked toward the horizon. When she had first advised Molili to get medicine to help her, she had thought of a horn that was already full. She had never dreamed of suggesting a new victim. Where was this person, completely unaware of the horrible end that was awaiting him—or her?

They talked long over this thing that had suddenly come to bring black clouds into their minds. Tselane decided to ask her father-in-law about it. That night when they had eaten and were sitting round the fire in the hut she was baffled by her father-in-law's attitude when she asked him about the uses of medicine.

"Why do you ask about medicine now?"

"I was just thinking about it."

"One does not think about these things without reason."

He looked away. Tselane could not understand the expression on his face. Did her father-in-law know that the Chief was going to make his own medicine?

"Must every chief have a lenaka?" she asked.

"If he finds it necessary. Fortunately, Majara's father has a strong lenaka and besides that our village has been doctored. What would he want medicine for?"

Tselane's thoughts were in chaos. Doubt crowded her mind. Must she tell them about Molili? Must she speak about her part in this?

It was with a heavy heart that she bade the old people goodnight and went to her own hut.

A peaceful quiet fell upon the huts. Every now and again the night wind brought the laughter and talk of people in other huts, but soon only the crickets and the howling of a stray dog disturbed the mountain stillness.

Tselane found no peace. Alone in her hut her thoughts kept coming back to this thing for which she held herself responsible. Molili had not believed. She had argued her into accepting the possibility that medicine might help. She had suggested it and kept on until Molili had promised to speak to her husband about it. Majara would kill some woman to get diretlo but she, Tselane, would really be responsible for the death of this woman and her child. Those were disturbing thoughts that kept sleep far from her. If only Khama had been there to reassure her; Khama would bring peace to her mind. She wondered where he was and what he was doing.

Tselane feared because she knew what was going to happen, but soon wild whispering brought fear into every hut. Where people gathered, diretlo was the first topic they discussed. There were many ideas but no one was sure of the facts. It was a terrible thing that was going to happen to some woman in a kraal far from theirs, but it was inevitable; it had to come sooner or later.

Those who had already adopted the Christian faith tried to argue the people out of their belief in the necessity for murder, but lacked the courage to say that they would report the matter to the police. The others soon learned not to talk when any of these people were near. Some said that it was idle gossip started by a few beer drinkers in search of something spicy and interesting to talk of.

"Some people hear the horse neigh but they cannot see him grazing. They do not know what they are talking about," the old people said.

"But it is true. I was on a visit to Teyateyaneng and there nobody goes out after dark. They are afraid to walk when the sun has gone to sleep."

"My mother has her kraal at Mokhotlong and there they put bars on the doors at night. The stranger does not find a place to sleep in her kraal."

"At Leribe and Butho-Buthe they keep vicious dogs, for who shall know who the next victim will be?"

"Children, why do you talk of these fearful things?"

Old MaPhépa felt the fear which was in everybody's heart but said talking only made it worse.

"But, MaPhépa, you were in Kosa's hut when the stranger told us of the chief who wanted twins and got the diretlo from such a child and soon afterwards his wife had twin daughters."

"I know, I know, but it is a terrible thing."

"I wish I could get some of the medicine they have behind the mountain. They say that a teacher disappeared and now the people in that kraal all have such clever children."

"At Phorrong, Maobane Leboea sold her husband for eighty pounds and sat there while they took his blood. They then threw him into his own goat kraal so that people finding him in the morning should think that thieves had tried to steal his goats and that he had been killed when he wanted to stop them."

"Hau! Hau!" came from all sides. It was hard to believe these things and yet the people who told these stories were sure of their facts.

The kraal of Majara had been a happy one before now. People had come to his beer parties. Song and laughter could be heard where his huts nestled on the side of one of the higher peaks of the Maluti. The young men of his kraal were strong; those who came back from the mines and the other places where they worked for the white people were rich. They brought wonderful presents back to the kraal for their Chief and their relatives. From the time that Majara had started his village, he had known only happiness and prosperity. There was enough water in the fountains on his side of the mountain to provide for his cattle, the people and the horses; the mealies grew well and bore in abundance; there were many small children strong and healthy in each hut.

This happiness and peace had now left them. People went about their tasks quietly. Nobody sent a child or woman on an errand that would take them far from the village. The little cowherders kept the animals on the slopes where they could see the village. When the sun had set, children were called into the huts, where people spoke in whispers. Men looked at one another with suspicion, wondering whom the Chief had chosen for the deed. Anybody who was seen talking to the Chief or old Metlae immediately came under suspicion. There seldom was a beer-drink now, with the usual bickering and fighting. Family men stayed at home and the young bloods remained sober.

Metlae had foreseen this. He had expected that people would whisper and talk, that fear would walk the footpaths to the village and sleep in the huts of the people, making them wary and suspicious. He was waiting for the time when they would forget and go about their tasks in the normal way. The pain that the sting of the bee brings does not last long, and fear soon dies when nothing happens.

During this time when people whispered of diretlo Tselane seldom went to fetch Molili at her hut. "I shall wait for you in the donga," she had suggested to Molili.

"I could finish my work early and then come for you. But why don't you want to come to our hut any more?"

"My body is becoming very heavy, my cousin, and it is difficult for me to climb the hill on the other side of the donga."

She could not tell Molili that she feared Majara. It was as if her body had a strange fascination for him. In the beginning when he had looked at her like that, she had forgiven him because she remembered his yearning for his own child. He used to come out of the hut to greet her when she arrived, and suddenly he no longer appeared although she knew that he was in the hut. This was more unsettling than his behavior when he was with them, and she therefore decided not to go for Molili any more.

They were quieter now when they went to the lands to work. People seldom sang, and if they did it was the mournful song of lost harvests and plague. Nobody talked of medicine when Molili was near. It was only after the fifth week had seen the light of day and was lost again that people sat around their fires at night and spoke of their cattle and their sons who were working in the places of the white people, and not about medicine any more.

Children played again after sunset, and young girls dared to walk alone to meet their promised husbands and sweethearts near the stream or the big rocks on the far side of the village.

6

THIS WAS the time that Metlae had waited for. During the five weeks in which people had looked at him only when his eyes were turned away from them he seldom got the six men together. When things were normal and people did not speak of medicine any more, he spoke to them.

"We meet in the Chief's hut as soon as the women have gone to the lands. See that you do not go with one of the others."

He had spoken to them a few times in his own hut but never about the actual murder. He had informed them of the power they would have afterwards, of their importance as men who held the secret, but more than that they did not know. That a woman was chosen and that they all knew her had been kept from them and they were eager to hear the details at last.

Molili hardly left the hut that morning when Metlae turned up at the Chief's hut. He was dressed with even more care than before and it was hard to see his withered body under the mass of stinking skins and the other paraphernalia of his trade. He was anxious to discuss a few things with the Chief before the men came. His new-found dignity and importance made him bold. Even the Chief now had to obey him and give whatever orders he wanted.

"I salute you, Morena."

"Dumela, Metlae."

"The young men will be here any moment."

"Have you thought of everything?"

"Everything. Today I shall tell each one what he has to do; the time is getting short."

"Are you sure that none of them have shown signs of weakness? Are they all willing to do this thing for me?"

"I have tested them many times but this morning I shall do so in your presence. We must be quite sure that we are not at the last moment betrayed by one who has the liver of a rat."

"It will be difficult to get her alone. She never walks to other kraals and does not go to beer-drinks."

"Leave that to me, Morena. When the time comes my bones will tell me what to do and how to get hold of her."

Majara smiled in contempt. He had thought of a plan and nothing that the bones could say would be better.

"The Chief does not believe me?" Metlae was pained.

Majara took no notice of his remark. He said: "I have thought of a good way to get her. I shall go to her hut in the night and tell her that my wife is ill and is asking for her. She will get up immediately and come to her cousin. You and the men will wait in the donga and there bind and gag her and take her to the cliffs near the caves. Nobody will hear you."

"The plan is not a good one."

Immediately anger flashed in Majara's eyes. "Why?"

"There may be somebody sleeping with her in the hut. The next day the story will be told that you came for her."

"If there is somebody in the hut we must postpone it to the following night."

"This thing cannot wait. When the time is ripe it must be done or not at all."

"What do you mean?"

"I must doctor the men; my medicine will not be laughed at and told to wait. I instruct the men today; tomorrow they will be doctored to protect them from the police and tomorrow night the deed must be done."

Majara felt excitement at these words of the witch doctor. How often he had looked at the strong and graceful figure of Tselane and remembered the words a young chief had told him how a woman like that had more power to rouse you than having ten other women. The young chief had told his story with so much relish that, remembering his words, Majara already experienced some of the thrill that was in store for him. As chief he would be the first and would have all the joy of her fighting spirit about which his friend had told him.

Metlae was watching the Chief and saw the smile in his eyes. He knew what Majara was thinking. For the last few nights such thoughts had kept him awake too. He thought over the details of the murder in those wakeful hours, and the thrill of having a young woman after all these years had turned his mind to water in the darkness of the night. He envied the chief who would be first but he would not give way to his right of being second. The young bloods would argue that he was too old but he'd show them! He waited until Majara said: "Let it be as you say. We cannot wait any longer; we have wasted enough time already."

"It was necessary. Women are like hens who cackle a long time after the egg has been laid and then forget about the egg. The time for the chicken to see the light of day has now come. I shall instruct the men as soon as they are here."

Metlae had hardly finished speaking when Sobeti hurriedly entered the hut. He looked back again as if expecting to see somebody following him.

"Is anything chasing you, Sobeti? You look like a rat running before the cat," the Chief teased.

"Dumela, Morena. It's my mother. She has not gone to the lands today and she saw me leaving."

"Did she see you entering my hut?"

"No, I slipped in when she was looking the other way."

"Where is your father?"

"My father has not come back yet from the old Chief's place."

"When did he leave for my father's kraal?"

"He left yesterday when the sun was still behind the mountains."

Metlae and Majara exchanged looks. Sobeti's father was a councilor, perhaps the most wily of them all. Councilors inform their chief when they leave the village. What business had taken Sobeti's father to the old Chief's kraal? What was it he wanted to discuss with Majara's father? Did he go there to talk about the things that were being said in his son's village?

RaPalla arrived and sat in his usual place where the Chief could not look directly at him.

"Did you see the others coming?" Majara asked.

"They are coming, Morena, I heard them."

Majara's impatience was rising. Did the men lie like dogs in the sun to warm themselves before answering his orders? He was on the point of sending RaPalla to call them when they arrived one after the other. They saluted the Chief and then sat down to wait for Metlae who had already started mumbling and shuffling his bones and stones.

Metlae was out to impress them; he must make them cower before him. He strewed the bones and then started jumping up and down and mumbling until froth stood at the corners of his mouth. He looked at each man in turn as if he wanted to bring their thoughts to the surface where they could be plain for everyone to see.

Like the loud hissing of a snake when suddenly trodden on in the footpath, he whispered: "Who is the man of whom the bones say that he has strange thoughts in the night?"

The men moved uneasily. What was coming? Was he going to smell one out and make an example of him?

"We are waiting to hear the orders of the Chief; there is not one among us who is not eager to obey," Seiso said.

"Seiso has spoken well. Is it true that you all think this thing?"

"It is true," they answered in unison and looked at their Chief. Majara nodded to show that he accepted this statement and waited for Metlae to continue.

The old man was taking his time. At last he said: "The person we are going to take is a woman."

He waited for the reaction. None of the men showed any sign of realizing what that meant. Metlae smiled. How young they were.

They had not heard a great deal about these things. They did not know what was in store for them.

RaPalla was the only one who was married and who had children. Perhaps the idea would be distasteful to him because he was a good husband to his wife and a good father to his children. But Metlae must tell them about the joy that was awaiting them to whet their appetites and make them eager for an experience they would never have in their lifetime again. He said: "I see that you sit like the small dog when he is born and has his eyes closed so that he does not see and know the world around him. You do not understand."

The men looked guiltily at each other. What was it that they did not understand? Metlae waited for the right moment when they were all looking at him again.

"The woman will first give you pleasure before we take diretlo."

Pitso drew his breath in sharply. He had only experienced the thrill of a woman's love in the proper way a short while ago and the thought of it gave splendor to Metlae's words. Passion showed on every face, and when Metlae was quite sure that they understood and were eager in their expectancy, he continued.

"You will be told later whom we take. We walk tomorrow night."

"Will it be far?" Mokwena asked the question.

Majara looked at Metlae and waited. The moment he feared had arrived. From now on doubt and anxiety would walk with each man.

"No, Mokwena, we will throw sand in the eyes of the police. The old people went to a kraal far from their own to get diretlo. The white people know this. We will stay in our own kraal."

His words had an unexpected effect. RaPalla rose before he had taken control of himself; Mofokeng and Sobeti both uttered a loud "Hau!" Pitso and Mokwena were so taken aback that they could only stare open-mouthed. Seiso was the only one who showed no feeling at all. There was a blank expression on his face and Metlae made a note of that. Seiso would be the one to cut off the first piece he needed.

"You kick like the unbroken horse when he comes under the saddle for the first time. Why? I have thrown my bones many times and they have always told me this is the right thing I want to do. We want the diretlo to bring a son to the Chief's hut. This woman is heavy with child."

"Is she young?"

"Young and strong."

"We'll have to be careful; they are sometimes stronger than wild animals when they are young and unwilling."

Metlae answered quickly: "We'll bind her before she can do anything. Because of the child we'll hold her on her side but that will not make your pleasure less."

The panic which had shown on their faces left them.

"The medicine will be made from the fat of her kidneys which we will melt and mix with the burnt powder from her right eye, left ear, the soles of her feet, her right breast, the place where we had our pleasure, and most important of all, the same parts from her unborn child."

Horror filled their eyes and made their mouths dry.

"Now listen carefully. Each one will get his special job and when the time comes he must not hesitate. It must be done quickly and surely; no blood must be wasted."

All six men sat speechless, hardly breathing. A tension had mounted in the hut with each word which Metlae had uttered and this caught them up and strung their nerves, until they were taut like the strings of their guitars when the night is cold.

"Seiso, I have chosen you for the first cut. You will cut off her right breast when the time comes."

Seiso blinked and tried to swallow against the knot which seemed to have come into his throat but he found no voice to answer.

"Answer him, Seiso!" Majara's command jarred on their nerves.

"Yes, Morena, I heard. I must cut off her right breast but—"

Metlae interrupted him. "I shall see to it that she does not bite or scream. I shall take the rags to close her mouth."

In turn Metlae told each man what he had to do and then turned to RaPalla.

"You are the oldest of the men and you will take out the child. You will cut the same parts from the child."

RaPalla felt nausea rising in him until he had to hold his hand over his mouth not to vomit. It was too much. He did not possess the liver of a rat but this thing he could not do.

Majara looked at RaPalla and saw his wild reaction. What would RaPalla do when he heard who the victim was? It was a wise move when he had chosen RaPalla. As Khama's cousin he would have to keep quiet because Khama would not hesitate to murder any person on whom suspicion fell when he heard what had happened to his wife. When Tselane was young and RaPalla was still unmarried, everybody saw him walking around for days without food and hardly speaking because she had refused to give him her scarf and had given it to his cousin. Perhaps it would now give RaPalla joy to take revenge. He would not know who it was until they had bound her and then it would be too late to withdraw or do anything about it. Perhaps his old love would return to make him unwilling at the last moment but then he'd only share her fate.

Majara watched RaPalla closely. Time seemed endless like the cold in the nights when snow falls softly and quietly to numb you and make your thoughts slow. RaPalla looked wildly from the Chief to Metlae and back again.

Metlae was watching him, waiting for the next move. The other five men sat tense and taut watching the play of feeling that was surging among the Chief, RaPalla and the witch doctor.

"Your heart has now turned to water but it will soon be over and then you'll find joy in the deed," Metlae said, remembering the reaction he had felt when he was chosen for ritual murder and the effect it had on him. The same would happen to these young men, although RaPalla now looked as if he had met death face to face and could not find a way of escape.

"Do you obey? Are you willing?"

Majara addressed RaPalla impatiently. He was eager for Metlae to finish.

"I am willing. I shall do what the Chief asks of me," RaPalla said with difficulty.

"I knew I could trust you, RaPalla. Men who will one day be worthy councilors must prove their worth before they are chosen."

He dangled the prospect of becoming a councilor in front of RaPalla to break down his resistance. The other five looked on with envy in their eyes. To none of them had the Chief promised so great an honor but they did not mind. Their futures were assured. One whispered word in the right direction and the Chief would have many questions to answer to the white people. They held the secret in their hands and he would be good to them whether they were councilors or not.

Like a bird caught in a trap, a thought had suddenly started beating its wings in RaPalla's mind. Who was this woman they were speaking of? Metlae had said that she was young and strong and that she was expecting a child. There were not so many women expecting children in the village who answered to that description. There was Mafata, Dikeledi, Mamokwena and Sebetle, there was— Suddenly his heart contracted. There was Tselane! But it was impossible! They could not think of taking Khama's wife. Khama was away but when he came back and heard of this he would kill the whole village. Khama was good and honest but quick with his knife when things did not please him. He loved his wife and was only waiting for the day that he could hold his son in his arms. This thing must not happen. They were doomed if Tselane was taken. He felt a weakness in the pit of his stomach. Nausea made him loath to speak but he must find out, he must make sure.

"Does this woman know the Chief's wife?"

"She knows the Chief's wife."

"But what about her husband? He will not allow her to go out alone at night. How shall we get hold of her and what shall we do when he starts looking for his wife the following day?"

Majara's eyes narrowed. RaPalla was clever. Was he asking these questions because of the things which were speaking in his heart? Metlae answered shrewdly: "Her husband will not know, of that you can be sure, RaPalla."

"But her people. She will not be living alone."

"You ask too many questions. The witch doctor has spoken and you will obey."

RaPalla was quiet. The wish to speak had left him. His mind felt numbed. His old love for Tselane that wanted to protect her, to keep that which was evil from her, rushed over him. But he must be wrong. It could not be Tselane.

Metlae's voice interrupted his thoughts.

"You will be doctored tomorrow to protect you and to make you ready for the night. Let not a rat gnaw in your hearts and bring thoughts of doubt. Everything will be as the bones have said and at the right moment you will see and know what to do. That is all."

7

RAPALLA left the Chief's hut with the others. They were eager
to get away. What they had experienced there made them long for
their own beer pots from which they could drink deeply and forget
for a while the thoughts and fears which were making their chests
small with anxiety.

RaPalla walked back slowly to his hut. His thoughts gave him
no peace. The rat about which Metlae had spoken was in his heart
and speaking to him. There was no time to be lost. If they were
thinking of Tselane, he had to warn her. If the Chief should suspect
or get to know that he had warned her, it would mean instant
death. But Tselane must not be taken. Kindly, beautiful Tselane
with her wonderful laughter, she whose only wish was to bring
happiness to others, whose every thought was of her husband and
the child she was carrying for him, how could they dream of taking
her!

At his hut he took the beer pot but quickly put it down again
without taking a drink. He must keep his mind clear, he must think;
his thoughts must not be slowed with beer.

He sat down on the sleeping mats but immediately got up again. Perhaps the women were already coming back from the lands. He looked at the sun. It was still climbing the skies, it would be a long time before they returned.

He opened the pail of porridge his wife had left for him, took a handful but found no joy in eating. Thoughts were making his head dizzy but the one name kept repeating itself—Tselane, Tselane. The more he thought of everything, the more convinced he became that they had meant Tselane and nobody else. He must warn her. He must tell her to go to her husband in Worcester. This decision brought peace to his mind and he stretched himself out on the ground in the sun to sleep.

"RaPalla, wake up; RaPalla, drink your motoho."

Seaka his wife was standing next to him. RaPalla blinked in the afternoon sun and then took the small pail with the thin porridge. He drank deeply and then got up.

"Where are you going?" Seaka asked.

"I am going to speak to Tselane about the cattle which Khama said must be sent to her father's kraal."

Seaka had been present when Khama and RaPalla had spoken of this so she let him go in peace.

Tselane saw him coming and shouted happily to him. "Dumela, RaPalla, my cousin, I was just going to throw this motoho away. You must be thirsty. Come and have a drink."

They laughed. Tselane would never throw good food away and they both knew this. RaPalla drank some of the thin porridge she offered him, wiped his mouth with the back of his hand and then handed the pail back to her.

"Your days are nearly full, Tselane."

She smiled with tenderness. "If only Khama were here!"

RaPalla looked up quickly. "Why don't you go to your husband?"

Tselane laughed loud and long. How could RaPalla say something so utterly stupid? She who had hardly ever seen a white person besides the missionary and the white trader. How could she go to the city of the white people where Khama worked? It was ridiculous even to think about it.

"RaPalla, you talk like a man who has had too much beer. I never knew that my mafi was so strong."

"Your mafi is not strong but it would be good for you to go to Khama. He longs for his child."

"I know." There was a tender little smile round her lips. Didn't she know how much her husband was longing for his son? She looked for a long time into the fire before she replied:

"When the moon is full again I have to go to my mother's kraal; it will be my seventh month. I cannot speak the language of the white people. What shall I do when my child comes? My child must be born in my mother's hut and nowhere else. By the time that Khama comes home again our son will be strong and big and won't cry in the night to keep sleep from his father."

"That is as you say, Tselane." RaPalla found no other words with which to answer her.

Her brightness and gaiety made it even more impossible for him to believe in the thought which had come to him. He soon left her to return to his own hut. Once there, away from the spell of her personality, doubt made him restless. If Tselane was to escape she was to go that night and not later. If the Chief had someone else in mind, it would not matter if Tselane was not there. Whatever happened he must try to get her away from the village during the night. Carefully he thought of each one of the women who was pregnant, but Tselane remained the only suitable one that the Chief would choose.

Seaka looked at her husband and was at a loss to understand him. He used to be so happy and never spoke a cross word to her or the children but during the last few weeks he had become quiet and morose when at home. He often left the hut without telling her where he was going to, and when he came back he never spoke of the place where he had been. The evil thought had come to her that she was no good any more, that he was courting another girl. If he wanted to take another wife, she must suffer in silence and bear with him. They had four children already. She was luckier than most of her friends whose husbands had already brought one or more wives into his kraal. RaPalla had so far not once spoken of taking another wife. She gave him his food and sat quietly waiting for him to finish. The children never addressed him, and as soon as they had eaten they left for their own hut. Seaka cleaned the plates and spoons, put the leftover food away and then rolled out the sleeping mats. She was tired from working in the sun all day and eager to rest. In vain she waited for RaPalla to come to her sleeping mats. He loosened his blanket and lay staring into the heart of the fire. What was he thinking of?

"RaPalla, why don't you sleep?"

"I have no sleep. Don't worry about me. You can go to sleep. I shall not come tonight."

Seaka felt disappointment. Were her suspicions correct? But he had never left the hut during the night. Perhaps his thoughts were of other things and not of a woman.

RaPalla's thoughts, however, were with another woman. A madness had come to his mind which blinded every other idea which came to him. Tselane must be warned, she must get away, she must go that night. There was not a moment to lose. If he waited until morning, she was lost. Once they had taken her he would be unable to fight for her life. They would both be killed.

Suddenly an agonizing thought left his mind weak and numbed. Why had they included him when they knew that he did not believe in witchcraft and that he knew the ways of the white people? They knew that he had loved Tselane, that he had promised Khama to look after her and yet they had chosen him for the deed.

Had the wily Metlae foreseen that he would be quick enough to realize who the victim would be without being told her name? Were they hoping that he would warn her so that she would try to get away during the night and that they would then easily get hold of her? Was that what they were waiting for? Were they watching his hut to see when he would get up to warn her? Would he be playing into their hands if he warned her? Death could not be many hours away from him if this thing was so.

RaPalla sweated and tossed and turned. Indecision and doubt drove him to distraction. What must he do? Perhaps he was only imagining that they had chosen him so that he would warn her. He would lose his life in any event because he would never stand by and see her being murdered. The only possible chance was that he was mistaken and that they were not watching him.

The night had walked to meet the early hours of the morning when his anxiety burned like the red-hot coals on the hearth and gave him no peace. Quietly he got up. Seaka heard him going and suspicion tortured her. He was going to spend the rest of the night with his mistress, that was why he did not want to make love to her.

RaPalla's thoughts were very far from love and love-making when he hesitated outside his hut. If courting death was love-making then indeed was he on his way to one of the wildest orgies he had ever hoped to partake in.

He stood for a few seconds in the pitch-darkness which surrounded his hut. He listened to the night sounds. Every muscle and nerve in his body was taut. Those who had reason to walk by night would be quiet by now and those who had to rise early were still enjoying the last few hours of peaceful sleep. If he wanted to save Tselane, now was the hour.

RaPalla's muscles contracted, his mouth became dry. Little spirals of fear chased up and down his spine and made his knees weak. Years of superstition, of belief in the witch doctor and his craft, of obedience to every wish of the Chief, made action difficult.

In his imagination he heard Tselane's fearful screaming when Seiso lifted the knife for the first cut. He saw her beautiful face contorted by insane fear, and saw the reproach in her eyes when she recognized him, a look that would follow him to his grave. He would never know peace again. RaPalla shuddered.

Somewhere in the outskirts of the village a cock crowed. The knowledge that dawn would soon be approaching goaded him to action. Quickly and silently he ran to Tselane's hut on his toes.

He listened at the door to make sure that she was alone. By her even breathing he knew that she was still sleeping. He knocked twice. Immediately there was quiet. He pushed the top part of the door a little to the inside.

"Tselane, it's me, RaPalla. Open the door."

She was quiet for so long that he feared someone might come and find him there.

"I must speak to you. Open the door."

"What do you want at this time of the night?" She was thinking of RaPalla's vow when they were both still unmarried that he would one day still have her, even if he had to wait for years. That afternoon she had noticed the intent way in which he had looked at her.

"I have come to save you. Listen to me."

There was immediate movement on the other side of the door.

He heard her taking off the latch and slipped in quickly, closing the door quietly behind him.

"Tselane, before daybreak you must go to the house of the missionary."

RaPalla did not believe in the church himself and he had never been baptized or confirmed but in this darkest hour the protection the missionary could give her seemed the only safe haven for Tselane. There Metlae and the Chief would not be able to get hold of her.

"But why must I go to the Moneri?"

"My cousin, you have heard the people whispering of medicine. I do not speak idle words; you must go."

Fear as she had never before experienced it grabbed Tselane in the stomach and took all rational thinking from her head. She fell down on her sleeping mats and started weeping, moaning and groaning hysterically. Just for a moment RaPalla did not know what to do. He had not expected such a reaction from her. But time was precious; there was not a second to lose in idle sympathizing. She must be jerked to action. He seized her by the shoulders and slapped her face hard once, and then again.

"Tselane, you are not a child. Stop your nonsense. Do you think that I risked my life to come here just to look at a whining woman who does not know when danger is overtaking her? Get up!"

Brought to her senses Tselane obeyed mechanically.

"Where is your money?"

She pointed to a place in the floor and RaPalla quickly dug up a tin. He took the money out and handed it to her.

"You may need that. Is your pail filled?"

"Yes."

"Here, drink some water." He held a billy can to her mouth and when she had drunk he put the pail of porridge in her hand which she had prepared for the following day. He bundled her clothes hanging over the stick in the corner into a skirt and balanced it on her head.

"Wait."

RaPalla opened the door a little and went out. He tried to pierce the darkness to make sure that nobody was waiting for Tselane.

He heard nothing and saw nothing. He opened the door a little more to let her out.

"Run, Tselane, and do not stop before you see the house of the missionary. The light will soon be coming in the east but you know your way. May the spirits of our ancestors run with you."

Without a word Tselane disappeared into the darkness and was lost to him.

RaPalla felt dizzy with relief. He had a feeling of urgency to reach the safety of his hut and the warmth of his wife.

Out of breath he reached his hut. Looking around once again he quietly went in. He did not go to his own sleeping mats but lay down beside his wife. He pressed her to him. He wanted to feel the security of something that still was as it used to be before all this had started. Seaka put her arms around him. He could not have been with a mistress. He had not been away long enough and having spent his passion on another woman he would not feel like coming to her, his wife. She did not ask him where he had been. That he had come back to her was all that mattered. RaPalla sighed. Tomorrow would bring many cares and sorrows when it was found that Tselane had disappeared during the night but he had done his duty by Khama, his cousin. Even if he had to pay with his own life, Khama's wife and child would perhaps be safe.

With Seaka tenderly stroking his body and holding him close to her, he at last fell asleep.

8

THE SMELL of dung and wood fires hung heavy on the morning air when MaKhama woke up. Her old husband was still snoring softly on his side of the fire which had long gone out. She put her hand out to feel the ashes but there was no warmth left in them. She pulled her blanket a little closer. The morning air was chilly on her withered old body. She listened intently for sounds from Tselane's hut but she heard nothing.

"'Ntate." She spoke softly. It was time her husband woke up. "'Ntate," she called again.

The old man stirred and turned over. "Have you seen the new light, MaKhama?"

"No, it must still be very early; I do not hear our daughter."

They both smiled. Tselane was the best daughter-in-law any parents could wish for. With the first light of day she was usually up to prepare their morning meal for them. She was obedient to their every wish and soon she would fulfill their dreams and give them the grandson they were longing for.

"I wonder. She must be feeling a little lazy this morning."

"Let her rest, MaKhama; I am not hungry."

"But they start on new land today. They must leave early."

"It is time that Tselane does not go to the lands with the other women. Her body is big and heavy. Khama would not like this."

"You speak like that just because she carries your grandchild. When I was carrying my children I had to work on the very day on which the child saw the light of day for the first time. Tselane is young and strong and she must work."

They spoke of Khama and his child, of their cattle, of Tselane's visit to her own parents but every now and again they stopped to listen for her.

"I shall go and start the fire."

MaKhama got up, pinned her blanket round her shoulders and went to the outside cooking place. She kindled the dung fire, washed out the three-legged pot again, filled it with water from the big calabash and then sat patiently waiting for the water to boil so that she could stir in the mealie flour for their porridge. She hummed a little tune and kept on looking at Tselane's hut.

"Hau, my child, are you sick or just lazy?"

She wiped the tears caused by the smoke from her eyes and stirred the mealie meal into the water. She went into the hut to fetch a piece of lard she had saved from the previous day.

"Our child must be sick today. Her hut is still closed."

Khama's father got up quickly, swung his blanket round his thin body and ran to Tselane's hut. MaKhama was at a loss to understand her husband's queer behavior. What was biting him? She followed at a quick pace. "What is the matter? Why do you look like that?"

Anxiety wrinkled the face of the old man. Not three days ago he had been to a beer-drink and there a man had said strange things when he had drunk too much. He had spoken of medicine and of a woman who was with child. Dark foreboding made the arm tremble that he lifted to knock on the door.

"Tselane! Tselane, speak to me."

There was no answer. He opened the door and looked in. The fear which had sprung into his heart when his wife told him that Tselane had not come out of her hut flowed over him like water in a thunderstorm, and like the lightning the thought of what could have happened struck him dumb. He sat down on the low step and held his head. Tears coursed down in the wrinkles on his face and fell on the hard-baked earth. Bent in his grief his pathetic old figure brought the deepest anxiety to his wife when she saw him thus.

"Why are you crying, RaKhama?"

He mutely pointed to the door. MaKhama entered and when she did not see Tselane, she came out again.

"You must go and look for her."

"Where shall I look for my daughter and her child when the mountains are quiet and the winds do not speak?"

His words struck terror into her heart. Was this the truth? She had taken part in the whispering—but it could not have happened! She threw her hands up and shrieked in horror and in agony. At a quick run she set off to the nearest hut to spread the news. Perhaps Tselane would be there, perhaps she had gone to another hut.

"Have you seen my daughter? Have you seen Tselane?"

Everywhere she asked the question and soon people started rushing to Tselane's hut to make sure for themselves that this terrible thing was true. They talked wildly and loudly. They made all kinds of suggestions but deep down in their hearts each and all struggled with a cold premonition which left them unwilling to utter the words that would express their fears. Had they not all been whispering about medicine? Had fear not walked on the mountain and among their huts for weeks now? Calamity had befallen their village; disaster had overtaken them and turned the light of their happiness to darkness.

Seaka was stirring the porridge when the first person passed her hut with the news. She put the spoon down and rushed into their hut.

"RaPalla, get up! Get up immediately."

RaPalla turned over. Why must Seaka wake him up when the light of day had not even come properly? Full realization of what he had done the night before made him sit upright.

"What is the matter, Seaka? Is one of our children sick?"

"No, it's Tselane. They say that she has disappeared."

"What? Is this true? Where do they say she had gone to?"

"Nobody knows, but—"

RaPalla knew what she wanted to suggest and hurriedly interrupted her.

"Does the Chief know?"

"I don't know but you must go and tell him. You are Khama's cousin and he asked you to look after Tselane."

RaPalla quickly put on his trousers, fastened his blanket into position and left his hut. Fear made him cold. If he went to the Chief first, the Chief would not suspect him. If they had, however, waited for him to warn Tselane, he was walking to his death. Certainty must be swift and final. He could not wait for the first move to come from the Chief and his witch doctor.

With a wildly beating heart he knocked on the door of the Chief's hut. Molili opened the door and came out closing it behind her.

"Dumela, Molili."

"Dumela, RaPalla."

"Is the Chief awake?"

"No, he is still sleeping."

"Our Chief must be tired."

"He is very tired. He slept little last night."

RaPalla felt his knees giving way under him. The impulse to rush away and save himself overpowered him. Then it was true: they had watched him. Metlae's bones had told him that Tselane would be warned. They had waited for her. Agony gripped him and made him speechless.

"Your eyes look queer, RaPalla. Are you feeling well? What is the matter? Here, drink some water."

Molili passed him a cup of water but wondered what had suddenly come over him. How could she tell RaPalla why her husband was so tired and why he had slept so little during the night? That whole week her husband had been like a man who was suffering from fever. He refused to eat and hardly ever spoke to her. On the few occasions when he had made love to her, it was with a violence bordering on frenzy. Whenever his passion was spent he had pushed her away from him as if her presence was repulsive to him.

She had suffered more than he had. Deep down in her the feeling had been growing that he was changing. His love was turning to hatred because she could not give him the child he so badly wanted.

During the night his behavior had been particularly strange. They had gone to bed early but there was no question of sleep. He rolled and tossed about on the mats. Sometimes he sat upright; then he drank some water; then he took her in his arms only to push her roughly from him again. Sometimes he started speaking only to break off in the middle of a sentence, leaving her to guess what he could have meant. Once he dozed a little but soon made the weirdest sounds as if he was struggling with a nightmare. It was only towards dawn that he had fallen asleep and was still sleeping peacefully.

Molili took the cup from RaPalla and waited for him to say something. He moved a step towards her and looked fearfully at the door behind which Tselane's murderer was sleeping.

"Tselane is not in her hut; she disappeared in the night."

Hardly had he finished speaking when Molili fell down in a dead faint at his feet. The strain of the last few weeks, the sleepless night, the message of Tselane's disappearance, were all too much for her.

"Help, Morena, help!"

Seeing Molili like that unnerved RaPalla. He knelt down and lifted her head. Majara, who had been already half awake, rushed out of his hut.

"What is the matter? What has happened here?"

He took his wife from RaPalla and gently rubbed her forehead. She opened her eyes and immediately started weeping.

"Why are you crying, Molili? What has he done to you?"

Molili did not answer but kept on sobbing heartbrokenly. Majara turned to RaPalla for an explanation.

"It is Tselane. She has disappeared."

Majara dropped his wife's head and got up. It was plain to see that the news had upset him. RaPalla's heart rejoiced. For the moment both he and Tselane were safe; the Chief did not know about her disappearance.

"It is a lie." Majara found it impossible to accept anything so upsetting.

"It is the truth, Morena."

Majara turned to his wife whose sobbing had become louder

with these words of RaPalla. "Stop your weeping. Nothing has happened to Tselane. We'll find her."

Such determination sounded in these words that fear started gnawing at RaPalla's heart again. The Chief would let Metlae throw his bones to find out who had warned Tselane. They would then torture him until he said where Tselane had gone to. The Chief would not rest until he had found her. Once a victim was chosen it was seldom that he escaped.

RaPalla waited anxiously for the Chief to say something. Majara, however, was looking uncertainly about him, for the moment at a loss to decide on action.

"I have only heard it from other people. Let us go to her hut to make sure," RaPalla said.

Majara went into his hut to get his blanket. Without saying anything to Molili, who was still sitting on the ground moaning softly, he called RaPalla to follow him.

At Tselane's hut they found practically the whole village gathered. Everybody was talking excitedly but as soon as they saw the Chief an uncomfortable silence fell on them and they made way for him to reach the door.

MaKhama and her husband were still wailing loudly over their loss. Their bright future, the wonderful happiness which had been within their grasp, had been shattered; to them the end of things had come.

"Dumelang." Majara greeted his people in general.

"Dumela, Morena." With trembling voices the two old people saluted their Chief and got up to stand in front of him.

"Didn't you hear anything in the night?"

"We heard nothing."

"Did you see a stranger in the village?"

"No stranger slept here."

"Did Tselane go visiting last night?"

"Tselane was not the kind who walked at night," MaKhama said proudly. Her daughter-in-law was above reproach. She never walked alone and never at night.

Majara was quiet for some time. "Is her blanket still here and has nothing been taken from her hut?"

So overcome were her parents by their grief that they had not looked at these things. "We do not know."

"Let us make sure. We have to find Tselane."

The way in which he said this placed the icy hand of fear on RaPalla's heart. Would there be escape?

The old people entered the hut first and the Chief and RaPalla followed them. Her parents were stunned. Her pail of food, her blanket, her clothes and money were gone. It was only too obvious that she had known what she was doing. She had prepared and had not told them!

The Chief uttered a loud curse. He was sure now that Tselane had been warned. His face looked cruel and angry, and startled the old parents even more. Majara was sure that Tselane was hiding somewhere but there was nowhere she could hide that he would not find her. He looked searchingly at RaPalla whose very soul shook within him.

"Come."

The Chief took no more notice of MaKhama and her husband but roughly commanded RaPalla to follow him. Once outside the hut and away from the other people he stopped.

"Tell the other five to come to Metlae's hut. Today the miserable spider will have to prove to me that he knows what he is doing. If he cannot smell out the one who has done this, he will die."

RaPalla put his hands behind his back so that the Chief could not see how he was shaking. Then he had been correct. Tselane would have been the victim; they were waiting to take her.

But what if the things he had learned from the white people, that the witch doctor had no power of divining things, were not true, and Metlae would be able to tell the Chief what he had done? Would it not be safer to run to the Moruti and ask for his help? But it was too late now, he would have to wait for his fate to overtake him.

Stunned, Metlae sat in front of his hut. From the time that he had heard the news he had known that Majara would come to him to solve the riddle. His good fortune was that the Chief could not suspect him of warning Tselane; he had too much to lose—his cattle, his reputation, everything.

His great moment had gone forever. How he had bargained on

his power after the medicine had been made! Never again could the Chief disobey him. Now everything that he had planned for all his schemes was lost.

The Chief would expect him to say who had warned the woman. He knew his own limitations only too well. People might believe in his mumblings and the things he said but he alone knew on what he based his words. With closed eyes he thought of the various ways out but none seemed acceptable.

"Metlae!" The Chief spoke loudly and angrily.

The old man jumped up and nearly pushed his face into the Chief's in his eagerness to attend.

"You miserable liar, child of a spider!"

Metlae stood back. The Chief had lost control of himself. Metlae tried to be dignified but his dignity was not enough to shield him from the anger which flamed in Majara's eyes. The Chief seized the old man by his monkey-tail necklace and roughly pushed him into the hut.

"Your bones told you many things but not this. Why didn't they tell you that Tselane would get away?"

Majara was shouting. He pulled on the necklace until Metlae's eyes started from their sockets and the fear of death shone in them.

Metlae tried to say something but fear made his tongue unwilling.

"Speak!"

Majara flung Metlae from him so that he fell on his sleeping mats. He tried to get up again. First crouching and then standing he pulled himself to his full height and spoke with a tone which for the moment had the power to bring Majara to his senses.

"The day will come when the young Chief will remember this. No man, be he chief, can do this to a medicine man. The bones do not forget. They will not be laughed at."

"They will surely be laughed at if you cannot find the man to-day who has done this thing. She must be hiding somewhere. You must tell me who it was that told her to go away."

"The people have been whispering a great deal. Perhaps she heard these stories and was frightened and went away where she could not be found."

Metlae was thinking quickly. It would be no easy matter to accuse one of the six men when they arrived. If he tried to stall and say that he would know on the morrow there was less hope for him. A knife made no sound in the night and an old man's heart was easy to reach under his meager flesh. He must think of a way out immediately. There was no time to be lost.

RaPalla with the other five arrived. On the previous day they had felt themselves heroes, men who held life and death in their hands. As they filed in now they were scared; one of them would be smelled out by the doctor, innocent or not. They eyed each other with suspicion. Distrust filled every corner of the hut. Metlae had laid some green sticks on the fire, for smoke was a good thing to hide the feelings that burned in the eyes.

Majara was standing. He commanded the others to sit down in a semicircle around Metlae. RaPalla found it hard to control himself. He looked nobody in the face. He kept to the background. He was Khama's cousin, and he had asked many questions on the previous day. Metlae would not hesitate to point to him. His heart was beating suffocatingly. Surely they must see the fright on his face. They all watched Metlae. He was shaking his dirty bag of bones with his eyes closed and mumbling all the time. With a loud "Hau!" he strewed the bones out in front of him. Every man watched the lie of the bones as if he could understand what was happening. Anxiously they waited for Metlae to speak.

"The one who warned her wears a dress."

So unexpected were these words that the men involuntarily looked up at Majara. Relief was in their eyes. RaPalla felt the smile tugging at his mouth but forced himself to look serious.

"Metlae, are these the mumblings of a man who had lost his senses? Does a mad dog know more than my medicine man?"

Metlae did not answer but scooped up his bones again. His wily mind had foreseen in a split second how he could save himself and the six young men sitting there in front of him. One must be guilty, of that he was sure, but he dared not point out the wrong one.

Like a person possessed, like the mad dog the Chief had spoken of, he jumped up and down and snarled like an animal, crouching low over the fire and clutching his bag to his thin bosom before he ripped the side and flung the bones in all directions.

He had his eyes closed while the men were looking at him, but once the bones were on the ground he knew that they would all be looking at the lie which could mean death to one of them, and in that moment he quickly opened his eyes and as quickly closed them again.

He had only one wildcat's claw in his bag and that was lying at the Chief's feet. If he could turn things so that it would seem that the Chief were responsible, he would be saved. Without opening his eyes and making the men believe that he had never looked at the bones, he mumbled: "The person at whose feet the wildcat's claw is lying is responsible."

Wildly each man searched for the claw. There was consternation when they saw where the claw had fallen. Majara jumped forward, crazy with anger.

"Imbecile, the claw is lying. Why would I do this thing?" He stretched out his hands as if to strangle Metlae but the clever old man bent low over his bones.

"Put the claw apart. I must throw again and ask him why he said this mad thing."

He threw the bones, then sat like a man in a trance. Time seemed to be standing still, and only fear and suspense breathed in the hut where the thick smoke caused their eyes to smart.

"The bones say that the Chief has spoken in his sleep."

Metlae whispered these words but dared not look up. Majara was silent. They had seen how he had stiffened.

From the time that he was a small child he had spoken in his sleep and more than once Molili had teased him with things which he was supposed to have said. Metlae knew of this weakness and his clever mind had made use of the only loophole that was left to save him from certain death.

He was thinking of saving himself but not of the consequences his words would have for Molili, the Chief's wife.

There was a deathly quiet in the circle round him. Anxious faces were turned towards the Chief, waiting for his next words. They were careful not to show the relief and happiness they felt at those words of the witch doctor.

"Liar! Do you dare say that I am responsible? Take your stinking bones and throw them again."

Metlae took the bones and muttering incoherently he threw them at his own feet.

"She is hiding; the place is far from here. It will be a long time before we see her again."

"But where? Where is she hiding?"

Majara's impatience brought fear to the men watching him and his medicine man, and panic into RaPalla's heart. Metlae scratched among the bones, took two or three away and then contemplated them for a long time.

"They say that the Chief will do well not to look for this woman. Medicine from a person who got away has no power. We shall have to choose someone else. The bones also say that the matter must rest until the warm weather comes again after the snow has been on the mountains."

"You talk like that because you are afraid. When the warm weather comes again I want my son in my hut. See that you find a new victim."

Majara did not wait for Metlae to speak. He left them abruptly without waiting for them to salute him. In him thoughts were rushing like the water down the mountain after heavy rains.

He tried fighting the cruel, hard feelings against his wife which were slowly taking possession of him. How dared she do this thing? The whip was the only thing that was good enough for a woman who could listen to her husband's talking in his sleep and use his words against him.

Frustration, disappointment, a feeling of failure and of losing face, made him eager to get to his hut to find out the truth.

The warnings of his parents came back to him. Was this the work of his father's medicine? Had his father's witch doctor thrown his bones or had Sobeti's father done this? He'd break the person who was responsible and in the end he'd still get Tselane in spite of Metlae's words that the diretlo from a victim who had once escaped was no good. He wanted Tselane! For weeks his dreams had been filled by her form; his nights were full of thoughts of her passion and now everything was flat.

At his hut there was quiet. The pots were singing on the fire but there was no sign of his wife.

"Molili!" he shouted her name.

She did not answer. He entered the hut and when his eyes became accustomed to the dim light he saw her on the sleeping mats still sobbing in her sorrow.

To Molili it was quite clear that the men had taken Tselane in the night for diretlo. Majara's behavior during the past week, his uneasiness during the night, all the talk in the village for weeks—everything pointed to the fact that a murder had been done while they were sleeping.

Her heart felt heavy with her sorrow for Tselane. She had been her friend from childhood, her cousin, the best woman one could hope to find. How could her husband think of bringing happiness to their hut by taking Tselane?

Majara stepped nearer to her. Loathing, fear and suspicion made her shrink into the farthest corner away from him. Panic stood in her eyes when he came nearer. She winced and Majara saw how she tried to get away from him. A cruel light came into his eyes.

"A woman must not try to get away from the man she has wronged."

Molili looked up quickly. What was he speaking of?

"Why do you cry when you know what you have done?"

He seized her by her shoulders and roughly pulled her to her feet so that she stood in front of him. She did not answer. She was at a loss to understand him.

He slapped her across her cheek with his flat hand. "Answer me. Why did you do it?"

"Why did I do what?"

"Why did you tell her to go away? Where is she? Tell me that!"

Majara was slowly losing control of himself and Molili feared the lot that was awaiting her. She started crying again. He shook her violently.

"Metlae said that I talked in my sleep and that the person who warned her wears a dress."

"What could your talking in your sleep have to do with Tselane? You often talk in your sleep but nobody would be able to understand what you are saying."

"But you warned her."

"Warned her against what?"

Majara did not reply immediately. Even at that stage he found it difficult to utter his plans in words.

"Don't ask questions. Answer what I have asked you."

"Yesterday when we came back from the lands Tselane still spoke of the things she was going to do today. How could I know why she went away from her hut? You know that I did not see her again after we came back from the fields."

Molili started sobbing again and Majara knew her well enough to realize that she was speaking the truth when she said that she did not know why Tselane had gone away. He roughly pushed her from him and sat down on the sleeping mats.

"Don't worry, I'll find her."

Molili fell on her knees beside her husband.

"Majara, please leave her, let her be. This terrible thing you could not do. The Moruti—"

"Don't talk like the wind that rushes through the mealies. I know what I am doing. The whole of Basutoland must be laughing at me because I cannot bring a son to follow me and my medicine man is a fool who cannot make medicine that is strong enough."

It was the first time that he had acknowledged to her that he was going to make his own medicine and find his own diretlo.

"You will be hanged," she said.

"And who would know about my comings and goings if the wife I married does not tell them?"

Molili winced. He still did not believe her that she had nothing to do with Tselane's flight. "Majara—"

He did not let her finish what she wanted to say but pushed her away from him.

"Go and cook the food; I am hungry."

Molili got up and went out. Even if Tselane had died her grief could not have been more poignant. Of one thing she was sure: Tselane had not been taken. If God was good she had probably got away to her mother's kraal or to other relatives in a kraal far from theirs. But where would she be? What agony she must have suffered fleeing in the night from her own people, alone and afraid?

Molili wiped the tears from her eyes and stirred the mealie meal into the water.

Majara sat in his hut where he could see her small figure bending over the pots. His wild, mad mood was passing. He was sure now that his wife was innocent. Who then had warned Tselane? Had she listened to the people's talk and taken fright?

Perhaps it was a good thing that she had escaped. If his wife cried like that at the thought of his medicine she would only bring a monstrosity into the world and no normal child. Perhaps the old people were wise when they said that diretlo must be taken from a kraal far from their own.

He was determined to make his own medicine. He'd not go against tradition again. Metlae must be careful this time. The medicine man must choose well because he would not suffer disappointment again.

Molili brought their plates and the pot with the porridge into the hut. She went to her usual place on the left-hand side of the hearth and dished out the food. Her cheek was still smarting and she kept her eyes averted. Majara had every right to slap her but it was the first time since they had been married that he had made use of this right. She toyed with the food but could not eat. Once or twice she felt her husband looking at her but she did not lift her eyes.

"Why don't you eat?"

"I am not hungry."

They were quiet for some time.

"You need not go to the lands today." In a sudden rush of remorse for his cruelty he meant to be kind. Molili looked up quickly. She sensed the change and was eager to make up with her husband.

"We start on a new land today."

"I don't think that many women will be going to the lands."

A silence entered the hut that made the air heavy to breathe. Molili struggled with her decision to beseech her husband not to go through with his plans and Majara was trying to find words with which to make good the injustice he had done his wife. He loved her. It was only in a moment of madness that he had forgotten himself and had injured her.

Molili lacked the courage to express her thoughts and when they had finished eating, Majara lifted the pot for her. To his mind that was sign enough that he was not as angry as he had been and that he still loved her. Molili recognized the gesture and smiled faintly. She went to the outside cooking place but her heart was still heavy in her.

9

TSELANE moved quickly through the village, her footsteps light upon the ground. All around she heard the sounds the people made in their sleep, yet in her terror she felt they were all awake, watching her, ready to take her prisoner at the last moment. She scarcely breathed, so great was her fear, and her eyes, dazed and stunned, stared blindly straight ahead into the dark night. As she passed the last hut, she trembled with a sudden chill, then broke into a fast run.

She ran as long as she could, until the heaviness of the child in her sent sharp pains across her back. She stopped and leaned against a tree to rest, and the cold night air bit deep into her lungs with each gasp. She did not want to pause too long, and after a few moments she picked up her pail of porridge and the bundle of clothes and hurried away.

She had the feeling of eyes upon her back. Often she glanced nervously over her shoulder to be sure she was alone. The shrill cries of night birds startled her and the call of owls brought sweat to her neck. She could not think clearly, she could not reason, yet she knew instinctively that if the others pursued her they would expect her to follow the footpath. Impulsively she turned off into the bush, into the thick darkness where the tall growth shut out the stars.

She tripped and fell and thorns of bushes cut into her face. She scrambled to her feet and rushed onward, using the back of her hands to brush away the blood that trickled down her cheeks. She began to cry, soft whimpering sobs catching in her throat and stinging tears clouding her eyes.

On and on she went, tripping, falling, and there were moments when she had only enough strength to crawl. Fat vines brushed against her; she knew that any of them might have been a snake but she was unable to feel a fear of them. Once she heard a soft cough nearby: a night animal. She froze in her steps, held her breath and waited, and when she heard no more she resumed her rush through the veld.

She wanted desperately to rest, but the only rest she permitted herself was when she fell. She would roll on her back and lie there briefly, staring at a patch of sky, and when she was able again to bear her pains and her aches she struggled to her feet and went on.

At times she knew she was lost. Only her instincts guided her through the bush towards the mission, miles away, where RaPalla had promised her she would be safe. The thought of safety was enough to goad her forward at moments when she felt she could not take another step.

The night was purple with dawn when Tselane saw the clearing just ahead. She quickened her pace towards the cluster of houses which looked so unreal in the morning haze. There was no one in sight. Tselane opened her mouth to cry out, but all the strength was gone from her. Her mouth filled with the sickening taste of vomit. She took one more step, then felt herself falling.

She was next aware of the warm sun upon her, and when she opened her eyes she saw standing over her three white children. Kneeling beside her was a white woman. In a language she did not understand she heard the woman say the words: "Quick, Jean-Pierre, call Papa."

Then the woman loosened Tselane's blanket and the black shawl around her waist. Tselane tried to sit up, but the woman said in Sotho: "No. Wait until my husband comes; we'll help you. Have you come far?"

"Yes, Jefreu," Tselane said.

"Alone?"

The word reminded Tselane of her aloneness and she buried her face in her blanket and began to weep uncontrollably. She felt the white woman's hand upon her, gentle, comforting. When she tried again to sit up, the woman helped her. Tselane saw a man coming from the big house and she recognized him as the missionary who had been to her village several times. He was carrying a glass of water, which he handed her without speaking, and she drank eagerly.

Then Pierre le Brun asked: "Do you know who I am?"

She said: "Yes, Moneri."

"And what is your name?"

"Tselane."

"Tselane, will you be able to walk if we help you?"

"Yes, Moneri."

To his wife the missionary said in French: "Let's take her to the rondawel, Simone. After she has had some rest, she can tell us what has happened."

They took her to the small hut which stood near the big house. The one room was sparely furnished: a bed with mattress, sheets and blankets, a small table, an upright chair, and on the wall a picture of Rouen. They helped Tselane to sit on the bed, then Simone le Brun asked: "Have you eaten anything this morning?"

"No, Jefreu."

"Then I'll fetch something for you."

Simone left the rondawel and soon returned with some porridge which had remained over from breakfast. Tselane took the plate and started to eat in the slow manner which was considered polite by the Basotho. Pierre le Brun took the children and left. Simone went to sit on the chair to remain with Tselane but did not talk to her. Between spoonfuls of porridge Tselane looked at Simone with eyes that revealed nothing. At last she put down the spoon.

"Have you had enough?" Simone asked.

"Yes, Jefreu. I shall rest now. I am so tired."

"Good. Let me fix the blankets for you."

"It is all right. I shall lie on the floor."

"The floor is cold and it will be bad for your baby."

Tselane looked at the bed. She had never before in her life slept on a bed. Her mother had a bed which Khama had sent from Worcester after their wedding and once when she had visited her mother she had sat on the bed. But to sleep on it—she was fearful of soiling the neat white sheets.

Simone said: "Come, Tselane; it will be better for your child."

Tselane stood by while Simone prepared the bed, then, reluctantly and with discomfort, she got into it, stiffly and awkwardly, avoiding Simone's eyes. But when it seemed that Simone was about to leave, Tselane sat up and looked at her. Simone said: "I shall stay with you; don't be afraid. If I have to go away I shall lock the door on the outside. Nobody will get in."

Tselane lay back again and Simone sat on the chair at her bedside. She could see that Tselane was fighting hard against the sleep which weighed on her eyes but at last exhaustion forced her to surrender the struggle and soon she was fast asleep. Simone got up quietly and locked the door behind her. She went to the big house and found her husband in his study, and she sat down with him.

Pierre le Brun asked: "Do you think she will be all right?"

"It is hard to say. Have you any idea what could have brought her to us?"

"Not the slightest," Pierre said, shaking his head. "I have never seen her before, and she definitely does not belong to our church."

Simone frowned. "Then her fear must have been terrible to bring her here alone and in her condition."

"She will probably talk when she has had time to relax."

"What could it be? Do you think that her husband mistreated her and that she ran away from him?"

"My dear," said Pierre, "you know that no Mosotho woman would ever do that. There must be some other reason."

Simone got up and went to a window and looked out at her garden. She said: "In all our years among these people nothing like this has happened. We must help her, Pierre, but I wonder how we will know that we are doing the right thing?"

"We must pray for wisdom," Pierre said simply. "Perhaps it is not as bad as we fear."

After noon, Simone le Brun went to the rondawel to see whether Tselane was still sleeping and found her sitting on the floor against the wall.

Simone asked: "Do you feel better now?"

"Yes, Jefreu," said Tselane. "Is the Moneri here?"

"Yes. Why?"

"I would like to tell Moneri why I have come."

"I'll call him." Simone hurried into the yard to get Pierre. When the two came back into the rondawel, Tselane was sitting with her face buried in her blanket, and when she looked up at them her eyes were damp with tears.

"Did you want to speak to me, Tselane?" Pierre asked.

"Yes, Moneri," she said. "My heart is like stone and I have a great fear."

"Do not be afraid here; nothing will happen to you."

There was a silence before Tselane said abruptly: "Our Chief has no medicine. He wants to make medicine."

She said the words quickly, eager to get the bitter taste of them from her mouth. Pierre le Brun closed his eyes in quiet pain. This he had not expected; this he had feared during his first years as a missionary; when there had been no sign of it for a long time he thought perhaps his presence and his instructions to the people had ended the custom of ritual murder, but now he knew he was wrong.

Tselane watched him anxiously, new terror in her as she saw him pale. What was he thinking? Was he afraid too? Would he refuse to help her now?

Pierre asked: "Are you from the village of Majara?"

"Yes, Moneri."

Pain made small lines on Pierre's face. He remembered the young chief well, and especially his wife Molili. How was it possible that people who had listened to his sermons, who had heard of Jesus and who had been baptized could fall back on their old pagan customs? Molili was a Christian. Was it possible that she could have known about the diretlo and still have consented to let something like that happen to a woman of her own village?

He asked: "For what did Majara want the medicine?"

"My cousin Molili cannot have children," Tselane explained. "The Chief must have a son and he wanted the medicine for her."

"Did Molili know?"

"I do not think she knew everything."

"And you were the one chosen to provide the medicine?"

"Yes, Moneri."

"Who told you?"

Tselane looked away, her face suddenly glum. Pierre knew the expression, and he knew he would never be able to bring her to tell him. He also knew now that, under the circumstances, he could not keep Tselane at the mission. Long ago he had learned that once a diretlo victim had been chosen the people involved in the murder would not stop until their plan had been fulfilled. Surely sooner or later the village would learn that Tselane was at the mission; the Chief would send men to get her, and then there could be serious trouble that could completely disrupt the mission work.

Pierre asked: "Where is your husband?"

"In Worcester. He works in the factories of the white people."

"Did he go to school?"

"No, Moneri, he cannot read or write."

"Does he sometimes write to you through other people?"

"Only when he sends the money."

"When last did you hear from him?"

"He sends his money every month. I buy cattle for him, but I have not bought any for three months."

"Do you have the money with you now?"

"Yes, Moneri."

Pierre felt relieved. Obviously there was only one course of action he could suggest to Tselane, but he did not have enough money to help her carry it out. But she had money; he had now only to talk her into it. He asked: "Would you like to go to your husband?"

Tselane stared at him, astonished. How could the white man ask her something like that? How could she leave the mountains and go to the city of white people? Her first child must be born in her mother's hut and nowhere else. Though she feared going to her mother's kraal because Chief Majara might find her there, it had not occurred to her to go anywhere else. Did the Moneri not know, after all his years among her people, that this was the custom?

Tselane turned her face away and did not answer Pierre. He said: "If you go to your husband he could look after you. You cannot go back to your village and you cannot stay here."

A long silence, then Tselane said: "But I haven't got a horse. How many days on horseback would it be?"

"It is too far to go on horseback," said Pierre. "Worcester is many hundreds of miles from Basutoland. I shall go with you to Mashai where you will get the airplane to Maseru, and from there you travel by train. In less than one week you will be with your husband."

Hau, it could not be true; she could never travel like that. Khama had told her about the train, though she had never seen that thing. But the airplane. To fly like a bird. How often, seeing planes overhead, she had held her breath expecting the thing to fall. The mine boys told her stories of how it was much nicer to fly than to travel by train and that it was nothing. But that could not be true. She was not afraid for herself, but for her child. How could he fly when he had not even seen the light of day? No woman of her people had ever done such a thing. No. It was impossible. She could never do it.

Tselane pulled her blanket over her face and started to cry. Simone patted her on the back to comfort her and said to her husband in French: "Don't torture her any more. I think she has suffered as much as she can stand."

"But it is the only solution," he said. "If she goes back to her people her fear may lead to anything, and if they should murder her we would have that on our consciences for the rest of our lives. She is all right; she is merely frightened by the thought of going away from the mountains."

"That may be so," said Simone, "but why can't she stay here until her child is born and then her husband can come and fetch her?"

"And if the Chief comes and demands her? Anything might happen then. Once a diretlo victim is chosen he seldom gets away."

"But Tselane did get away," Simone insisted. "We must protect her."

"This thing has not been planned in one day," Pierre said. "For months they have been preparing for this, and what do you think will happen if they should find out that we are hiding her?"

"That cannot do anything to us."

"Are you sure of that? Let us give her time to make up her own mind." To Tselane he said: "We are going to eat now. Think about what I have said. There is a plane every second day and I shall ask the pilot to see that you get safely on the train."

Still sobbing, Tselane did not answer. Pierre and Simone went out and left her alone.

The rondawel suddenly seemed much larger, and filled with loneliness. On cold winter nights when Tselane was still a small child she had had the same loneliness which now stole over her. When snow was falling and there was no sound she had felt cut off from everyone, completely alone. Then she would long for her mother's warmth and the stuffy closeness of the hut where her parents slept. If only her parents, or Khama's parents, could be with her now.

Her child stirred inside her and his movement made her think of Khama. Should she go to him? How would it be in the places of the white people where nobody would speak to her and where she would be alone with the strangers around her all day, where people slept on beds and had no fires in the middle of the room to make the hut friendly, where things were cold and white and nobody went out to work on the lands? Yet Khama seemed happy there, and with Khama she would have peace and safety. When he knew why she had left the mountains he would understand and be good to her. And she must leave the mountains: they had been the only world she knew, and now they held death for her. Yes. It would be best. Go to Khama.

There was a knock on the door and a servant entered with her food. He said: "Peace, sister, are you alive?"

"I am alive."

He placed the food on the floor in front of Tselane and left without speaking further. Tselane pulled the plate to her and began eating, her mind deep on her decision to go to Khama.

10

LONG after midnight Tselane still lay awake, considering all that had happened to her. In just a few hours her life had been totally changed. At this hour the night before she was stumbling through the veld, and now she lay quietly between sheets in a soft bed, and in the morning the missionary would take her to the plane. In a few days she would be with Khama. How stunned he would be to see her, and yet how pleased. She would have much to tell him, for in just one day she had done many new things. In midafternoon, Pierre and Simone had returned to the rondawel to ask Tselane what she had decided to do.

"I shall go to my husband," she said, "if Moneri will speak to the man of the big bird."

Pierre seemed relieved, but Simone still wore a worried frown. She said: "I'm sure you don't want to sit here all day, Tselane. If you like, come with me to the kitchen; I have to prepare the evening meal."

It was the first time Tselane had ever entered a white man's house.

The kitchen was large, with tables and chairs and cupboards and an iron stove that burned wood and had pipes to carry the smoke outside. On a table in a corner was a five-gallon container of water with a spigot, and Tselane was fascinated by the way Simone drew water merely by turning the handle. Two Mosotho girls helped Simone; Tselane sat quietly in a corner and watched everything. She was impressed by the familiarity the girls displayed with the kitchen and towards Simone, and she wondered if one day she would be able to act that way towards the white women she would meet in Worcester.

At one point Pierre looked into the kitchen. Simone said in French: "I don't think Tselane should eat with the others. They may question her, and if they find out about the diretlo there may be a problem."

"As you wish," Pierre said, then to Tselane: "Would you like to have your meal here in the kitchen tonight?"

"Yes, Moneri."

"Good. Then you can join us at night prayers later."

Soon the Mosotho girls were carrying platters of food into another room, then left the house for their own quarters for their own meal. Simone fixed a plate for Tselane and put it on the table in front of her, arranging a knife and fork. She said: "Eat well, Tselane, for you have a long trip and need your strength."

Alone in the room, Tselane stared at the plate and at the knife and fork. Hau, this was strange food indeed, soft and juicy, and she knew she could never pick it up neatly in her fingers. She presumed, because Simone had given them to her, that she was expected to use the knife and fork but she did not know how to manipulate them. She gave the fork a try or two, but either she picked up nothing or the entire plateful. She sat still a moment, listening, until she was content that the others were far enough away not to see her, and then she began to eat with her fingers, quickly, frightened, gulping down the food to get rid of it before anyone could return. She dried her hands secretively on the underside of her blanket, then sat back to wait.

In a while the women returned, Simone and the servants, to clean up after the meal. Tselane watched silently. They did the dishes, put away what food could be saved, and the servants took the rest away with them when the work was done. Simone said to them: "Prayers in ten minutes." They said: "Yes, Jefreu."

"Now," Simone said to Tselane, "I have just time to wash the children before prayers. Will you mind sitting here alone?"

"I will be all right, Jefreu," Tselane said, and Simone left.

Tselane waited. Certain objects in the kitchen caught her eyes, and she was curious to examine them closer but she felt she had better remain where she sat; maybe the Jefreu would not like to have people snooping around her house. Shortly Tselane heard the voices of the mission servants as they gathered at the kitchen door, waiting to be brought in for prayers. Phrases Tselane caught held no references to her. The talk was light, vague, and there was laughter and the giggles of young girls.

Then Simone returned and opened the kitchen door. "Come in now," she said, and to Tselane: "Come along, my dear."

They went through the house, passed three rooms, then entered the missionary's study. Pierre was standing with his children. He waited until everyone was in the room and quiet, and then he began to read from a thick black book. Tselane did not understand everything he said, but his voice was sad and the words he said were sad too, and Tselane wondered why anyone who seemed as good a person as the Moneri should be so sober about his religion. But she knew she would never be able to understand the many odd things white people did, and she listened, her eyes downward, as the others were doing. Then Pierre finished reading and lowered himself to the floor; all the others likewise knelt. Pierre closed his eyes and began to talk in a soft, husky voice, almost unintelligible to Tselane. She was startled to hear her name, as he said: "We pray thee, O Father, to go with our sister Tselane and to guard her from evil. Keep thy hand of protection over her."

Hau, they were praying for her to the Christian god. What should she do now? She knew nothing of this god, except the few things Molili had said, and to these she had not listened with much attention. She did remember that the Christian god was supposed to love everyone and help them in their troubles. But he had not given Molili a baby when she wanted one; why should he now help Tselane, who had not committed herself to him? Surely the Moneri knew this; maybe this part of the white man's religion Molili had not explained. Perhaps Khama would be able to explain.

When the prayers ended, everyone got to his feet, nodded to the missionary, and left the room in silence. Simone said: "Pierre, start the children off to bed. I will take Tselane to the rondawel."

They walked across the garden to the small hut. Simone went in first and lighted the candle. "Put that out before you get into bed," she said. "And have a good sleep."

"Yes, Jefreu."

"God bless you."

Simone went out, locked the door, and Tselane heard her footsteps soften away. She stood for a moment in the flickering light, could not think of anything to do, snuffed out the candle and went to the bed.

Falling asleep, she thought: yes, there will be many things to tell Khama.

When the first cock crowed, Simone knocked on the rondawel door, then opened it. "Tselane, time to get up," she said. "Come to the kitchen when you are ready."

Tselane got up hurriedly. She had not undressed the night before and now she quickly tied the black shawl around her waist and then pinned her blanket into position. She tidied the bed and took her bundle and the pail for her food. She saw Pierre saddling two horses and found Simone in the kitchen dishing up warm porridge.

Simone said: "You must eat well. It will be some time before you can eat again. I shall fill your pail for you."

Pierre came in rubbing his hands. "Chilly this morning. Coffee ready?"

He drank a cup of warm coffee and then went into his study to fetch some money in case the girl did not have enough for her air fare as well as the train ticket. When he came back Tselane was waiting for him. Simone went with them to where the horses were stamping the ground and snorting in the cold morning air. Pierre brought Tselane's horse to the kitchen step to make it easier for her to mount. Simone held the horse's head while Pierre assisted Tselane and handed up her bundle.

Then Simone came round when Tselane was seated to say farewell. Just for a second she had the awful feeling again as if they were sending the woman out to meet an unexpected danger. She pressed Tselane's hand.

"God bless you, Tselane, I shall pray for you. Go well, my girl."

"Stay well, Jefreu."

Simone watched them riding away into the early mistiness of breaking day. Most Sotho women were good riders and Tselane was no exception. She sat well and rode well. Before they disappeared Pierre turned round and waved to his wife. Simone went into the house but the picture of Pierre and the Mosotho woman riding away into the mist stayed with her. Two lonely figures in the mountain vastness—the one fleeing from a danger that meant certain death and the other soon to return.

The surefooted ponies picked their way confidently along the footpath that led to Mashai: four hours' traveling before they could arrive there but they must arrive before the plane because the pilot did not know about her and might leave before they arrived.

Pierre watched Tselane and saw how she tried to pierce the half-light of dawn, as if expecting to meet other riders. To take her mind off her fear, Pierre started talking to her.

"Do you also believe in the power of medicine, Tselane?" he asked.

She remained quiet. What was the use of telling the white man about the things that the medicine of their witch doctor could do? He did not believe and never would. The white people were clever but that was one thing which they would never understand.

Pierre waited but when she did not answer he continued: "I cannot understand how you people can believe that a few drops of blood from a person, who is as sinful as we all are, could have the power to do miracles. Jesus gave all His blood so that we may live, and yet people can't seem to grasp that." Pierre realized that the woman probably did not understand what he was saying. But rather than trying to convince her, he was actually looking for words with which to make the Chief see light when he went to speak to him.

After a time Pierre became quiet too. The snorting of the horses and the sound of their hoofs on the earth were the only sounds that disturbed the mountain stillness. Pierre was riding in front and Tselane immediately behind him.

Pierre pulled his horse in. "Whoa, Pétain." Then: "We are stopping here for a while. I want to rub the horses down."

There was a big stone near the path and he helped Tselane to dismount there. Pierre took the saddle off his horse and Tselane immediately did the same. He took brushes from his saddlebag and started brushing the horses down.

"Why do you do that, Moneri?" Tselane asked.

"When I go for a long ride, I always brush them down every hour. At the end of the ride they are still fresh and not so tired."

"You must tell the people. They love their horses too."

"Will they listen, Tselane? I tell them many things and they turn the other way."

"But to this they will listen."

"And when I speak to them about medicine?"

"We cannot help that, Moneri. Our ancestors have taught us about medicine and the good things it can do for us. They knew; they heard from their fathers many, many years ago."

"But how did they explain it? Where does the medicine get the power to do miracles?"

"The white doctor also gives medicine that heals."

"But that—" Pierre broke off suddenly. Two horsemen came round the bend and Tselane jumped up, ready for flight.

"Peace, men. Are you alive?" he greeted them.

"Peace, Moneri. We are alive. We are on our way to Mashai."

"From where do you come?"

"The village of RaKhoali. We go to the mines."

"Do you take the airplane?"

"We fly today."

"Go well, men."

"Stay well, Moneri." They had only looked at Tselane once but did not ask any questions. She did not greet them but sat with her face sunken in the folds of her blanket.

When the horses were brushed they mounted. In the east, light was beginning to show red against the mountain and far down in the valley the first sounds of day were in the air. The mists were fleeing before the light of day and mountaintops became clear and villages could be seen on the slopes. How lovely the country was! Pierre looked back along the path they had come. Every time he had to travel in the early morning he marveled anew at the beauty of this wild untouched roughness—barbaric grandeur more magnificently beautiful than anything he had seen anywhere.

As so many times before, he looked at the toy villages with their little conical huts and thought about the lives of the people who lived there. Their days were long hours of enjoyment of the sun and the goodness of the earth; they lived free from the cares and the worries which civilization brought and yet the struggle to bring this civilization to them occupied the thoughts of men. Would they be happier? Would they thank those who forced them into a different way of living which perhaps offered them less than the old and from which they would find it hard to turn once they had become used to it? Pierre remembered the words of one of their old sayings: "If a man does away with his way of living as his fathers have taught him and throws away his good customs, he had better first make sure that he had something better to replace them."

So deep in thought was Pierre that he looked up surprised when Tselane spoke to him.

"I see the big bird," she said. "It must have slept at Mashai."

Pierre looked ahead and saw the plane on the landing strip, with several people waiting for the flight. What was he to do if they had already paid their fares and there was not a seat to be had? They broke into a canter and soon came to the plane.

Pierre was greeted from all sides. "Dumela, Moneri."

Tselane stayed with the horses and scarcely looked up. Fear as she had known when she had stepped out of her hut to flee into the darkness of the night again filled her.

Pierre walked to Dick Stone, the pilot, who was speaking to the two men they had met on the mountain. "Good morning, Mr. Stone."

"Good morning, Padre." Stone turned briskly back to the two men as if there was not a second to be wasted. Pierre waited until Stone had counted the money and had given the men their tickets before he spoke.

"I must ask you to do me a great favor," Pierre said.

Stone did not answer but looked at Pierre, who said: "I have brought a woman from the mountain who must go to Maseru today."

"I am sorry, Padre. She'll have to wait. I am loaded and cannot take another passenger."

"But this is urgent; she has to get away."

"These men have all paid their fares. How am I going to ask one of them to stand down? I am in a hurry, if you'll excuse me."

The pilot turned and walked towards the front of the plane. He looked across and saw Tselane standing with the horses. His first thought was that the missionary must be crazy to ask him to take a woman in that condition on a flight to Maseru.

Pierre followed him. "If I speak to the men and one is willing to stay, will you take her?"

"Under no circumstances. I am not allowed to take women in her condition on board."

"But this is an exceptional case."

"It cannot be so exceptional; I am sorry," Stone said curtly. "All right, men, come on." The passengers immediately filed up to the steps.

Pierre became desperate. "This woman has been chosen for ritual murder."

The pilot did not listen. He was taking the little slips of paper, tearing them in half and giving one half to the passenger and putting the other carefully in a notebook.

Pierre said: "This is your responsibility as well as mine. If this woman is murdered she will be on your conscience because she can only be saved if you will take her."

"I told you, Padre, I cannot take the woman."

"Mr. Stone, I must beseech you. It is imperative that she goes today."

Stone did not answer.

"Could I speak to the men?"

"I cannot take a pregnant woman."

"I shall take all responsibility with your company for whatever happens on the way."

"Padre, please, I have told you I dare not take her."

"But let me speak to the men."

"All right, go ahead. See for yourself that nobody will give up his seat." Stone was red with impatience. These bloody missionaries! They thought they had power over everything.

Pierre started speaking quickly in Sotho to the men. They listened quietly but as soon as he had spoken a babble of protests broke out.

"I must get to my work."

"I am already late and will lose my job."

"I came three days ago, I cannot stay."

Each one had a good reason why he could not stay. Pierre watched them carefully and listened to their protests. One young man was standing a little apart and he was the only one who remained quiet.

"Where are you going to?" Pierre asked him.

"Maseru."

"To work?"

"No, but I have sold my only cow so that I can fly in the big bird." His lips trembled and tears stood in his eyes: the other men were all older than he was and they would make him stay. He had seen his only cow being led away by the man who had paid him the money and his heart had felt like breaking but he wanted to do something that no one else in their village could do. He wanted to fly and prove to them that he was a man. Five days he had walked over the mountains and slept in the cold to come to Mashai. He was the envy of every young man in his village. From the time that the first airplane had come over their village he had dreamed of going to Maseru and now it seemed that they were going to leave him behind.

Pierre asked: "If I give you the price of your cow, will you let the sister go?"

The young man hesitated. It would mean another two days to wait but then he could buy his cow back and have the flight as well. Pierre saw his hesitation and took the money out of his pocket.

"How much did you get for the cow?"

The pilot cut in: "You can discuss that when we are gone. I am in a hurry."

"Does that mean that you will take her?" Pierre asked.

"I'll take her but I wash my hands of her."

"Will you let her sleep with your servants tonight and see that she gets on to the train tomorrow?"

What next? Stone wanted to refuse the request but there was no time left to argue. He was already a few minutes late and black clouds were rolling in from the east.

"All right, Padre, all right, only tell her to hurry."

"Come, Tselane," Pierre called. "You will go to Maseru and Mr. Stone has promised to see that you get safely on the train to Bloemfontein."

Panic-stricken, Tselane could hardly get up the few steps. Pierre handed her the bundle and pail with her food when she was seated.

"Fasten your belts," Stone called from the pilot's seat.

Bewildered Tselane looked around. What did the man with the red face mean? Pierre stood on the steps and showed her how to fasten the safety belt. Tselane did as she was told but she felt uncomfortable and very frightened. One of the men they had met on the mountain sat on the seat next to her.

"Will you keep an eye on her?" Pierre asked him.

"Yes, Moneri."

"Go gently, Tselane. God will look after you and bring you safely to your husband."

"Stay well, Moneri." Tselane was trembling all over and Pierre hurriedly climbed down. Stone was getting everything ready and hardly looked at Pierre again. He was annoyed that the missionary had forced the woman on him. He clambered into his seat and got ready to start.

As soon as the engine roared Tselane buried her face in her blanket. She folded her arms over her body as if to protect her unborn child.

"Hau, my little one, don't be afraid. Soon we'll be with your father. Lie still, my little calf. We are both afraid but this thing must be."

She tried desperately to comfort herself by speaking in her mind to her child. Khama had once told her that you were only afraid of the things of the white people as long as you did not know them, but that once you had looked in their face and seen them for what they were, you were no longer afraid. Khama was so clever because it was just like that. The big bird roared, but it was nothing to sit inside him. Once she ventured to look down on the mountains and the green fields of mealies slipping by under them. She could see the villages clustered on the slopes and, as they were nearing the lowlands, the huge red dongas and the barren brown earth made her glad that she was from the mountains where things were green. Hau, she would not like to live in these barren places. The people must be poor, for where did they find water and grass for their cattle?

The plane passed near the top of a mountain and fear returned to Tselane. Hurriedly she hid her face and returned to the safety of her blanket.

When she looked up again she could see the houses of Maseru. The men started speaking excitedly and shouting above the roar of the engines. They were excited, but in Tselane's heart there was only panic. Moneri had said that the white man would see her onto the train, but would he? What if he left her there with the men?

When the plane touched down she got up stiffly with the men and clambered down. Stone called: "Wait there at the gate, girl. The missus will fetch us."

The men walked in a bunch to the native houses on the edge of the airfield. Tselane stood alone and forlorn among the petrol drums at the gate, her bundle and her pail beside her. Little children, stark naked, came from the houses to see who had arrived and greeted her with a shy "Dumela." Tselane greeted them but turned away from the men who came to pass the time of day.

Soon a woman in a big car stopped outside the gate. Dick Stone walked to the car and called out to Tselane: "Come, girl."

The white woman asked: "What made you bring a woman in that condition with you?"

"The missionary in the mountain. He cooked up a tall story that she was wanted for ritual murder and must go to her husband."

"It was a risk you took. She looks far gone to me."

"I refused, but there was no shaking him off and into the bargain we have to give her a sleeping place and see her onto the train."

"That's cheek; I am playing tennis tomorrow morning. Anna can see her to the train."

"I promised to see her right so I suppose I'll have to make sure that she gets onto the train. She can sleep in Anna's room with her. These black bastards can sleep twenty in a room, if need be."

Tselane reached the car and Dick opened the door for her. She had seen pictures of cars but had never been near one. She hesitated.

"Come on, get in," Stone said.

She heard the impatience in the man's voice and with a wildly beating heart she got into the car, muttering: "Spirits of our ancestors, save me. Spirits of our ancestors, save me."

Through the native location, down the dip and into the big street they roared. Tselane tried to make herself small in the corner of the seat. Men of her village had told her of the big buildings, of the glass windows that were bigger than her hut, of the houses built of stone where many white people lived, but the pictures they drew were nothing compared with what she now saw. Motorcars flashed past, big buses lumbered down the road, the big green "Hallelujah" bus, crammed full of natives, nearly bumped into them. People on horseback stopped at the shops and laughed and talked before they went in. Wonder filled Tselane when she saw all the things in the shop windows where the man stopped, telling his wife that he was going to the post office across the road to get their letters.

Tselane felt as bewildered as the first time that she had gone to the trader's store with her mother. There had been so many new things which she had never seen before—mirrors, cloths, brightly colored sweets in glass jars, shoes and scarves, until her mind had become too tired to absorb any new sights. The things she now saw left her as speechless and breathless as she had been on that day. She felt all tight and small inside.

Soon the white man returned and gave the letters to his wife. They talked and laughed and took no notice of Tselane. At the house the man hooted and a big fat woman came out of the house. He said: "Anna, take this woman to your room and see that she gets onto the train for Bloemfontein tomorrow."

"Yes, boss. Come, sister. Peace. Are you alive?"

Tselane could not find her voice to answer.

In the servant's room, Anna gave her a wooden box to sit on. It was a small room with a bed, two wooden boxes on top of one another to serve as a table, and another wooden box to sit on. There was a small stove on which Anna was cooking food. The room felt stuffy and warm and smelled of the food Anna was cooking.

"Put your bundle by the bed," she said. "Have you come far?"

Tselane said the name of her village, but Anna was born in

Maseru and had never been to the mountains. These people from the mountains were strange. They spoke slowly and moved slowly. She had never liked them. The women were not so bad but the men were like dumb sheep when they came into Maseru.

"I must go to work in the house. Stay here," said Anna.

Anna moved towards the door and Tselane got up to follow her. In the room next to Anna's she could hear men talking, and she was afraid. On the mountain, people told fearful stories of the men in Maseru. It was said that they had asked a woman's name and before she had time to reply they had her on the ground. They said that the men from the town were different from those in the mountains. Perhaps they would not molest her but she was afraid, afraid to be left alone in the strange room.

Anna said: "You must stay here. The missus does not want other people in the house."

"I could help you with the work."

"Have you ever been in a white man's house?"

"Only yesterday in the kitchen of the Moneri's house."

Anna laughed loudly. Hau, these ignorant people from the mountains! "These houses are different, my sister. You would not know what to do. You stay here in my room."

Tselane drew back into herself and sat down on the floor with her bundle next to her. How long would this agony go on before she got to Khama? She felt tired and strained and soon, in spite of her fear, she dozed a little.

11

TOWARDS noon Anna came back to her room. Tselane looked up eagerly, but did not speak because Anna's face looked cross and she was muttering to herself.

" 'Anna, press my dress. Anna, clean my shoes. Anna, tell Jonas to wash the car quickly. Anna, clean the bath for me and, Anna, don't cook lunch, we eat at the hotel. Anna, throw away the dead flowers. Anna. Anna.' Do they think Anna has ten hands?"

She took the pot of food off the stove and banged it onto her table of boxes, saying: "The white people are mad; you must never go and work for them. From the time that I get into the house it is 'Anna, do this, Anna, do that, Anna, come here, Anna, go there.' The missus does not lift her hand. She only makes mess and Anna must clean up."

Tselane listened to Anna's tirade and made no comment. Anna dished out some of the stew into an enamel plate and handed it to Tselane. For herself she took a big plateful and started eating.

"I have my afternoon off and I am going to the location. If you want to you can come with me," she said.

Tselane did not want to go among strangers but she was afraid to stay alone in Anna's room. "I do not know the people of the location," she said.

"We go to Maria's place. Maria is a good friend of mine; lots of people come to her. You will like Maria. We always have a good time there." Anna hitched up her heavy bosom with one hand and wiped her small pug nose with the back of the other hand. There was an expression of pleasure on her fat face. She smacked her thick lips and looked cunningly at Tselane.

"Maria is not expensive. Only three pennies for a cup. Do you like your beer sour or strong?"

"I do not drink."

"But you have money?"

"Only to pay for the train and to buy food on the way."

"Why did you leave the mountain? Is this your first child? You will be lucky if you get onto the train with your body like that. The white people do not even take their own women on a journey when they look like that."

Anna looked up surprised when Tselane dropped her spoon with a loud clatter. There was an expression of hurt and fear on Tselane's face.

Did the Moneri know about this? Did he know that the white people would make trouble and perhaps refuse to take her on the train because she was heavy with child? What would she do if she came to the train and they refused to take her? How would she get back to the mountains? She had no horse and it was too far to walk. The man of the big bird did not want to bring her to Maseru and he would never take her back now that she was there. Tselane's mind darted from one awful possibility to the other. Tears came into her eyes.

Anna became flustered when she saw the reaction her words had on the young woman. She said: "I'll go to the window to buy the ticket, don't worry. They need not see you. Just carry your bundle on your stomach and made your blanket big. They will never know. How long is it before your child will come?"

"Two months, if the old women spoke a true thing."

"Does your husband know that you are coming to him? Who told you this mad thing, to go away from your mother's hut?"

"My husband does not know and the missionary said I must go to him."

"Why?"

"Because—"

"Anna! Anna!" Anna's missus called impatiently. They had not heard the car coming back, and Anna got up hurriedly. The missus said: "Anna, I forgot to tell you that I am having friends in tonight to play bridge. You must come home early because we have to eat early. When you come back, get the things ready for baking crumpets. The Johnstons are coming and they like your crumpets."

"Yes, missus."

The car drove off and Anna slammed the door of her room, grunting: "I knew she had something else in her pail when she told me that they would eat at the hotel. Because I need not cook lunch I must come home early. They get quickly where they want to be because the car rushes for them but Anna must walk to the location and it is far. 'Anna, come early; Anna, bake crumpets.'" Anna spat the words out.

When she had spoken to her missus she had smiled and had spoken pleasantly. Tselane could not understand this. Anna hated her missus and yet she stayed there and made the missus think that she was happy to work for her.

"Why don't you work for another missus if this one is so bad?" Tselane asked.

"They are all the same. I have been here a long time now and I do what I like. My missus thinks she is the best missus in the world and that she is so good to us. You must hear her sometimes when she reads in the paper of the other people who do bad things to the black people. She talks and talks and tells everybody how there will be trouble if people do not stop behaving as they do. In winter she even makes clothes and collects money for the poor people in the location but that is only to be smart with her friends and to speak at the church when they have big meeting. You people of the mountains will never know what it is to work in the houses of the whites."

"The Moneri and his wife are not like that."

"Missionaries are paid to have white hearts. Every month we pay money for the church, why?"

Tselane only looked at Anna and waited for her to answer her own question but Anna was already busy taking off her neat green uniform and cap and putting on a brightly colored floral frock. She knelt in front of her bed and fished out a pair of low-heeled brown shoes. She slipped them on her bare feet and took the jar of vaseline from the shelf. She rubbed some of it on her face and arms until they shone. Her hair was tightly plaited against her head in neat little black worms running from her forehead to the back of her head. On top of these she pressed a small red felt hat with a black feather and put on shiny earrings and a shinier necklace. Tselane watched her with interest. Hau, these people of the town were so smart, they had such wonderful clothes just like white people. Anna took a small mirror from under her pillow and looked at herself.

"We go now."

Anna locked the door of her little room securely and they walked through the back yard and the garden to the front gate. There was nobody at home so she made use of the front gate.

Jonas was watering plants in the front garden. "Oho, Anna, going to Maria again? See that the beer does not sting and make your head a pumpkin again."

"You go to hell, Jonas. You know I don't drink."

Jonas laughed loud. "That you say every time, and every time you come home stinking of Maria's bad beer."

Anna made a sound between a snort and a cough and waddled through the garden gate, holding it open for Tselane to follow her.

They were halfway down the street when a lorry stopped beside them. Anna, a woman in her early forties, not bad looking and always gaudily dressed, had many friends among the men who worked in the town.

The driver asked: "Are you going to the location? Hop in; I'll take you there."

Anna giggled. The driver of the lorry was one of her special friends and his little favor might earn him her good will on a night when he had no money to pay her.

"Hau, Michael," said Anna, "I shall not forget your kindness. I must be back early today."

"Why? This is your afternoon off."

"I know, but I must be back early."

Anna got into the cab with the driver, and said to Tselane; "Get in the back, sister. There is not room enough for us both with Michael."

Tselane looked bewildered at the huge lorry and did not know how to get into the back as Anna had ordered. She looked helplessly at them and saw Michael whisper to Anna.

"All right, come and sit here at our feet," Anna said.

Tselane got in and tried to make herself fit into the small space at Anna's feet. Anna had one leg on the other side of the gear lever and every time Michael changed gears, which he did more than was necessary, Anna giggled and protested laughingly, but Tselane could not see what was happening since her back was turned to them. Of one thing she became sure. The thing she was thinking in Anna's room was true. Anna was not a good woman. She was of the same kind as Katila in her village. But where were they taking her? What was she going to see in the place they called location?

The road was rough and bumpy and every time the lorry jerked, Tselane prayed to the spirits of her ancestors to guard her and her unborn child. She held her body tightly and spoke to her child in her mind not to be afraid. Her own fear and bewilderment made her unable to understand the things the other two were talking about.

At the location the lorry pulled up suddenly throwing Tselane against the front.

"Open the door, sister," Anna said. "We are here."

Tselane looked at the door. She saw the handle but dared not touch it. Michael leaned over Anna pressing himself against her fat bosom and opened the door. Tselane got out and waited for Anna, who was still speaking to Michael. At last she clambered down and the lorry roared away.

Tselane looked about her and a feeling of revulsion filled her at what she saw: dirty little shacks of planking, sacking and pieces of corrugated iron; unwashed children in filthy rags and the women lazing around in the sun doing nothing but scratch themselves and now and then scold the children; pigs, hens and dogs wandered around looking for something to eat.

Hau, it was good to live on the mountain and not in the town. In their village the huts were clean, the ground always swept and the yards smeared with dung to keep them neat and clean. Things were kept in their places and not lying around in the sand as here among these houses. Tselane looked along the street and saw houses on the far side that were neat and well built like those she had seen at the airport. Why did Anna come to people who were so dirty and lazy? Yet she must stay with Anna: there was nothing else she could do.

"Come," said Anna.

Anna took no notice of the people standing nearby and did not greet them. How strange that was. In the village you greeted everybody.

At a little house, better-looking than the rest, Anna stopped and opened the door without knocking. It was dark inside. There was a window but a piece of blanket was stuck in the broken window-panes. The house smelled musty of stale smoke and bad beer. In the room into which they came there was a table littered with dirty cups and plates. A vase with bright paper flowers stood in the middle of the table and on the wall there was a picture of the royal family plastered against the wall with stamp-edging. There were three battered chairs and in the one corner stood a small iron bed, still unmade.

A heavy voice came from the next room: "Who is there?"

"Maria, you old mother of a fat cow, why are you so lazy today? Your bed is not even made. What did you do last night?"

"Anna, come in here. I am busy. Big things on for tonight."

"I have a mosadi from the mountain with me."

"I am coming."

Maria came to the door of the room from which she was speaking and just for a second Tselane got the wild urge to flee, to get away. She was in a place where she knew she had no business to be. The woman was even fatter than Anna and looked so dirty that it was hard to know what the color of her dress must be.

"Peace, Mosadi," she greeted Tselane.

"Peace," Tselane greeted her, and pulled her blanket closer around her. The woman eyed her and Tselane got the same feeling she always had when she had to pass the witch doctor's hut in her village. She shivered.

"Come sit, sister," Maria said. "Let me give you something to drink."

Anna sat on one of the chairs. Tselane looked for a place to sit on the floor as she was used to, but the floor was so dirty that she reluctantly took the other chair. Maria took two cups from the table and disappeared into the other room. She came back with the cups brimful of beer.

"Sixpence," Maria said.

Anna looked at Tselane. "You said you have money, sister."

Tselane's hand shook when she took out the rag in which her money was tied. She fumbled among the loose change and handed over the money.

"Maria's beer is good. Drink, sister," Anna said. She lifted her cup and drained the last drop in four big gulps. Tselane watched her spellbound but did not drink from the cup offered her.

"Oh, I forgot," said Anna. "You said that you do not drink. Then you won't mind if I take yours too." And she took Tselane's cup and emptied it as well. She fumbled for her handkerchief which she kept safely in the sweaty recesses of her big bosom and took out a shilling. She placed it on the table and Maria once more went into the other room and returned with a saucepan full of beer."

"We drink alone today?" Anna asked.

"The others will soon be coming."

No sooner had Maria spoken than a woman's face appeared at the door.

"Come in, Sebo, come in," Maria cried gaily, and soon the room was half filled with dirty bedraggled women who each took out her money as she came in and placed it on the table.

They chattered mostly about things which Tselane only half understood. They looked at her suspiciously and suddenly Tselane saw in her mind her little white goat walking among the cattle. She must look like that too, alone and alien among these people.

The afternoon wore on and Tselane felt more lonely and out of place as the wild talking and gesticulating went on. The sun was still high when Anna got up.

"Are you going now? You must be mad!" said the woman named Sebo.

Anna swayed a little and looked at the woman who had spoken to her. "I must go. The white bitch said I must come early."

"Are they having a party?"

"No, why?"

"I just wanted to say I'll come and help you. Those glasses are too many for one woman to wash."

"*Sies*, Sebo, you think I'll let you help me again? Last time she gave me hell when she caught you drinking the leftovers from the glasses. You remember?" They all laughed shrilly. "You were so drunk by then that you told her to shut up and get out of *your* kitchen. The white people were no better. Hau, the glasses they broke, the good drink that fell on the floor and Anna had to wipe up. Anna had to clean the bathroom." Still talking, Anna walked to the door and told Tselane to come.

Tselane's heart was sad. She had not known people who talked like that and behaved like that. What would the missus say if Anna came home in that condition? It was with a heavy heart that she walked along the dusty road at the swaying Anna's side.

The sun was still hot and soon little rivers of perspiration ran down her body under her warm blanket. A weariness, different from the way she felt when she had been working hard in the hot sun all day, took possession of her. Her thoughts darted around in her mind like a frightened trapped hen in a hut.

She had been so happy with her people on the mountain. Four days ago she had known nothing of the things outside her village and now strange things were crowding in on her, making each new morning seem like the slaughtering place where the oxen are taken. She had the rope round her neck and must follow: there was no way out.

"*Gh*, the missus will row and shout and say that I am drunk. I am not drunk; I only paid one shilling."

Anna was getting her arguments ready. True, she had paid only one shilling out of her own money, but being a special friend of Maria's she had got much more than the others for her money, and several of the other women had paid for drinks for her too.

The town seemed to be so far away. In a way Tselane was thankful for the walk in the fresh air because it was sobering Anna, and by the time that they passed the tennis courts she was walking faster and straight. It was getting late and she did not want to annoy the missus. In her room she quickly took off her finery and dressed herself in her uniform and cap.

"Stay here, sister," said Anna, "and if Michael comes before I am back tell him to go away and come later. No, tell him I said he must come tomorrow night. I must stay in the kitchen until late tonight."

She left abruptly for the kitchen as the car pulled up.

Left alone, Tselane sat on the floor against the wall and sank her face in her blanket. Her thoughts were far away in the mountain with her people. Her child was stirring more than usual and was hurting her. In front of Anna's bed there was a tattered little mat. Tselane pulled it from the opening under the door through which the wind was blowing and she lay down on it to rest for a while. She fell asleep and only woke up when there was a knock on the door.

Michael opened the door and walked in. Tselane jumped up and stood in the corner farthest away from him. Her beautiful face looked even more attractive in the half light. That afternoon Michael had noticed her exquisite features, the lovely full mouth, the young graceful neck, her firm young breasts, and thoughts of Tselane had been with him ever since then. He took a step towards her and smiled. Fear made Tselane's mouth dry. She tried to speak but no sound came. Michael put out his hand to touch her. Tselane screamed, short and sharp.

"Go away," Tselane said. "Anna said you must come tomorrow."

"I don't want Anna. I came to see you."

Terrified, Tselane screamed at the top of her voice. Michael cursed and made for the door.

Anna had heard Tselane's first little scream and realized at once what must be happening. She put the things down with which she had been busy and ran to her room. She reached the door just as Michael tried to get out. She raised her arm and slapped him with a flat hand across his face. Michael pushed her and threw her over. He jumped across her and disappeared into the dark. Anna picked herself up and went into her room. Tselane was weeping hysterically and Anna searched her mind for something to say.

"The dog. The filthy black dog. Why he comes and does a thing like that? All right. Anna lock the door. Nobody will come."

"Anna!"

Dick Stone's voice spoke outside her door and sounded angry. She opened the door. "What the dickens is going on here? Who screamed like that?"

"It's the girl from the mountain. She got a fright."

"It's that Michael. I saw him running. You tell him from me that if he comes here again, I'll shoot him. Make no mistake about that."

"Yes, boss, I'll tell him."

"Tell the girl to shut up."

"Yes, master." Anna fumbled on the table for the matches and lit a stump of candle in a broken bottle. "My sister, come, sit down, don't cry. Tomorrow you will be on the train and everything will be all right."

Tselane was still shaking and sobbing. No man save her husband had ever touched her. And she with her body heavy with child. How could a man think of touching such a woman?

"He did not mean a thing," Anna said. "He would not have thrown you on the ground. Michael likes pretty faces and he just wanted to touch your pretty face. That is all." Anna tried to sound convincing but she did not succeed. She knew Michael too well. "I'll bring you something to eat. Here, drink some water."

Tselane sat down and watched the flickering shadows on the whitewashed wall. The dried-out flowers Anna had in a jam jar threw a grotesque shadow and the more she looked at it the more it resembled Metlae when he was dressed in his ceremonial outfit. Children laughed at him then because all the other medicine men dressed like any other man but Metlae was still one of the old ones who had been to Swaziland from where he had brought all the things he wore. Tselane tried not to look at the shape. She cowered into her corner. The things seemed to be growing, to become bigger and reach for her. Were all these things Metlae's doing? Was he following her with his witchcraft? Was it because she had escaped them that he was doing this to her? Had he been sitting in his hut muttering against her ever since she had left?

Her child kicked and Tselane took this as a sign that the witch doctor was even influencing her child. She clasped her arms round her body and her lips moved in silent prayer:

"Spirits of my ancestors, guard my child, don't let the medicine man bewitch him. Save me and my son. Bring us to Khama."

From the house loud laughter drifted on the night air. Tselane listened and envied the white people. They had a house to live in and they were not afraid of anything. They knew all the things and they had no witch doctor, no chief that they must obey. How lucky the white people were.

Complete exhaustion overcame her and although she fought against it, her eyes closed and sitting propped up against the wall she fell into a deep sleep.

It was very late at night when Anna woke her to eat.

"Come, sister," the fat woman said. "They have eaten. Now we can eat all the leftovers." She placed a plate of strange-looking things on the table and offered some of it but Tselane hesitated. She did not recognize anything except the small pieces of bread.

Anna said: "They say the name of these things is savories. They eat lots when they drink and play cards."

"Did you make them?"

Anna laughed. "Never! My hands are black and they think I am dirty. That is why they make them themselves. But Anna can cook and make crumpets all right. The missus and Mrs. Johnston made these."

Tselane enjoyed the strange food but it was not filling like porridge. When she had eaten she was still hungry and ate some of the porridge Simone had given her in her pail.

"I am sleepy," Anna said with a big yawn. "I'll soon be asleep."

Anna took off her uniform and she was soon fast asleep. Tselane lay on the mat on the floor and covered herself with her blanket but sleep would not come to her. Her fear of the train journey and the strangers she would have to come into contact with kept her awake.

At last the night of agony was over. Tselane watched Anna dress to go and make the early morning coffee. Anna said: "I'll ask the missus to give me the morning free so that we can get to the station in good time. It is a long walk. Perhaps the boss will take us there in his car."

Anna's hopes of being taken to the station by car were shattered when she saw the missus driving off soon after breakfast to play tennis. She went into the kitchen to prepare the vegetables so that she would only have to cook them when she came back.

Dick Stone came into the kitchen and said: "Tell the girl that I shall take her to the station."

"Yes, boss, but I will have to go too."

"Why?"

"She is alone. She does not understand the train and she will not know what to do."

"Then it is time that she learns."

"Yes, my boss, but Anna must go too. I promised her."

"All right. You just want to go for a ride but don't waste my time at the station with your talking. We have to get back to fetch the missus in time. I am going to town now to get the car. See that you are ready when I come back."

"Yes, my boss."

Anna hurried to her room and soon was dressed in her gay frock, her brown shoes and red hat. Tselane got her bundle and her pail ready and stood waiting with a wildly beating heart. When would all this end? She was beginning to feel numb from all the anxiety and fear and she wished that she had stayed on the mountain or had gone to her mother's hut, there to await her fate. At the station her fear bordered on panic. She held her bundle in front of her as Anna had instructed her but an overwhelming urge to run and never stop again overcame her when the huge black monster came to a puffing halt just at the place where they were standing. Anna talked to the people on the platform; laughing and having a good time, never dreaming what was going on in the mind of the woman who stood so stiffly at her side.

"You see there at the back?" Anna asked. "Just wait until the train stops, then we go there and find you a seat. Hold on to your ticket, sister, the white man throws you off the train if you haven't got a ticket." Anna was joking but Tselane clutched the little ticket in awful fear of such a calamity befalling her. Anna went on: "And don't you speak to strangers on the train. The tsotsi also ride the train and when you sleep they get off and take your things with them."

Tselane stood taut and stiff. She trembled a little and her nostrils trilled like those of a horse which stands ready for flight. The huge engine was belching coals, blowing steam and smoke until the sight of it dazed her.

The train jerked to a standstill and immediately bedlam was loose. People ran about trying to get in and those who wanted to get out shouted and swore, laughed and greeted relatives who had come to meet them. Milk cans clanged as they were loaded and workmen shouted and jostled the passengers. Anna elbowed her way through the crowd trying to make a way for Tselane who was pushed this way and that way, too frightened to resist. She frantically clutched her bundle and held on to her pail. For a moment she lost sight of Anna's red hat with the black feather and panic made her heart faint.

"Here, sister, here," Anna shouted above the clamor of the pushing crowd. Tselane went to her and followed her into the train.

They came to a compartment where an old woman was sitting in the corner, snugly wrapped up in her blanket. Her face was wrinkled into a smile and her kindly eyes greeted them when Anna spoke to her.

"Are you alive, Mother?"

"Peace, Mosadi, I am alive."

"Is there a place here for our sister?"

"There is a place."

"Will you keep an eye on her, Mother, for she has not gone this way before."

"I shall. Don't be afraid, my child. We are all sick with our thoughts when we have to take the train the first time."

She smiled and her smile warmed Tselane's heart. Here was a woman like MaPhépa, MaKhama, and her own mother, kind, good people with hearts as white as the snow that fell on the mountains in winter.

Tselane sat down on the hard wooden bench and put her bundle at her feet, while Anna was busily talking to the men in the corridor. There was the sound of a bell and Anna pushed her face into the compartment.

"Go gently, sister."

"Stay well, Anna. Thank you that you have helped me."

Anna disappeared. There was a sharp whistle and the big black monster became alive. Tselane closed her eyes. The train jerked and blew its whistle loudly. There were shouted farewells and soon they rushed clacking over the rails on the way to Bloemfontein.

Tselane felt her inside turning to water when first one, then two, then another stranger entered the compartment and sat down. How long would she have to stay with these people? She had heard that they would sleep in the train too. What about these strange men then? Tselane pressed herself deeper into the corner and looked at the old mother sitting in her corner quietly reading her Bible. The old woman looked up and seeing the fear in the younger woman's eyes she smiled and touched Tselane's hand.

"Peace, my child, the worst is over," she said. "It's only getting into the train for the first time that frightens you; you'll soon feel better."

Tselane tried to smile but she could not believe that the old mother was saying that which was true.

12

CONVERSATION in the crowded compartment was slow. The air was heavy with the strong smell of stale smoke and unwashed bodies. Tselane sat quietly in her corner watching the strange new country passing by. How was it that they in the mountains never thought that the flat land below would look like this?

One of the men addressed the old woman but Tselane did not hear the question. She only heard the old mother saying: "We wait there for three hours."

"And if the train is full we wait until tomorrow." The man with the bright red cap said this.

Tselane looked at them in alarm. What were they talking of? Wasn't the train they were on now taking her to her husband?

"Mother, don't I stay in this room until I get to my husband?" Tselane asked. The men looked at Tselane and smiled at her ignorance.

"No, my child," the old woman said. "At Marseilles we get into another train. That train will take us to Bloemfontein and there you have to wait until tomorrow morning for the train from Gaudeng to take you to Worcester."

Tselane was shocked. Where would she stay in Bloemfontein? Would she have to go to another location and perhaps experience worse things than she did with Anna in Maseru? "But where shall I sleep?"

"You can come with me. I am going to my white child but she will let you sleep at the house."

Horror stood in Tselane's eyes. What was the old mother talking of? Her white child? The old woman saw the disbelief on the young face and smiled serenely. She said: "I only call her that. Her mother died when she was born and I brought her up. She married a doctor in Bloemfontein and every year I come to spend a few weeks with her." The wrinkled old face was wreathed in smiles at the prospect of seeing her white child again.

Hau, it was strange. Tselane wondered at the people she had met. Anna stayed with a missus that she hated, yet in spite of that she did not go away but stayed year after year. This old mother had stayed with one family all her life and she loved the white people. How was she to understand this? Were the white people not all the same? She asked the old woman about this.

"No, my child. They are not all the same. Basotho all have horses but some treat the horses well and others don't. We all work for the white people and some are good to us and others are very bad. They think that because we are black we have no feelings."

"You are wrong, Mother." Everybody in the compartment looked at the man who had spoken. There was a sullen vehemence in his voice and hatred burned on his face. He had come in after the other men and did not wear a blanket as they did. He was dressed in a neat European suit, he wore glasses and shiny black shoes, he carried a new leather brief-case and his hat was perched at a slant on neatly brushed hair. "The white people are all the same. They hate us just because we are black. They hate us, too, because they are afraid. This is our country and they know it."

"My son, this is God's country. Did we buy it from Him or did the white people buy it from Him? We all live here because He is good to us."

"You have lived too long with the white farmers; that is why you say things like that. They have taught you to say those things."

"Your tongue has learned to speak many words quickly. The child who tries to run before he can walk properly falls on his face and gets hurt."

The man did not answer this remark but started speaking like one who has said the same words many times before. "Our chiefs are quite capable of looking after our affairs. Why must the white people make laws for us which do not suit us?"

Tselane shuddered. This man was talking like the wind that comes up the valley and stirs the dry leaves on the mealies but does not move the plant. The chiefs! If the white people were no longer there to stand guard over the chiefs, how many people on the mountain would be used for medicine? Now the chiefs were afraid of the white police but to whom would people like herself flee when the white people were there no longer?

The man said: "The time will come when we will chase the white people into the sea and take what belongs to us."

Tselane was bewildered. How could the man say things like that? What did they know about the things of the white people? Look at the train. What black man could make a train and let it go? If they chased the white people into the sea, who would teach them about such things?

The man did not wait for an answer from the rest of them but continued, looking at the men sitting opposite him. "The mines are rich. We have to take the gold out for the white people and what do we get for it? A small pay and bad food. If the mines belonged to us we could have all that gold and money."

"I work in the mines and I am quite happy there," a man said. "I like it."

"How long have you been there?"

"This is the third time that I go back."

"And do the white people treat you like a human being? No. Don't come and tell me that because it is not true. Even if we had the money we could not go into their hotels and ask for a bed to sleep. We cannot enter their churches and we cannot go to the same places as they do. And why? Just because we are black and not white like they are."

Tselane thought a long time about these words of the clever man.

In the village the cowherd does not sit and drink beer in the chief's hut. Some Indians, who were as black as they themselves were, came to live near their village and the people did not mix with them. The white people must feel like that too. They were not the same as the natives so why must they mix with them? The natives must go to their churches and the white people to theirs. She smiled a little at the absurd thought of her going into the places of the white people, to mix with them just like another white person.

The man watched her closely and when he saw the smile on her pretty face he said: "You smile because you think that I am talking nonsense but that is just because you have lived in the mountains and know nothing of these things. You people of the mountains make it difficult for us. You are so satisfied with the little that you have and are so happy to stay on the mountain that you don't care about anything else."

The old woman looked up quickly, saying: "The people of the mountains are the only happy ones. Leave her alone; she has only just come among the white people and does not know anything of the things you think about. Not everything that you say is good, my son. We are still like little children; there are many years before us in which we must learn from the white people. Perhaps the time will come, when both you and I are dead, that our children will know the things that we must know before we are the same as the whites. You people now speak many words that do not help our people."

"My mother, you are old. We who are still young know what we are talking about."

"And we, the old, will suffer with the young. Idle words have never been any use to anybody. We must work and work hard and the children must go to school."

"And where are these schools that you are talking of? Do the white people give us enough schools?"

"And if we chase the white people into the sea as you have said, where will we get schools then?"

"We'll take their schools."

"And the teachers will be swimming in the sea and they won't have time to teach the children."

Everybody laughed, but the man in the neat suit became angry.

"It is because our people talk like this that we will never get anywhere. You laugh when there is nothing to laugh about."

"We are happier this way. But do not let us quarrel; rather tell
us of the big city where you come from."

The man did not answer but got up angrily and went into the
passage. When he had closed the door the man who had said that
he worked in the mines looked at the old woman and said: "There
are many like that one in Gaudeng. Everywhere they speak to us
and tell us to hate the whites and join their movement. There are
some white people, too, who tell us these things, but we do not
listen to them because a man who talks against his own people is
less than a dog."

"When I was in Bloemfontein the last time, I heard these things
there, too," the mother said. "I wondered then what these whites
were thinking that tried to be with us and not with their own people.
I am sure they are hiding something in their pails of which we now
know nothing."

"When the time of trouble comes, their pails will be smashed
too. There will be no time to look inside a man's pail to see whether
he is for the black people or against them."

"My son, you young people talk so wildly of a time when things
will be smashed. What are you thinking of?"

"I do not know, Mother, but at night in the compounds men
talk strange things."

Tselane looked from one to the other and the old woman realized
how frightening the things must be that she heard. She did not
know the outside world and, on the first day away from her country,
people spoke of trouble and killing. She laid her hand on Tselane's.

"My child, the days that still lie under the mountain of the future
are perhaps good days. Do not listen too much to the talk of the
people." The train whistled shrilly and jerked to a standstill. "Come,
we must get out."

Tselane followed the old woman and together they went to the
little waiting room to await the arrival of their train. The men who
had been in their compartment walked to the far end of the platform. At noon Tselane offered her companion some of her porridge,
which was now cold and hard. They ate slowly and by the time
that the train arrived they had also eaten some of the food which

the old woman had brought, and were ready to get in. It was a mad scramble again but helping each other they were soon seated.

Tselane watched the flat country through which they passed and asked the old woman about Bloemfontein.

"Is it bigger than Maseru? Are there many white people and such big houses?"

The old woman laughed, showing her small teeth which were worn nearly to the gums. "Maseru is a tiny, tiny piccanin against Bloemfontein."

Tselane tried to form a picture of such a place but her thoughts were interrupted by the entry of the ticket examiner. He was a tall stern-looking man. It was plain to see that his patience had been tried to the extreme by the time that he came to them. People were so afraid of losing their ticket that each one hid it well and the white man had to stand and wait until they had searched through all their pockets and purses before they at long last produced the precious piece of cardboard.

"Hurry up, I haven't all day to wait for you," he said repeatedly.

One man he had spoken to fumbled about in his pockets but he could not find his ticket. The examiner moved on to the next man. Others held their tickets up, glad that they would not make him wait. In her eagerness to please the man Tselane gave her ticket before he was ready to take hold of it. Just then somebody opened a window and the ticket vanished on the gust of wind that swept through the compartment. There was a gasp of terror. Tselane leaned far out as if she could get hold of the ticket, her most precious possession.

"Imbecile!" the man said. "Why couldn't you hold the thing tightly until I could take it from you? I am sure that was not the right ticket at all."

Tselane was so overcome by fear that she could only shake her head. She did not answer but all the others in the compartment started speaking at the same time. "It was the right ticket, we saw it."

"Keep your big mouths shut!"

"You had the ticket in your hand, basie," the old woman said with dignity and respect. "You'll have to give her another."

"Keep quiet. Don't tell me what I have to do."

He slammed the door after him and left a void of stunned silence. Then like the birds in their mealielands when harvest time drew near, the people chattered, each one louder than the other.

Tselane was shaking. What was going to happen to her now? Anna had said that the white man would throw her off the train if she had no ticket. Was that really going to happen? Her mind was in chaos. She had gone dry. She felt feverish and unable to think clearly.

How they came to know of it, who spread the story, was hard to say, but soon there was not a single passenger in the coach who did not know of her predicament. There were wild stories of unfairness and when the ticket examiner came again those in Tselane's compartment glared at him in sullen silence and all along the corridor people got out of his way as soon as they could. He opened the door of Tselane's compartment. Sullen defiance hit him in the face, but with callous indifference to the tension that pervaded the room he spoke to Tselane.

"Don't get off the train at Bloemfontein. Wait until I come for you."

He did not explain the reason for this command but left them abruptly. Resentment and wild speculation lashed the air with each sentence that leapt from mouth to mouth. Tselane took no part in this talk. One sentence was repeating itself in her mind, casting a shadow even over her fear of the ticket examiner.

Metlae! It was the work of the witch doctor! Why didn't the wind blow any other ticket through the window, only hers? What thing would Metlae do against her next? Would he pursue her until she could not bear it any more but had to return to the village?

Her child kicked her and in a sudden fear she clutched her side.

"Spirits of my ancestors, don't let him do it. Not here!" she prayed. "Don't let him make my child see the light of day in the white man's train!"

The thought had never come to her before that the witch doctor would have the power to make her give birth before the time, to punish her, but now the thought blinded her. She looked wildly around her. Sweat stood on her forehead.

The old woman looked concerned at her. "My child, this is a

bad thing that has happened to you but Miss Sannie will speak to them. You'll see, everything will still be all right."

At last Bloemfontein came in sight. Tselane looked through the window but hastily pulled her head back. What she saw was bewildering and confusing. So many houses, the trains pulling in and out of the station, people rushing around, bells clanging, whistles sounding, while people shouted their welcomes and farewells.

Those in her compartment gathered their bundles and blankets ready to get off. Panic-stricken, Tselane looked at the old mother when she too took her small suitcase and her blanket from the rack.

"Are you going, Mother?"

"I am just going to stand on the platform for Miss Sannie to see me. I shall stay here until the white boss has told you what to do."

The train stopped. Tselane was left in her corner alone and afraid. The old woman stood in front of the window and suddenly waved wildly with her arms. A slim young white woman with a pretty face, brown hair and blue eyes came rushing up to her. She put her arms round the old woman and said: "Selina, I am so glad you are here. Come, I've got the car outside, let us go."

"No, my little one, we have to stay here for a while," the old woman said. She looked down the platform. "There they are coming."

"Who?" asked the white woman.

"The man from the train. The child there inside has lost her ticket. Why does he bring the policeman? She did not do anything wrong. We all saw her ticket but it blew through the window."

The ticket examiner, a police constable and an inspector came to the window. "Come, woman," the policeman said.

Tselane was unable to move. She sat like one paralyzed and could only look at them with her big frightened eyes.

"Didn't you hear me? Come!"

Selina stepped forward. "Excuse me, basie, what are you going to do to her?"

The man was on the point of being rude to Selina when he saw Mrs. Nel. To her he said, "I tell you, ma'am, these blacks were sent to try us."

"What has happened?" Sannie Nel asked.

"She said she had the right ticket but we'll have to keep an eye on her until she comes to her destination."

Selina had spoken to Tselane and was helping her onto the platform.

The trainman said: "There she is, Inspector. You'll have to make sure that she gets onto the Cape train tomorrow morning at seven."

"Miss Sannie," said old Selina, "could she come with us?"

"Certainly, but what about her ticket now?"

The inspector said: "We'll give the examiner on the Cape train her papers and when she arrives in Worcester the police will meet her at the train."

"But they say she had the right ticket."

"That we'll have to find out from Maseru. These people are becoming so shrewd you have no idea what they get up to. If she is going to sleep at your house you will have to make sure that she comes to the train in the morning. She must not miss it."

Tselane did not understand a word of what was being said and clung to Selina's hand. The old woman comforted her. "It is all right, my child, Miss Sannie will see to everything."

The three men left and Sannie immediately started talking gaily to old Selina about the farm. She took them to her big car and Selina got in front with her. She saw to it that Tselane was comfortable at the back and then drove to her house. Aloise and Paul, the two Nel children, were playing on the grass when they arrived. They left their toys and ran with glad cries to welcome old Selina. The old woman sat down on the grass and hugged the two small children. There were tears in her eyes.

"My piccanins, my little white piccanins. Hau, you have grown!"

"What is Oupa doing on the farm?" Paul asked.

"Oupa said: 'Selina, you give Paul a big kiss from me.'"

Selina hugged the little boy to her again and for the first time Tselane smiled. It was a true thing that Khama had said to her. If you are good to the white people, they are good to you, too. Just look at the old mother with the white people and their children.

In the servant's room Tselane sat on the floor. She was unspeakably weary and the fears of the morning gave her no peace. What was the white man going to do? What did he say about the ticket? Selina had told her that she would be able to get onto the train, but what would she do if they came and asked her for the ticket?

It was late before Selina came from the big house and brought her food.

"Eat, my child, don't worry about tomorrow," she said. "Miss Sannie will take you to the train; everything will be all right."

In spite of Selina's reassuring words Tselane slept very little. Again and again the face of the ticket examiner appeared before her, and in the background the grinning image of Metlae mocked her. In her mind her dreams became reality and even when lying awake the triumphant smile on Metlae's wrinkled face remained before her to remind her of the calamity that had overtaken her.

Long before seven they got up and went into the kitchen where Selina prepared fresh porridge to fill Tselane's pail.

"You must not buy food on the train and let the people see that you have money. Today you cannot trust people; they steal even from the poor."

When they were ready, Sannie brought the car to the front door and waited for Tselane to get in. At the station the same white man who had spoken to Selina the previous day came to them.

"All right, girl, get in," he said. "Don't get off the train along the way."

He walked off. Tselane was trembling. Selina helped her into her compartment and handed her her bundle and her pail. She took the young hands tightly between her own.

"May the spirits of our ancestors and the good God watch over you. Go gently, my child."

"Stay well, Mother."

What little courage Tselane had felt now left her when Selina got off the train to stand on the platform. She looked at the strange women around her and the urge to get off and stay with Selina overwhelmed her. A bell clanged, the train whistled sharply and started moving away.

13

SHE SAT in her corner on the hard wooden bench of the compartment and looked at the people around her. The atmosphere was warm and stuffy. Dark thunderclouds hung in the sky and although the sun was scarcely up, it was warm already.

Opposite her sat a woman who was wearing glasses and high-heeled shoes. She had on a smart frock like the white people and a smart hat on her head. She looked at Tselane with a smile of contempt on her lips. These raw people from the mountains with their blankets and their bundles! They must really be made to travel separately. She turned the page of the book she was reading and did not greet Tselane in the usual way.

Tselane felt awkward and did not know what to do with her hands. She tried to hide her feet under the seat so that the woman with the shiny high-heeled shoes should not see her dusty, flat, black tie-shoes. What would this grand and clever woman say when she heard that she had no ticket?

There were three other women with them who wore European

dresses but with their blankets over them. They spoke a language which Tselane could not understand. At last the woman sitting next to her spoke to her in Sotho.

"Are you going far?"

"To Worcester."

"That is a long way. We are not going so far but she is." And she pointed to the woman with the glasses who did not look up, and Tselane felt frightened of her.

In her excitement that morning she had forgotten to ask Selina to show her the place where she could relieve herself and it was now urgent for her to go. She looked around at the other passengers and then leaned over to the woman who could speak Sotho.

"Mosadi, where does one go to the bushes here?"

The woman smiled. "Come, I'll show you."

They walked down the narrow passage to the lavatory where the woman showed Tselane what to do and promised to wait for her. "You mustn't stay long. Each person can only stay little time. It says so on the paper behind the door."

When Tselane came out she had not put her blanket over her shoulders but carried it over her arm. Her companion's eyes became big in alarm.

"Quick, Mosadi, put your blanket on. Don't let them see you!" She looked about them to make sure that nobody had seen Tselane's figure. "Mosadi, how long is it before your child comes?"

"Two months; why?"

"How did you get onto the train? The white man will be very angry because we must not travel in their trains when the time is near. I don't know what will happen if a black woman should have her child in the train."

Tselane quickly pinned her blanket into positon to hide her figure. "Mosadi, but why should my child come now? It is still a long time."

"How did you come from the mountains to the train? You must be tired, and in the seventh month it sometimes happens when we are tired."

"I am very tired but I am strong. I don't think that it could happen."

"Let us pray that you will be saved from that. Have you got

medicine with you?" She looked around furtively as she whispered the question.

"Medicine?"

"Yes, you people can get it so easily from your doctor in the mountains. My mother brought hers from MoKhotlong and nothing ever happens to her. Has your chief got a strong lenaka?"

Tselane, who was walking in front, stopped suddenly. She clutched the window bar and swayed a little. The woman hastily put her arms round Tselane's waist.

"What is the matter, sister, why do you look like that? Wait, I'll get you some water."

"It's all right, Mosadi," Tselane managed. "I'll walk to our room."

The woman helped her along the passage and in their compartment she quickly told the others how she had feared that Tselane would faint. The woman with the glasses said: "You must tell her that she must not have her baby here. I don't want to have anything to do with such things. Why did she not stay in her hut instead of coming on a journey?" She pulled her skirt closer as if she wanted to protect herself from contact with such a person.

Tselane could not understand what the woman was saying but she could make out that the woman was dissatisfied about something concerning her because they all looked at her. She closed her eyes. If only she could forget the witch doctor and the power of the medicine. She was sure that from the time that she had escaped he had only busied himself with things that would bring her hardship and calamity. He was cursing her and her child because they had spoiled his plans. Would her child be normal when he came? She had heard stories of a witch doctor who had cursed a mother and when her child was born he had two heads.

She pressed her hands to her sides. The child was stirring and was hurting her. Then she sat back and tried to rest.

Towards noon the ticket examiner came for the first time.

"Tickets, please," he said.

Tselane closed her eyes. Would the man understand? The woman who could speak Sotho had come to her destination and had got off the train. Only the woman with the glasses remained with her.

"Tickets, please." The man spoke impatiently. The woman with the high-heeled shoes spoke too. Tselane answered in Sotho that she had lost her ticket but they did not understand her.

He addressed the woman with the glasses. "Can't she speak English? I am sure she got on the train without a ticket. These stupids think they can get a train ride for nothing, just like everything else they get. Ask her where she came from."

"I cannot speak her language. She got on at Bloemfontein."

"But where does she come from?"

"If you look at her clothes and her manners I must think that she comes from the mountains in Basutoland. These people are still so ignorant." She spoke with disdain.

The ticket examiner looked at the woman and cursed her in his mind. He greatly preferred the raw natives to these half-baked city types who thought themselves better than the rest of their sort. Impatiently he started speaking to Tselane who only shook her head, too frightened to trust her voice to speak. They would not understand. The man was getting angrier with her. He took a sheaf of papers from his pocket and started looking through them. This must be the woman they referred to who had lost her ticket and was on her way to Worcester.

"Are you going to Worcester?" he shouted at her.

Tselane had not understood the question but because he had spoken of Worcester she nodded. Without a word the man went away and panic made Tselane wonder what would happen now. Was he going to come back? Selina had said that she would be safe on the train but the man looked so angry that she was sure everything was not all right.

Towards seven o'clock the first low rumblings could be heard in the west of the storm which had been threatening all day. There was a light in the passage but in their compartment it was dark. A sudden flash of lightning lit up the darkness and Tselane shied away from the window. In her village in the mountain there were often thunderstorms and she was not afraid, but sitting securely in your hut was different from rushing along in a train.

The lightning was followed by crashing thunder that shook the atmosphere. Tselane covered her face with her blanket. One crash followed another, lightning played on the veld and chains of it stood on end, ripping the inky darkness of the night. Rain such as she had never seen before started beating against the window and pattered down on the roof. Wasn't the train going to fall over? It was impossible to believe that they were safe rushing along like that in the storm. Tselane clutched the seat and held on until her arms ached and her body felt cramped.

Suddenly she sat bolt upright. A sharp pain had thrust its way upward through her body. She held her breath. She must get to the lavatory to relieve herself. Painfully she got up and struggled down the passage. The lurching train flung her now against the windows and then against the doors of the compartments.

Inside the lavatory she fastened the latch securely. At last she was safe from the ticket examiner, for although he had not come again she was sure that he would come back before they went to sleep.

Tselane nearly shouted in her agony. Another searing pain shot up her body. She clutched her sides and sweat started on her brow. She put her hands under the weight of her unborn child and tried to hold him.

With regular intervals the pain started coming and going. A fire burned within her. Agony such as she had never known before made her writhe, and she bit her lips until blood came from them, to stop a scream of pain. She tried to think of things that could give her courage. She must try to hold the child back who was struggling to get out.

She mumbled meaningless words about the ghosts of her ancestors; she tried to remember the words Pierre had read from the Bible. If only she had known more of the God Molili had told her of, and who the Moneri had said would protect her!

The world became black in front of her. Out of the darkness that enveloped her two huge eyes were looking at her. Metlae! She struggled to push him away but he held out his thin, bony arms with the fingers like claws, waiting for her to deliver the child that he had willed to be born in the white man's train. The eyes disappeared and she was now in the big bird, falling down and down but never reaching the earth. The night started rushing past her until the sound of rushing water remained her only conscious feeling. She was on the floor, everything was wet. Slowly she came back from the mists of unconsciousness to hear her child thinly wailing.

She struggled to a sitting position. The old women had instructed her what to do if the child should be born in the veld when she was alone. This she quickly did and untied the black shawl to wrap the baby up and make him quiet.

She was too weak to get up and take a sip of water to cool her burning lips.

What must she do now? What would the white man say when he saw her there? The train shuddered and rocked. She slid about on the wet floor unable to steady herself. She hit her head against the washbasin. She grabbed the edge of the basin and tried to get up. Her mind became a blank and she was unable to think clearly.

Suddenly there was a loud knock on the door.

"Open the door. What are you doing in there?"

Tselane did not understand what the man was saying but she recognized the voice of the ticket examiner. Frantically she looked about her. Where could she hide the child? What must she do with it? She heard the man inserting a key and knew that he would open the door as he did the door of their compartment when he came to ask for their tickets. The only thought that occurred to her was a searing anxiety to get rid of the baby before the man could enter the room.

With a frantic effort she struggled up to the window and when the examiner opened the door he saw her pushing the child through the small opening of the window. She fell backwards on him.

"My God!" the man cried. "Are you mad?"

Looking at the floor, the man had realized instantly what had happened. He rushed down the passage to pull the emergency brake.

With a jerk and crashing of wheels on metal rails the train shuddered to a stop. The conductor answered no questions thrown at him but rushed to get a light. He walked along the rail in the darkness with the rain and thunder beating down on his bent shoulders. At last he found what he was looking for. He picked up the black bundle but there was no movement. The child was dead.

He hurried back to the train. In the first class there was a doctor who was a passenger, and the man said to him: "I am sorry, Doctor, to bother you, but won't you come and help me? A woman has given birth to this child in the third class. She has fainted."

"Is the child alive?"

He handed the child to the doctor who examined it quickly, then said: "Put it down here and lock the compartment. Where is this woman?"

They put the child on the seat and when the compartment was locked they hurried down the passage where people were crowding to find out what had happened.

In the lavatory the doctor took one look at Tselane and then ordered the two bedding boys to carry her to an empty compartment.

"Give the signal to start," he said. "We must get her to a hospital as quickly as possible."

The train was soon moving at full speed again and at the first stop the conductor telephoned the police of the next town.

"There has been a murder on my train," he said. "A Mosotho woman killed her child. Will you meet the train and bring the ambulance?"

"Sure. Murder did you say?"

On through the night the train sped. Numbed by pain and her experience Tselane lay with her eyes closed. She still felt the softness of the small body and heard his weak little cries. She saw his quivering lips but they became contorted and evil and Metlae leered at her, smiling in his triumph. Tselane shrieked and groaned.

The doctor leaned forward and laid his hand on her forehead. He had nothing with which to help her.

"Come now, my girl, try to get some sleep."

Tselane looked at him, her eyes wide with horror and pain, but with no idea of his words or of the thing that had happened.

14

AS THE train neared the town of Beaufort West, the sound of its whistle stirred activity on the platform. The ambulance was there, and now the two attendants opened the back doors and pulled a stretcher halfway out. Then two policemen arrived in a car, and in a moment a doctor came from the hospital. Together the five men stood in an important little circle, hands on their hips, occasionally speaking softly to each other, their eyes northward, watching for the train. There were many others on the platform, watching for the train. Natives, like children who knew they had no right to ask questions, dallied as near to the five men as they dared, openly eavesdropping and rushing back to their friends each word they caught. White people, especially those who had no standing in the town, pretended not to be too interested; occasionally they shot brief glances at the five men, glances which were mildly curious and which said that if the matter were at all important they would already know about it. But others, like a shop owner or a rich farmer or a man who frequently spoke up at town meetings, tried less to hide their curiosity. They strolled calmly to the five men, said good morning and chatted idly before they asked their questions.

"Who is sick on the train?"

"We don't know. Some woman gave birth to a child on the train. That is all we heard."

"It is a white woman?"

"No, a native."

"These people have no sense. Why did she travel in that condition?"

"I've heard that she tried to throw the baby through the window?"

"Yes, she did. It was killed."

"Good God. How dreadful. Murder."

The word flashed down the platform and people strained their necks to hear more. Women, white and black, walked from one group to another to spread the news.

A hush fell on the crowd as the train drew to a stop, and as soon as the conductor was seen waving from the last passenger car the crowd moved along the platform in his direction. The two policemen tried to hold the people back, but they pressed forward to see what was going to happen next.

The doctor from the train stepped to the doctor from the hospital. They spoke in soft whispers and none of the bystanders could hear them.

"She has lost a lot of blood, Dr. Spiro," said the doctor from the train. "Her pulse is so weak you can hardly feel it. You must get her to the hospital as quickly as possible."

The crowd gasped when the train guard handed the policemen a black bundle. "The child," was whispered along the platform. A policeman put the bundle into a box he had brought for that purpose and hurried to the ambulance. Then the ambulance attendants pushed the stretcher through a train window and soon Tselane's unconscious form was lifted down. Police Sergeant Myburgh called out: "Make way, people, stand back. Please stand back."

But nobody moved. Dr. Spiro declared in a loud, tired voice: "This woman is dying. Will you please let us through?"

At the mention of death and the stern look on the doctor's face, the people moved away and stood silently watching the procession to the ambulance. Soon the siren screamed through the quiet streets and everywhere people turned to look, wondering who in their town could be so sick that the ambulance must speed like that.

At the hospital, the nurses were ready, and Dr. Naude was ready. When Dr. Spiro arrived, they all went to a small hot room and intently scrubbed their hands.

Dr. Naude asked: "Do you think septicemia would have set in already?" He was a young doctor and still afraid of death.

Dr. Spiro first dried his hands before he said slowly: "Perhaps it would be better for her if it has. If we succeed with her we will only be saving her for the gallows."

Dr. Naude looked surprised, then Dr. Spiro told him what had happened on the train, and the young doctor said: "But what is the use then?"

"Duty, Doctor, duty," said Dr. Spiro, and he sounded like a professor of ethics who was weary of the subject.

In the room where the surgery was done, all of them worked quietly for a long time, unmoved by the person who lay before them, not caring what she had done, where she was from, or what might happen to her should she live. Their job was to keep her alive, and they worked as skillfully as they knew, doing all that they could.

Outside, the two policemen waited in their car. Sergeant Myburgh sighed heavily and said: "I honestly do not understand these black people. The woman is a Mosotho and everybody knows how they love their children, especially their first-born and even more so if it is a son."

"I don't understand either," said the second policeman. "Unless the doctor can prove that the baby was already dead, she'll swing for this."

"The doctor on the train already told me the baby was alive when she threw it out the window," said Myburgh.

They looked at the hospital door through which Dr. Spiro was coming. He said: "Your prisoner is alive, Mr. Myburgh, and I think she'll pull through. But you'll have to wait until she is stronger before you can take her, and I think that will be the better part of two weeks."

"Thank you, Doctor," Myburgh said. "Will you come with us now to examine the baby?"

They left together for the police station.

In the ward Tselane slowly regained consciousness. The whiteness of everything around bewildered her: white sheets on the bed, white curtains surrounding it, a white woman in a white uniform. The woman held Tselane's wrist with one hand and with the other patted her cheek, saying: "Come on, now, come on, wake up."

Tselane became more aware of things around her and looked pleadingly at the nurse, asking in Sotho where she was. The nurse had to guess at the question, and she said the one word: "Hospital." Tselane closed her eyes again and the nurse, satisfied that she had come safely out of the anesthetic, left the bed and sent a native nurse to look after Tselane, saying: "Nurse Evalina, you are not to tell the woman what became of her baby if she asks you."

"I am Xhosa, Sister Greyling," said Nurse Evalina. "She is Mosotho. I do not speak her language."

"Oh, of course," said Sister Greyling, surprised as she always was that natives, who all looked so much alike, could tell at a glance that others were not of their own tribe.

At the bedside, Nurse Evalina wondered why Sister Greyling had given her such instructions. How was she to know what had happened to the woman's baby? She had not even known that the woman was there for a birth. Patiently, Nurse Evalina waited at Tselane's bedside to help her, if help was wanted. Tselane did not open her eyes again, and soon Evalina heard from her breathing that she was asleep. Evalina went to other patients in the ward, to speak to them and cheer them up. Most of them had been eagerly awaiting an opportunity to ask Evalina what was going on. They wanted to know the woman's tribe, what was wrong with her, where she came from, what the doctors had said about her condition. Evalina, knowing her people so well, smiled.

"She is very sick," she said. "That is all I know. You must be quiet now. We haven't a private room for her today, but tomorrow she will be moved out of here and then you can talk loudly again. She is a Mosotho and even if you can speak her language nobody is to talk to her. She is too sick to talk."

"Hau," they said, "hau." There was deep sympathy in their voices. Poverty and hardships they could bear, but sickness and death always filled them with awe. Poverty they had known all their lives and there was nothing one could do about that. But sickness. Only the white people with their injection needles and medicines knew how to fight that. The white doctors knew how to cut out the parts that brought pain, and with implicit faith and no fear they came to be cured.

It would be only a matter of time: the doctors would soon cure this woman too of whatever ailed her. Patiently, resigned, they watched Evalina as she went from one bed to the next.

Sister Greyling came in and quickly went to Tselane's bed. Evalina hurried over. "She is asleep, Sister Greyling."

"It looks like it, but you must not leave her alone." Sister Greyling felt Tselane's pulse; deep concern suddenly clouded her face. There was scarcely any pulse at all. "Quick, Evalina, call Sister Brink. Tell her to find Dr. Naude and ask him to come here."

Sister Greyling ran to get hot water bottles. Everybody in the ward sat upright. When the nurses ran like that it could mean only one thing: the patient for whom they showed such concern would die. Those who had been in the hospital for longer times had seen such concern on the nurses' faces often enough to know what to expect. Some clicked their tongues to sound their wordless sympathy; others stared wide-eyed at the screen behind which the new patient was lying, and those in the row opposite craned their necks in the hopes of getting a glimpse of Tselane.

Then Dr. Naude hurried to Tselane's bedside, followed by Sister Brink and Sister Greyling. He felt her pulse, listened to her heart, then shook his head.

Sister Brink asked: "What do you think, Doctor?"

"See that you get her warm as quickly as possible," he said. "I'll go and get the injection ready."

He left the ward, and the two nurses began putting the hot-water bottles to Tselane's body and covering her with thick blankets.

In the laboratory, Dr. Naude held the syringe up to the light to see that the fluid poured to the right mark. Out of the corner of his eye, he noticed the green cord which hung from the ventilator against the white wall. For an instant, the looped cord looked shockingly like a noose. The young doctor hesitated. His arms dropped to his side and he stared blankly at the floor, uncertain what to do next. A heavy truck rumbled by outside, stirring the doctor. He wrapped the syringe in a clean towel and holding it carefully he hurried out of the room.

15

IN THE village there was great fear and quiet terror. All that first morning, the people thought and talked only about Tselane. Everyone learned quickly about the diretlo, but they could not believe it. They had seen Chief Majara go to the witch doctor's hut early in the morning, and with him went the six young men, and the people wondered if perhaps they might be choosing a new victim, and after that the people spoke only in angry whispers. Hau, it was a terrible thing that had been planned. Tselane was well loved, and so were her parents-in-law and their son. Not even the fact that medicine was needed for the Chief's wife could warrant such cruelty as taking the good Tselane and her child for diretlo.

Old MaPhépa shook her head sadly and said to her husband: "Our Chief has done that thing that will speak to him in the night with a tongue of fire."

"You speak too quickly, MaPhépa. The Chief has gone to the witch doctor to hear what he has to say. He will be the only one to tell where Tselane has gone."

"And the six men who went there with him?"

"I suppose they were sent out to look for Tselane. I shall know tomorrow what the Chief thinks. Where we go to the trees my place is not far from his. I'll speak and hear what he answers."

"RaPhépa, don't put your old head where the bees can sting it. I tell you that the Chief did not look so angry for nothing."

The whole day they speculated. As RaPhépa had said, Metlae the sorcerer had foreseen that to divert suspicion from the men who had entered his hut with the Chief, he would have to send them out on the supposed mission of looking for Tselane. He had instructed them to make sure that everybody knew that they had been sent out to the villages round about and to Tselane's parents to see whether she had gone there. Because RaPalla was related to Khama he was chosen to go to the kraal of her parents. RaPalla did this but he passed the time of the day and said that he had come to bid farewell as he had to leave for the mines soon.

"Have you seen our child? How is she?" Tselane's mother asked.

"She is well, MaTselane. She told me that she will soon be coming here."

"Yes, her time is drawing near. Our old hearts are soft with the thoughts of the little child that she will bring to us."

RaPalla despised himself for the role he had to play and, as soon as was politely possible, he left them.

The other five also came back towards sunset to report that Tselane had not been seen by any person. In their young hearts doubt and fear stormed. They had been keyed up for the deed but now that they knew who had been chosen they were not so sure of themselves.

Sobeti met Seiso in the path coming from the direction of the villages near the traders' store.

"Have you heard anything?"

"Nothing, she has not been seen."

"I am not a rat but this thing I could not have done. Tselane and I used to play together, and I was chosen to cut off the first piece. I am glad she got away."

"I wonder who told her."

They were quiet for some time, each one busy with his own thoughts.

"Do you think Metlae said a true word when he said that the Chief had spoken in his sleep?"

"It is possible but I do not believe it."

"What do you think?"

"I don't know what to think but of one thing I am sure, I am not going to stay in the village very much longer. I am going to the mines' office tomorrow. I don't want to be here when Khama comes to look for his wife." Seiso spoke without realizing the effect his words would have on Sobeti. Sobeti had never thought of Khama coming to look for his wife when the news reached him that she had disappeared, but that thought now worried him. He pulled his horse up sharply; the horse reared up on his hind legs.

"Hau, Seiso. People have seen us going to the hut. They will think. When Khama comes they will point to us. I shall speak to my father and I shall go with you."

"What will the Chief say when he hears that we want to go?"

"He will say that we are running away and that we are going to speak about this thing."

"Do you think he will try to keep us in the village?"

"I don't know but if he does, I shall run away. Khama will ask no questions and he kills quickly with his knife."

"We have been chosen for this and the Chief will want us to stay to do the deed because he told Metlae to look for a new victim."

"That is true but I have lost my heart. I shall go away without the Chief knowing about it."

"Then he'll think that you warned her."

"Perhaps. But my father knows nothing of this and he has long ago tried to get me away to the mines. I shall now ask him to speak his mind to the Chief."

They rode into the village at the same time that Pitso and Mokwena arrived and people flocked round them eagerly waiting to hear the news.

"She has not been seen." The news was taken to Majara but he did not show himself to his people again.

In their huts that night, people were quieter than usual. They were stunned by the calamity that had suddenly befallen one of their people.

Sobeti's father sat quietly pulling on his long-stemmed pipe. That day, when he had gone to Majara's father to tell him of his suspicion that his son was planning ritual murder, the old Chief had laughed at him and told him that the young puppy would not dare such a thing without speaking to him and asking for his help. Now RaSobeti was sure that the thing he had suspected all along was the truth. Many times he had wondered about the change that seemed to have come over his own son and when his wife had one day told him that she had seen Sobeti going into the witch doctor's hut fear had gnawed his heart like a rat in the mealie basket, but he had not spoken to Sobeti. When he had been chosen to ride to other villages to look for Tselane, this fear had walked beside the old man anew, for this son of his who was always laughing had done many strange things already.

Sobeti sat on his haunches at the fireside and changed his position every now and again, looking at his father but lacking the courage to speak.

"What is it, Sobeti? You have something on your tongue which wants to come out," the old man said.

"I have, Father."

"Speak, let me hear this thing."

"I want to go to the mines."

The old man looked up surprised and asked quickly: "Why? I have cattle enough to pay for your bohadi. What do you want to go to the mines for?"

"Seiso is going and I would like to go too."

His father did not answer but pulled vigorously on his pipe. Seiso had also been chosen to ride out to look for Tselane. "When have you thought about this?"

"For a long time now."

RaSobeti looked speculatively at his son. This was the time to challenge him and hear more about the thing that had given him no peace.

"What were you doing in the witch doctor's hut?"

Sobeti was unprepared for this question and swallowed, trying to think of something quickly. "I went to buy medicine which will make your heart soft so that you will let me go."

"You did not go alone."

"No, Seiso and the others all want to go to the mines." Lies flowed from him as easily as always.

"RaPalla was seen with you."

"RaPalla had trouble in the mines. He wanted to know whether he must go again and he also bought medicine to help him against his boss-boy."

"When did you think of leaving?"

"When you have spoken to the Chief."

"I shall speak to the Chief tomorrow morning," the old man said sadly.

The light of day was already strong in the east when Majara got up. It was earlier than his usual time to go to the place of the trees to relieve himself in the company of his councilors and other men. He swung his blanket round his shoulders and left without speaking to Molili.

When he came to the trees many men were there already because they wanted to talk. When the Chief arrived and went to his tree which stood a little apart from the rest everybody became quiet. Tselane's disappearance was the one thought uppermost in each mind but nobody dared speak about it. If the Chief did not open the subject they must refrain from airing their opinions.

Majara was eager to hear what the people thought and after they had exhausted the topic of the weather and their health he said: "It is a strange thing that Tselane should leave the village without telling her people."

"Perhaps she has gone to the hut of her mother."

"I went there yesterday and she was not there," said RaPalla, who had taken his usual place so that the finger of suspicion could not be pointed at him.

"I shudder to think what Tselane's parents will say to RaKhama when they hear of this."

RaKhama had not taken his usual place. Too sick at heart over the disappearance of his daughter-in-law, he had not risen.

Phonya said: "And what parents could be held responsible for their daughter-in-law's wanderings in the night? Doors open softly and footsteps do not sound on the hard earth."

RaPalla looked at old Phonya and his heart started beating a wild tattoo. What did the man mean? Did he suspect that Tselane was told to go away? Did he know that medicine was to be made?

"Yes, footsteps are quiet in the night," the Chief said slowly, as if he were thinking seriously.

Old Phonya had, however, no thought of somebody warning her, because he was one of the few who did not believe that the Chief was thinking of making medicine. He said: "Women are sometimes queer during the time when they carry their children. Some get a craving for their husbands, which nothing can satisfy. There are many caves in our mountains. Who will know in which one she is hiding to satisfy her craving with some other man?"

Majara was shocked. That was something that had never entered his mind. Somebody else might do a thing like that but not Tselane. She was too proud and she loved her husband too much to think of going to a cave with another man. A woman who had no husband and did not know who was the father of the child she was carrying could think of that, but he had never heard of this thing among his people before.

"Tselane has not gone to the mountain for that, of that I am sure," he said.

"Where else? Messengers have been everywhere and she is nowhere. She could not have disappeared into the sky."

As if they were expecting to see her there, they all looked up at the sky and, to change the subject, old Sekwata said that a thunderstorm could be expected that afternoon.

"The fields are dry; we need the water."

Miles away at the mission station Simone le Brun also looked up at the sky, and she said to her husband: "There will be a storm this afternoon. Can't you postpone this trip until tomorrow?"

Pierre le Brun did not take his eyes from the horse he was brushing. "Tomorrow there will be another storm. What difference does it make?"

"The path along the cliff is slippery when it has rained."

"All the more reason why I must go this morning."

Simone stepped closer to Pierre. "You know I'm afraid, don't you?"

He glanced at her. "I wish you wouldn't be. I must go to the village and talk to the Chief. Tselane's been lucky; she's got away from him, but if he's determined to go through with this thing he will choose somebody else. Certainly you realize, my dear, that I must do everything I can to prevent that."

"He will resent you," Simone offered.

"I suppose so."

"Are you going to tell him that you helped Tselane escape?"

"I don't know yet what I'll tell him."

"I wish you wouldn't go." She almost begged.

Pierre put down the brushes and turned to Simone and said to her patiently: "Now, look. I am a missionary; do you think that means merely sitting here at the station and teaching prayers to children and handing out aspirin when the people are sick? You and I are supposed to be convinced that our way of life is better than theirs; that is why we came here. And if we're going to do our job properly we must teach them to break from their old pagan customs, and this includes ritual murders. Tselane is safe, but the others may not be. That is why I must go to the village and do whatever I can. If I don't, if I just stand here idly and let things go on, then I'm as guilty as Majara himself."

"I know you're right," Simone said helplessly, "but I'm so worried. Everybody in the village must know about the diretlo by now. I'm afraid of what might happen to you if you enter the village in the middle of it all. They might do anything to you."

Pierre tried to smile. "Nothing will happen. I surely won't do anything foolish. After all, I have a lot to live for, you know."

Simone smiled weakly. "I'll be praying for you all day," she said.

"That's all I need."

Riding toward the village, Pierre le Brun was not so sure that prayers were enough. His had been a life of prayers, but there had been many times when he wondered if he were succeeding at his work. There had been moments of excruciating doubts. Why was it that a man so eager to work only for God should be rewarded with such slim fruits of his efforts? Years before, in his youth at college, he had gay friends who chided him on his choice of a profession. They accused him of being swayed by books he had read, and they teased him when he insisted with naïve sincerity that he would achieve some good in Africa. And now what had he achieved? He had imposed on his wife and children a life which offered scarcely more comforts than the natives themselves had. Now and again he had managed to capture a heart, but most of his Christians he had inherited from the old missionary who had preceded him at the station. In many villages, like the one to which he was now riding, he had had practically no success at all. There were perhaps a dozen Christians in the village, mostly women who had married into the clan, and surrounded as they were by paganism and ruled by a pagan chief it was difficult for them to sustain their Christianity. Many of them fell away. Pierre had been most hopeful when Molili had married the Chief. He expected that, edified by Molili's conduct, Majara would follow her into the church. He did not—quite obviously—and now he had apparently influenced her to resort to paganism again in the futile hope that it would enable her to become pregnant. Slim fruits, indeed. Then why keep trying? Why continue to subject one's family to the heat and rain and monotony and, for Simone occasionally, to be sure, loneliness for the way life could be in Paris?

There could be only one reason.

Pierre le Brun had not found in Africa what he expected. The natives were not happy children who would flock to the mission for him to care for their spiritual and physical needs. They were a shrewd people, cunningly clever, perceptive, intelligent, quick. They had to be to survive, for their lives were heavy with fear, suspicion and pride. Paganism, with the power of the chiefs and the incredible power of the witch doctors, caused this, and as long as the people remained pagan they could never escape from it. Oh, there was something lovable in them, certainly, and if they felt at ease with you they could be utterly enchanting in a coy way that was delightful, but they would never give themselves to you completely, as a person might do in a big city elsewhere despite many of the same evils which existed there, because they never knew what it was like to live without some hint of distrust lurking in them. This was as true among themselves as it was in their relations with white people. It accounted, in a strange way, for their formalities with each other, the display of good manners which was at once a defense and a show of respect which could be charming, and it accounted, too, for the maddening ease with which they could lie, cheat, steal, even murder. No deed was evil to them if by performing it they were able to stay alive and out of trouble. The result of this was a constant tension which at times could burst into chaos, as well as a prevailing air of suspicion that needed only a word to explode into violence. White men, aware of this, often felt it wise to keep the African in his primitiveness, for there at least he seemed controllable, but to believe this was to disregard the history of the white race itself. The race marched forward only when all members of it were in step; men like Pierre le Brun believed that the entire human race could not advance as long as certain segments of it were denied the privilege of joining the parade. The goal, of course, was a kind of peace, and men like Pierre le Brun believed that the catalyst for it was Christianity. That was why, fundamentally, he had gone to Africa: To stimulate the influence which white Christians already there professed but did not display. If he could stimulate enough of it, then the sheer weight of Christianity would force the fulfillment of its own goal. There were any number of people, both black and white, who would lose out in any number of ways if this were achieved, men like Chief Majara. Actually they would not lose out if only they could be won over. With this in mind, Pierre decided to make the trip to the village. Where the footpath crossed the river he met some children making clay oxen.

"Dumelang," he greeted them cheerfully. The children looked at him wide-eyed and then abandoned their play to rush home shouting that a white man was on his way to the village. They had not recognized Pierre as the missionary, and the sight of a white man near the village was disconcerting. Grownups came from their huts and when they saw who it was they greeted Pierre, but remained at a respectful distance.

What was bringing the missionary to their village at this time of the day?

Pierre rode straight to the Chief's hut and sat there waiting for him to come out and invite him to dismount.

Majara was aware that something was amiss and hurriedly came from his hut. His eyes were bloodshot and had a wild look. He was morose and ill at ease. He looked at Pierre for a long time before he spoke. Then it occurred to him that the missionary was there in connection with Tselane.

"Dumela, Moneri. Are you alive?"

"Peace, Morena. I am alive." Pierre greeted Majara in the native fashion.

"I shall take your horse."

It was an invitation to dismount, and Pierre immediately got off. Majara called a youth to take the horse and lead it to water. He started walking to the place where he met his councilors and listened to the cases of his people, but Pierre remained standing. At the meeting place every man in the village had the right to come and listen to their conversation and he wanted to speak to Majara alone.

"What I have to say is for the ears of the Chief alone," he said. "Shall we speak in the hut?"

Majara turned round slowly. Pierre was struck by the young man's royal bearing and the figure of authority he looked even in his simple blanket which he had slung over his shoulders. The sullen look on his face became one of defiance. What was the white man after?

They entered his hut and he offered Pierre a low stool and placed it on the left-hand side of the fireplace, the place of the women. Pierre, knowing the customs, felt the insult but sat down waiting for Majara to be seated.

"I am waiting to hear your business," the Chief said.

Pierre's heart started beating uncomfortably. The moment had arrived. "My business has to do with a woman of your village. Tselane."

"I do not know where she is. You ask in vain."

"I did not ask where she is because I know."

Disbelief was clearly to be seen on the Chief's face. Pierre hesitated only a second and then continued: "She came to me because she was afraid. People whispered of medicine which you wanted to make and she was frightened. She is on her way now to her husband."

"How?" It was quite clear that Majara did not believe this. A woman in Tselane's condition could not ride on horseback to Maseru.

"She went by plane and is now on the train which will take her to her husband. But tell me, are the stories true which people whispered of your lenaka?"

"People talk many things. They also talk that which is sometimes not true."

"But it is true that you wanted to make medicine?"

Pierre realized that he was on dangerous ground. When Majara looked up he saw the anger in his eyes and he knew that he had perhaps made the wrong move to speak so openly. There was a suffocating silence. Majara shifted his weight and looked away.

"The missionary asks many questions."

It was plainly meant as a rebuke.

Pierre said: "Moshesh, your great and illustrious ancestor, invited the missionaries to come to his country to help him in times of need and to teach the power of prayer. If he trusted the missionaries to help him, why can't you?"

"I do not need help."

"Yes, you do. Your wife cannot have children and I can perhaps help you."

Majara looked up quickly. "In which way?"

"I shall ask the white doctor to come to my station and if you bring your wife there, he will help her."

Majara scratched on the ground with a small stick and it was hard to tell what he was thinking. Many were the stories he had heard of the things the white doctors could do but that they could help his wife—that was impossible. Diretlo, medicine brewed by his own doctor with diretlo, was the only thing that would help. Pierre waited patiently but when Majara did not answer he pointed out to him that with the help of God all things were possible.

A smile of derision crossed the face of the Chief. This God! When he had first courted Molili she had often spoken to him about the power of the God in which she believed. Why didn't He help her then to have children?

"Most of the people in my village do not believe in your God and they have children. They believe in the spirits of their ancestors and they seem to be doing better than my wife with her belief in the things the white people taught her."

"But if you ask God He will help you."

"My people do not ask the spirits of their ancestors for children; they just have them."

"Will you allow your wife to come and see the doctor when he comes to my station?"

"No!" The refusal was so blunt that Pierre could not believe what he had heard.

Majara was silent.

"Are you still thinking of taking diretlo?" Pierre asked. "You must think well before you act. God, who has power over life and death, will not forgive you this thing. You'll hear His voice on the mountain, and you will shudder because He will always remind you that He is waiting with His judgment on the day that you will stand before Him to answer for the life of the victim."

A loud thunderclap rent the air and Pierre saw his chance to make use of natural phenomena and the superstition of the natives to drive home his point.

"Did you hear His voice?" He was immediately sorry that he had resorted to this strategy.

There was contempt on the handsome features of the young chief. "God then only speaks in summer. Has He forgotten you in winter?"

"I did not mean that the thunder is His actual voice but that we feel His power in nature. In winter He speaks to us through the snow. Who sends the snow, the thunder and the rain? Have you ever thought of that?" Pierre stopped. Further speech was impossible, as such a loud volley of thunderpeals rumbled round the mountainside that no other sound could be heard. A lull came in the fury of the onslaught only to break out a few seconds later in greater intensity. A blinding flash of lightning hit the village, followed immediately by a thunderclap which shook the very earth under them.

Majara looked uneasily from Pierre to the dark clouds which were shutting out the daylight. He seemed to be thinking things over. It had never before worried him to think of a power strong enough to cause a thunderstorm like the one which now raged round his village.

Pierre watched him closely and wondered what thoughts occupied his mind. The low rumblings of the subsiding storm could still be heard in the distance but in the hut there was a deep oppressive quiet.

At last Pierre broke the silence. "What made you decide to go against the traditions of your ancestors?"

He had caught Majara unawares with such a direct question. Majara glared at him in silence.

Pierre went on: "Perhaps you did not think well what the consequences would be here in your own village, because sooner or later people would have found out where you got your diretlo for your lenaka, and your days as a chief that the people could love and respect would have been numbered. You know your own people and can imagine yourself how it would have affected them."

"It is not for the people to talk about the things their chief does."

"You are young, Majara, and we who are young are sometimes unable to judge beforehand how things will turn out. The whirlwind starts in the valley but who can tell where it will end and what it will do on its way? You were only thinking of your own wife, but what about this woman's husband? As chief of this village you would have had to answer him when he came back to look for his wife."

"My doctor has strong medicine."

"Not strong enough to hold out against a man who loved his wife and had lost her."

"You white people will never understand these things."

"Yes, it is rather hard for us to understand how the flesh of a human being who had no power to do miracles while the person was alive will all of a sudden be able to help you when the flesh has been burnt to powder."

"Our witch doctors understand these things."

"Your witch doctor understood so well that he allowed this woman to get away. That doesn't say much for his power."

Pierre could see that he had hit on something which had been worrying Majara too. Majara retreated within himself and sat sullenly staring at the ground.

"Believe me, Morena, I have come to you as a friend," Pierre said. "I do not condemn you because I have studied your customs and I know how you feel about these things, but times have changed since your ancestors started this custom. Won't you let me help you?"

Majara looked into Pierre's eyes and it was clear that he challenged Pierre to explain in which way he intended helping him.

"If you would only let me come here and talk to you so that we could get to know each other better—or come to my station—I am sure that you will later understand the things I want to tell you about."

Molili, who had come from the fields with the other women when the storm was nearing them, entered the hut and saved her husband from answering the missionary's plea.

"Dumela, Molili, daughter of Thotofeane," Pierre said.

"Dumela, Moneri." She did not look up. Would the Moneri greet her in such a friendly fashion if he knew what she had done? That she had consented to the use of medicine? She could not look into his face.

Pierre got up. "I must go now, for the rain will not be long in coming and I must pass the cliffs before the road becomes slippery. Shall I see you at the station for church on Sunday?"

He asked the question of Molili but looked at her husband for the answer. Neither of them answered. Molili did not answer because she dared not and Majara was silent because he had no intention of going.

"I am passing this way again one day next week on my way to Chief RaDitaba. I shall look you up." Pierre left the hut and Majara followed to see that he got his horse. While the Chief was speaking to the boy to bring the horse, Pierre stepped into the hut:

"Do not worry about Tselane, she is safe."

He left before Molili had time to recover from the shock of his words. She rushed out of the hut after him but he had already joined her husband and she was afraid to speak.

Heavy drops of rain started splattering in the dust when Pierre rode out of the village. Few people were outside their huts and those who greeted him did so quietly.

Pierre felt dejected and despondent. His visit to Majara had not been very successful. If only he could win Majara's friendship, the hope that Tselane could soon return to her people unafraid that the Chief would fill his own horn with medicine would not be so forlorn. Perhaps the fact that he had said that he would come that way again the following week would make the Chief consider before looking for another victim. Majara's belief in the witch doctor had surely been shaken to a certain extent because Tselane had escaped, but that was not enough. He must be made to realize the hopelessness of looking for help from a source that was unable to help him and could only ruin his life for him.

When Pierre had left, Majara called for his beer pot and drank deeply. He was annoyed. What right had the white man to come and meddle in his affairs? Did he go to the mission station to tell the missionary what he had to do? The white people in their stupidity knew nothing of the power of a chief's horn if the medicine was correctly made in the way his ancestors had always made it.

The white man was offering him friendship, but what would he do with his friendship? Would they ever drink together from the same beer pot? Would they hunt together or sit in his hut smoking their pipes on long winter nights, talking of the things their fathers had taught them? Would the missionary dance with them at harvest time and at the weddings of the young girls of his village? What good was a friendship when men could not enjoy their friendship in this way together?

Molili busied herself preparing their food. She felt an exciting happiness now that the Moneri had told her that Tselane was safe, but she was burning to know more. All morning in the fields her remorse had been bitter. The women hardly spoke of Tselane, at least not when she could hear them. She knew that they held her responsible in a way and she could not blame them. If she suffered, it was the just punishment God was giving her.

16

THE SUN was climbing down from his seat of high noon and the shadows were lowering to the valleys when Majara pulled his blanket close around him and left his hut to visit Metlae. He had been drinking steadily and in his befuddled mind Metlae's failure to see that Tselane would escape was the cause for his feeling of frustration and disappointment.

Metlae was in his hut, brewing herbal medicine and muttering all the time. He was not dressed in his ceremonial clothes but was naked under the blanket he wore. He sprang up when Majara kicked the door open. It was dark inside the hut and the Chief could not see the old man where he cowered against the wall.

"Metlae!" There was no answer. "Metlae!"

"The Chief makes a loud sound for an old man's ears. I am here; does the Chief want something from me?"

Majara laughed scornfully. " 'Does the Chief want something from me?' " He mimicked the old man and entered. "Even if I do want something from you, all that I shall get will be lies! Lies!" He was standing inside the hut now and glared at Metlae. "Have your bones told you already where she is?" His knowledge of what had happened to Tselane gave him pleasure in mocking the medicine man who would throw his bones only to tell lies.

"I told the Chief that she has gone to a far place."

"I want to hear more. Throw your bones again."

Metlae thought quickly. He had seen the missionary arrive and speak to the Chief and had wondered all the time whether the visit was in connection with Tselane. What was it that made the Chief so bold and scornful of his power? Things had started going wrong for him and one more slip might mean anything. He must be careful.

"The bones will not speak twice of the same thing."

"Let them then speak of a new one, of the new victim."

"They have said that this thing must wait until the snows have been on the mountain and melted."

"Then tell your bones that this thing cannot be. By then I want my son in my hut."

"The Chief will do well not to be hasty. The spirits of our—"

Majara sprang forward and grabbed the old man by his throat. "Stop your talking! Do as I say." He flung the bony old man down and glowered at him, his eyes red with anger.

Metlae took his bag but was shaking so violently that he could not untie the string.

"My medicine man is shaking when it is not cold," said Majara. "Perhaps the bones will be shaking too, and unable to speak."

Metlae threw the bones with a wild gesture and then sat contemplating them. Scornfully, Majara waited for the lies. At last the old man started speaking in a mumbling voice, completely oblivious of his visitor.

"They say that many days will pass before peace comes to this village. I see the black bird of death flying from the mountain. I see people leaving and others coming. There is a knife that is thirsty for blood. There are many horses and white people."

"Stop!" Majara shouted. "I don't want to hear your stories. Tell me about my lenaka."

Metlae looked at the Chief and with great certainty he knew that the day he had always feared had arrived. His era as medicine man for this young man was over. He would have to leave and find a new village in which to live. He gathered the bones and threw them again. Of one thing he would make sure; peace would not easily sit in this man's heart again. He looked at the lie of the bones for some time and then whispered: "They say that the Chief will never possess a lenaka."

Metlae was not prepared for the onslaught and fell flat on the floor when Majara sprang at him. Majara grabbed the old man by his throat and started strangling him.

"Liar! Because you have lost your heart now that your bones have lied to you, you say that I shall not have a lenaka. Perhaps diretlo from a medicine man would make the best and strongest medicine!" He laughed wildly. "Nobody has ever thought of that. A medicine man to make medicine from!" He pressed on Metlae's throat until his eyes bulged in their sockets. "Shall I possess a lenaka? Speak, tell me the truth!"

He let go for a moment and Metlae gasped for breath. He was too weak to speak. Majara got up and pulled the old man to his feet. His blanket had fallen off and he stood in his bony nakedness shivering before the Chief.

"Speak!"

"I have spoken. The spirits of our ancestors have seen and they tell me that I have said that which is true. The Chief will never possess a lenaka." Hardly had he finished speaking when Majara slapped him across his face with the flat hand.

"Sleep tonight on your lies. I shall come again tomorrow to hear whether the spirits of our ancestors have not changed their minds about my lenaka."

Metlae picked up his blanket after the Chief left and swung it round his shoulders. There was no time to be lost. He must pack up and leave before the Chief came again. He looked round his hut at all the little calabashes full of medicine, at the bottles and charms littering the place behind the fireplace, at the skins and animal claws that were waiting to be made into charms, and his heart was sore because he was too old and weak to carry everything with him. Slowly, with deliberate care, he started packing his most valuable possessions. He pulled on his thin trousers, and then threw some wood on the fire. He must prepare food to take with him and eat a good meal before he left. There was an evil light in his eyes as he made one plan after another for punishing the Chief before he went away. He had spoken of the black bird of death flying from the mountain, of a knife that was thirsty for blood; he would leave a sign at the Chief's hut which would give him something to think about.

There was not a sound in the village when Metlae at last opened the door of his hut to go. He had his bag slung over his withered old shoulder and carefully he picked his way to the Chief's hut. It did not take him long and, when he left, there was a smile of satisfaction on his wrinkled face.

The sky was still overcast; there was, however, a moon and by the varying light he found his way to a mountain cave where he would stay the night before he went on his way.

Molili rose earlier than usual. After the rain, hoeing and weeding would be easier and the women would leave for the lands as soon as the sun was up. She got up quietly but Majara was watching her. He could not sleep and had been awake since the first cock crowed. Molili opened the door but immediately jumped back into the hut. She put her hand to her mouth to check the scream that rose to her lips. She looked around at her husband and found him watching her.

"What is the matter?"

Molili pointed to the ground immediately in front of the hut. Majara got up to see what it was and stood back like his wife. There, spread out on the hard ground, was a dead lizard with four black stones in a straight line towards their door. The meaning was only too clear: death would visit that hut in four days, four weeks, or four months.

"This is Metlae's work," Majara said. "I'll kill him for this. Take the things away."

Molili had to obey her husband, although superstition, which she so carefully tried to overcome, made her tremble when she scooped up the bad omen. She walked to the donga and buried the stones and the lizard in some loose sand.

Majara had gone back to his sleeping mats. He'd wait until the sun was high before going to Metlae. For Metlae this would be the day of reckoning.

At Metlae's hut, Sobeti and Seiso were waiting anxiously for a reply to their knock. They had come to buy medicine to protect them. Sobeti's father had not spoken to the Chief yet, but the young men had decided to leave the village as soon as possible. Metlae must give them medicine to make them strong and to guard over them in Gaudeng. When there was no answer they knocked again. Everything was still quiet in the village but soon people would be getting up and the young men did not want to be seen at the witch doctor's hut.

"Let's open the door. He is an old man and he must be deaf."

They tried the door and to their surprise it opened. Bewildered, they looked around. The hut was empty. The fire in the middle of the floor had gone out and things were in great confusion on the floor. It was obvious that the medicine man had gone away. Immediately fear sprang into their hearts. What could this mean? Did the medicine man throw his bones and find out that there was danger and had he therefore gone away without warning them too? They looked at each other. Seiso was the first to speak.

"I ride today, I am not waiting. We must leave before the Chief hears of this."

They hurried back to their huts. On the way they had to pass the hut of RaPalla and on an impulse Sobeti called out to him when they were near his hut. Seaka was already up and she came to the door.

"We want to speak to RaPalla."

"My husband is still sleeping."

"Wake him."

Seaka was surprised at this command but went into the hut. RaPalla soon came to the door with sleep still heavy on his eyes. "Why do you come so early in the morning? What is wrong?"

Seiso whispered to him what they had found and immediately RaPalla was wide awake.

"We are leaving for the mines today. Are you coming too?"

RaPalla hesitated only for a second. It could mean only one thing;

something had happened which made Metlae flee. If they wanted to escape danger they had to go too.

"I'll ride with you."

They left the village separately. RaPalla took his son with him to bring the horses back, and nobody knew that they had gone until late in the afternoon when the story of the medicine man's departure was still striking fear in the hearts of everyone who heard of it.

Wild stories were being told and people held their mouths with both hands to show their utter amazement at the things that were happening. First Tselane had disappeared, then their medicine man had walked out on them and now RaPalla, Seiso and Sobeti had ridden away to the mines without the usual send-off and without saying goodbye to anybody.

Majara flew into a temper of great fury when he heard about these things. He spoke angrily to RaSobeti but the old man did not answer him. Sobeti must have had a very good reason for wanting to go away and his father was surely the last person to stand in his way.

The village seethed with speculation and fear. Men drank hurriedly and women forgot about the food they had to prepare. They walked hurriedly from one hut to the other, talking and listening eagerly to every scrap of conversation. Children left the clay they were molding into oxen and herds to stare open-mouthed at the grownups and their goings on.

The people who were Christians spoke quietly in their huts of the goodness of God who had seen fit to make the witch doctor go away at last. Now there would be hope for others to be freed of their belief in his chantings and medicines. The pagans lamented, for did not this mean that their village had now become weak, an easy target for any other village where the chief had a strong lenaka or the medicine man could make good medicine?

Khama's parents were the only people in the village who took no heed of what was going on. Their sorrow was too great; there was no room in their hearts for any other calamity. RaKhama lay dazed on the sleeping mats and his wife sat next to him. They had heard that the witch doctor had gone away so their suspicion that Tselane had been chosen as the victim for ritual murder became a certainty.

There was bitterness in their hearts. How could they ever stand before the Chief again knowing that he had done this thing to them? Where was their child? If only they could be sure that she was well, that she was safe and in no danger any more. A hundred times they had asked the same question of each other.

"Do you think she is still alive, MaKhama?"

The old woman wiped a tear from her wrinkled cheek. "Our child is strong. Let us hope that she is still alive."

In the hospital, Sister Greyling looked at Dr. Naude and asked the same question: "Is she still alive?"

The doctor felt the pulse again. "She is strong and it is possible that she may live."

The two nurses assisting him watched his face anxiously. Nobody spoke. The minutes ticked by. Suddenly Tselane's eyelids fluttered. She turned her head from side to side and it was obvious that she was struggling to shake off the darkness which had been enveloping her.

Dr. Naude felt the pulse and shook his head. "I must go to Number Sixteen. Send for me if she shows any signs of rallying." He started for the door but before he reached it Sister Greyling called him back.

"She has opened her eyes."

Naude came back and laid his fingers on the weakly beating pulse. "Go to Number Sixteen, Sister, and see whether everything is still all right. I'll stay here."

After half an hour Tselane's pulse had recovered to such an extent that Naude left her to attend to the other urgent cases. Walking down the passage his thoughts were still with Tselane. While waiting for her to recover he had watched the strong but gentle young face. What could have driven the woman to such a deed?

On the third day, Sister Greyling went to Dr. Spiro to report that Tselane was refusing to eat. "She just turns her head away and lies with her face turned towards the wall."

"Has she spoken at all, asked any questions?"

"Not a word."

"You'll have to make her eat. She is strong and young and her body has overcome the shock. She must only get well now."

Sister Greyling went back to Tselane, who had now been moved into a private ward. Tselane lay with her eyes open and watched Sister Greyling when she placed the plate of food on the bedside table. The sister tried to feed her but she turned her head away.

"Come now, my girl, you won't get well if you don't eat."

There was a knock on the door. Sister Greyling put the plate down and turned impatiently to the door. It must be the policeman again. She opened the door so that Tselane could not see who had knocked, and slipped out closing the door behind her.

The policeman asked: "How is the prisoner?"

"She is better," said Sister Greyling, "but she is still quite weak."

"Can you put a chair here at the door?" the officer asked. "Starting tomorrow it will be necessary for us to station a man to guard her."

The nurse frowned, displeased. "Must you?"

"It's the law."

"She won't try to escape, if that's what you're afraid of. I'm sure she's still too frightened to try that."

"We can't take chances."

Sister Greyling looked away. "There's something very sweet about the girl. I wonder if she really understands what she has done? Or do we? After all, none of us know the actual circumstances."

"I'm sure all that will come out at the trial, Sister."

"There'll be a trial?"

"Of course."

Sister Greyling's smile was sad. "Even so, what chance has she? Most of you policemen have so little patience with the poor blacks."

"You sound like a Kafferboetie, Sister," and from his grin it was obvious that the policeman was teasing.

"I suppose I do," the nurse said. "But I don't really believe they're all angels, the way the fanatics do. I do believe they ought to be educated, taught to live in this kind of world we've imposed on them, but I know some of them are hopeless and we'll never make any progress with them. Still, once in a while you meet one like this girl. You somehow know she is sweet and good. Yet you also know that she's done a terrible thing, and because she's so afraid of us she'll never be able to explain why, and because we'll have no explanations to listen to we'll go ahead and hang her simply on the facts we know." Sister Greyling turned back to the officer. "All right.

The chair will be here in the morning." She went back into the room and took up the tray again and tried to feed Tselane.

She filled a spoon with food and held it in front of Tselane's mouth. She smiled and asked Tselane to try just one spoonful. Tselane did not understand the words but the smile spoke to her and she opened her mouth. She took three more spoonfuls and then turned her head away.

This white woman was kind. She would like to help her but the food tasted bitter in her mouth and she could not eat more.

Each day Sister Greyling had a little more success. Tselane ate and walked a few steps every day. Sister Greyling held her arm and pulled a chair for her to the window so that she could see the flowers and the people walking in the streets.

"Soon you will be able to walk outside too." Sister Greyling smiled but was thankful that Tselane could not understand her, for she realized what it would mean when Tselane was strong enough to walk outside.

Every time the door opened Tselane saw a white man at the door. What did he want there? Sometimes when she walked to the window he suddenly opened the door and looked in. She had forgotten her fear a little but now it darted around in her mind like a flea that got in under her blanket. She tried to catch the flea to kill it but one little flea of fear became many and she shivered every time somebody entered her room.

Soon there would be no escape from them. She would be taken away. They would not let her stay in the hospital. At night when she thought of this a great darkness loomed up in front of her and she wept into her pillow.

Two weeks passed and her strength came back to her. Only her sorrow over her child and the fear of the white man who was at her door reminded her of the thing that had happened to her.

It was on a Monday that they knocked on her door just when she had eaten her food. The sister and two men came in. She had seen both the men at the door before.

"Come, girl, you must go now." The sister spoke kindly but the sound of her words shocked Tselane.

"No, they must not take me away, they must not. I want to stay here until my husband comes!"

These thoughts rushed through her mind but could not find her tongue. With big pleading eyes she looked at the sister. Her heart was pounding.

One white man came forward. "Come."

Tselane sprang up and ran to Sister Greyling. She took hold of her dress and clung to her.

"Tell her to come." The policeman spoke impatiently.

"It won't help, she does not understand."

Tselane looked from the one to the other. What were they saying? What were they going to do? Spirits of my ancestors, help. Help me! Her silent prayer died in her heart when the two men took her each by an arm and pulled her away from the sister.

The ox went quietly when the rope was around his neck. There was no escape; she had to go.

Without crying, without resisting, she walked down the long passage between the two policemen. They took her down a long hall to the steps, then outside to a waiting car. Tselane got in when the policemen opened the door, and she sat with her head lowered as they drove through the city. She felt the car stop: the door was opened and when one of the policemen touched her arm Tselane obediently got out. Again between the policemen, she entered a building and was taken to an office where several men gathered around her and looked at her and asked her questions, but she did not understand them. Then they took her away again, down another long hall, and she thought that now it was that they would hang her, and she grew nervous and afraid. One man opened a door and pointed for her to go in. She stepped forward slowly, her eyes half closed.

The heavy key turned in the door. Tselane swung round. She was alone in the cell. High up there was a small window through which the sun shone on the opposite wall. She tried to see the blue sky but it was impossible. She could not reach up to the window. She sat down on the mat and stroked the coarse blanket which they had given her. Her own lovely blanket, with the bright red flowers on the smoky-gray background and with the black braid, had been soiled on the train. Would they keep it for her? Khama had brought it to her on his last visit. Thoughts of her husband brought this thing which she had done to her mind. What would Khama say when he heard of it? If only she had gone to school so that she could write to him. But what would she write? That she had killed their child? That the witch doctor had willed her to have her child in the white man's train? She pushed her face into her blanket to keep out the sight of her child. She felt his warm body in her arms and held them out as if they could still hold his small head. Agony made her weep. She had fled and suffered to save him and then with her own hands she had killed him. Tselane cried out in her pain and the echoes of her cries bewildered her. She looked at the patch of sunlight against the wall but it had moved; it was only half the size now and soon it would be gone too.

What were they doing in the village? The sun was going down. Women would be calling their children to leave the fields and go home. She saw the procession of young girls with the calabashes and tins on their heads going down to the fountain to draw water. The little cowherds would be whistling and shouting to call their charges to go home. Thin spirals of smoke would be rising from the outside fireplaces where people were preparing the evening meal. She smelled the dung fires and the wonderful aroma of freshly made porridge.

In her imagination she stood high on the mountain and looked far down into the valley. The exhilarating mountain air filled her, making the cell smaller and smaller until the walls seemed to be drawing nearer. From the corners of her cell shadows crept in, and the loneliness and the quiet of the place brought the village and her people even closer to her.

The light of day had not completely gone when the key grated in the lock. Tselane stood up and away from the door. What did they want now? Were they bringing somebody else into the cell? A woman came in and put her food on the small table before she went out again. They had made some stiff porridge for her and had given her white man's food too. She took the spoon to eat but the food stuck in her throat. MaKhama with her wrinkled old face was perhaps serving food to her husband at that moment. What were the two old people thinking? Were they very sad? Did RaPalla tell them that she had gone to the missionary? Would they come and look for her? Tselane's heart ached with grief, and tears dropped into her plate of porridge she had on her lap. She put it back on the table and sat with her back against the wall, waiting for the night. In the hospital the night had never seemed to end and here it would be ten times worse.

Five times the little patch of sunlight was on her wall; five long lonely nights she had struggled through when at last they came for her and took her to another building. There were many people and they talked a great deal and wrote in books but she did not understand what was going on.

A native spoke to her as soon as the white man, who was sitting alone on the high chair, had said something but she only looked at them because she did not know what it was they wanted from her. The white man from the train must have told them that she had lost her ticket, that she had had her child in their train and what had happened then. Were they speaking of these things? It lasted a long time and when they took her back to the cell the little patch of sunlight was gone and darkness was already on the floor under the window.

One day followed another with a sameness that was dreary. Twice a day they took her to walk in the yard in front of her cell. Three times a day they brought her food. The doctor came to her and did not speak but felt all over her body and spoke to the policeman and the woman. Why did they do this thing?

She had heard many stories in the village of what the white people did to those who had killed somebody. Whenever she thought of this her throat seemed to close up and her thoughts left her and only a buzzing in her ears remained.

A few times the native who had spoken after the white man on the high chair came to her cell with a white policeman and the woman who brought her her food, and he talked to her, but she remained silent because she did not understand him. They became very angry and twice the native took her by her shoulders and shook her until she had cried out in pain and in fear. The white man had spoken sharply and the black man stopped shaking her.

What was it they wanted of her? Bewildered she had tried to ignore any person who came to her room after that. She refused to go for her walks. She only wanted to stay where she was and await her fate.

Many days passed, however, and nothing happened. The waiting made her weak and turned her heart to stone. All feeling left her and her insides felt hollow. She only wanted to sit against the wall and think of the village and the child that she had killed.

She did not hate Majara or the witch doctor. If Molili could only have had a child, nothing would have happened. She did not blame the Moneri for sending her away, she only blamed herself for leaving her country. She could have gone to her father's kraal. If Majara had come for her they could have fought; there were many strong young men in her village. Now she only had to sit and wait and wait until the white people had made up their minds. Why were they taking such a long time?

Did her parents know that she had gone away? Soon they would be expecting her: what would they do when she failed to come?

17

KHAMA stood at the doorway of the hut, smiling. "Dumela, Seaka," he said. "Are you alive?"

Startled, Seaka jumped to her feet, sending her sewing scattering across the dirt floor. It was a moment before she could speak. Then: "I am alive, cousin of my husband. What brings you back to the mountain?"

"The season is late and our work starts after a month; they have given us time to come to our homes," Khama explained. "Where is RaPalla?"

"My husband has gone to the mines."

"Already?" Khama was surprised and a little hurt. "He said he would remain here until after my child was born."

Seaka looked away, then dropped to her knees to gather up her sewing. "Yes," she said. "At first he thought he would stay longer, but we need the money."

He nodded, understanding. "Stay well, Seaka. I must go to the hut of my old parents; there will be joy when they see me. And

Tselane, too, will laugh when she comes from the fields. If you see her before I do, don't tell her that I am here."

He left abruptly, gaily, setting off at a quick trot for his own hut. His heart was full of love for his beautiful wife. He must remember to tell everyone not to mention to her that he was back. How surprised she would be to see him. Then he would take her in his arms and they would go to their love-making.

When Khama reached the fireplace in the yard of his father's hut, he stopped short. Why was there no fire? How could his parents let this happen? He glanced at the hut: the door was closed and there was no sign of life.

He called: "Ma! MaKhama!"

Nobody responded. Khama was puzzled. He tried the door but it was locked. This was strange. His parents only locked their hut when they went on a long journey. Where could they have gone? He went hurriedly to his own hut and found it locked too. Had his parents perhaps taken Tselane to her parents? But it was not the time yet. He had expected that Tselane would be in the hut for at least another week or two.

He stood for a moment in the yard, frowning, bewildered, trying to imagine what was happening. He heard voices nearby and walked toward them: the men were drinking beer and smoking lazily in the sun. When they saw him they sat upright and some got to their feet. They said his name in greeting, but he noticed the absence of welcome in their voices and saw the looks they exchanged.

He asked: "Have you see RaKhama and my old mother?"

"No," they said. "Not since last night."

Khama asked: "Do you know if they have gone away?"

"They have said nothing about it."

"Have they taken my wife to her parents?"

"We do not know."

Khama turned away impatiently and went back to Seaka's hut. It was empty. He called out loudly but there was no answer. He cursed softly. Now where had this woman gone to? What was wrong with everybody today? Someone must know what is going on.

From hut to hut he went, but nowhere was there a person who knew anything about his parents, and everywhere he got the feeling that people were not glad to see him. They did not look at him when they spoke and their words were few. What could have happened to them? When he had left to go to Worcester there had been warm friendship in their smiles and handshakes, and now suddenly he felt like a stranger to them.

He asked one group: "Has Tselane gone to her father's kraal?"

"We do not know," they said, "you must go and look."

Khama was at a loss to understand this. People always knew when a woman left the village to go to her mother. There was the send-off. There were the women who walked with her and her parents-in-law to see them safely on their way. How was it that people said that they did not know whether Tselane had gone to the kraal of her parents?

He did not wait to argue about this but ran to his small hut in which he kept his saddle. He shouldered his saddle and ran to the kraal. His horse whinnied when he heard Khama whistle for him but there was no time now to pat and play with his horse. Khama saddled quickly and set off for the kraal of his parents-in-law. He did not take the normal footpath but went along the short cut over the mountain which he used to take when he still courted Tselane. He spurred his horse on and more than once they slipped and nearly fell. He loved his horse but this was an hour when he could not spare the animal. The last stretch was a piece of flat land and Khama lashed his horse until foam flecked its sides.

At his father-in-law's hut Khama jumped from his horse and threw the reins to a young boy who was playing nearby.

"Khama!" his parents-in-law shouted when they saw him.

"Peace, are you alive?"

"We are alive, our child, but what brings you here? It is a long time before we expected to see you."

There was no time to waste. Khama turned to his mother-in-law. "Where is Tselane, Ma?"

The woman looked at him with great surprise and wondered at his question. "Why do you ask us this thing? She is with your parents. She must be working in the fields with the other women now."

"I have not been to the fields. I shall go there."

Before they could ask him more questions, Khama sprang on his horse. Tselane's parents were stunned. Why was their son-in-law behaving so queerly?

For the first time since his return, Khama felt fear. If Tselane had gone to the fields with the other women, then someone in the village would have told him so. He beat his horse to race it forward, already afraid in his heart that Tselane would not be at her work. Again he took the shorter route over the mountains, and because he did this he missed meeting his parents who were on the normal footpath between their village and the kraal of Tselane's parents, walking slowly, resting often, their years heavier on them because of the sad news they carried.

He saw the women in the fields from a distance and he saw that they paused in their work and pointed at him. He did not stop his horse until he was a few feet from them. They were working in single file; then, as if by agreement, they all moved away and left the old woman MaPhépa to face him alone.

He said to them: "I greet you, mothers; are you alive?"

"Helele, Khama. You ride with the wind," MaPhépa said.

"My thoughts spur me on. They are of my wife. MaPhépa, where is Tselane?" He looked along the line of unsmiling faces and frightened eyes.

"Khama," MaPhépa said, "that is a question which is dark as the night. I cannot answer you."

Khama jumped from his horse and came to stand in front of MaPhépa. "Your words are hidden in your pail. Open and let me hear."

"It is many days now that we woke up one morning to find that Tselane had gone away."

"Where has she gone to?"

"We do not know."

"And my parents?"

"What about your parents?"

"They are not in their hut and the door is locked."

MaPhépa's eyes widened, then she rolled them in terror.

"Why don't you answer me?" Khama demanded.

"What shall I answer you, my son, when my old heart has suddenly left me? I did not know about your parents."

Khama looked down the line of women and saw Molili. He called out to her: "Cousin of Tselane, you must know where she is. What has happened to my wife?"

Molili glanced at the others before she answered him in a small voice: "I do not know, Khama. I heard it from RaPalla. But she is gone and we have not seen her for many days now."

An anger of helplessness exploded on Khama's face; he wanted to shout at the women, but he knew there was nothing they would do for him. He swung himself onto his horse, hitting the saddle with a loud slap, then pulled the horse around and sped off towards the village. There was one man who would know, who would tell him. The Chief must have some idea where his people go; it was always that way; Majara would know what had happened to Tselane and the old couple.

Khama drew up his horse in front of Majara's hut and made noises to let the Chief know someone was there. Majara came out.

"Dumela, Morena," said Khama, "I greet you."

Majara returned the salute, then gestured to him to sit down on a stool opposite the Chief's outside the hut door. Khama's anxiety burned in him, but he knew he must conform to good manners and speak of other things first before he touched on the subject that had brought him. At last he could bear the suspense no longer.

"I have not found my wife in her hut," he said. "Does Morena know where she has gone?"

"It was a strange thing, Khama," Majara said intimately. "She went away in the night, never saying a word about her plans, not even to my wife, and you know what good friends they were. I sent men out the next day to all the villages but she had not been seen. I do not know what to think of this. It is hard to understand that a woman with her time so near would do a thing like that. Tselane has done a very wrong thing not to tell your parents about her plans."

"My parents are not in their hut." Khama made a bland statement and was surprised at the reaction his words had on the Chief.

Majara got up quickly. "They must have gone on a visit to your relatives near the store. Have you been there?"

"No, I have been looking for my wife. I must find her."

"Where will you look next?"

"I have been to her father's kraal. I shall ride to my uncle's hut and look there for my parents. They must know where she is."

Khama soon left the Chief to ride to his uncle's place. There disappointment awaited him. They had not seen his parents and they would not speak of Tselane. The fear which had tortured him in the afternoon—that something had happened to his wife—now gnawed at him as he rode back to his village in the night. There was still no sign of his parents. Their huts were quiet and closed. He unsaddled his horse, turned him into the kraal, and then sat dejectedly on the step of his own hut. He held his head and slowly tears of desperation came down his cheeks. He was painfully weary; the strain was becoming too much for him. At last he got up. He would go to the hut of old Phonya and eat there.

He neared the hut and heard the voices of many men speaking inside. This he had not expected. Why were the men all together? Such things did not take place at night unless there was great trouble. He stood there, hearing the low voices, unable to understand a word, his mind slowly fusing the scattered day into a clear picture.

They knew. They all knew. They had all lied to him. He could see it now. The sudden departure of RaPalla from the village, Seaka's fumbling surprise to see him, the evasiveness of the men and the obvious fear of the women—even the Chief's vague explanation that Tselane had left the village during the night: it all fitted together now: it was all lies. They knew. They knew what had happened to Tselane and they knew what had happened to his parents. It was his unexpected return that had stunned them; they had not had time to prepare better explanations, and now that he was back they were terrified. They knew what he would do to them—to all of them—if anything wrong had happened to the three people he loved. Now they were all in there, all the men, plotting what to do next.

When Khama stepped forward and kicked through the door of Phonya's hut every muscle of his body bulged with hate and violence. The shocked men looked at him.

"Tell me!" he shouted at them. "Tell me! Tell me where is Tselane! What have you done to her?" He thrust out a fist and crushed the face of a young man who was already too terrified to feel the pain of broken bones and ripped flesh.

"Tell me!" Khama screamed. He lunged into the room, grabbing at whoever was near.

The men scattered; some of them darted through the battered

door, others pressed themselves against the wall. Their cries of "We don't know" filled the air.

"I'll kill you!" Khama shrieked at them. "I'll kill all of you unless you tell me!"

The voice of old Phonya rose above the furore. "Stop, Khama! We are your friends."

Khama spun on him. "Friends? You have all lied to me all day. That is not for friends."

"We have not lied."

"Then tell me where is Tselane!"

"We truly do not know. One morning she was gone; that is all we know for certain."

"Why didn't you search for her?"

"We did. We looked one day and found nothing."

"One day! Is that all she meant to you? Is that all the wife of Khama meant?"

"We found nothing."

"And where are my parents?"

"That we do not know either. This morning they were not here. Their door was locked. Nobody saw them go."

"They would not just go! Why didn't you do something? Why didn't you go to Metlae? He could have helped you."

"Metlae is gone. He left the village a few days after Tselane disappeared."

Khama froze. He looked from man to man in the room, his eyes afire with unbelieving astonishment. A small fear curdled in the pit of his stomach, boiled up into his mouth and exploded into a crazed scream. He turned and ran out of the hut and across the village to the hut of the Chief.

He stopped close to the door and shouted: "Majara! Majara, come out! Come out here and tell Khama the truth! I tell you to come out here and tell me the truth, Majara, so the people can watch me kill you if you tell my ears what my heart fears."

There was a movement at the door. Khama moved nearer to see who it was. Recognizing, he called out: "Send out your husband, Molili, you who call yourself the cousin of my wife. Send out your husband!"

"He is not here," Molili scarcely whispered.

"Speak out," Khama commanded. "I have too much fire in me to hear your words."

"He is not here," Molili said louder.

"You lie, too," Khama said.

"See for yourself."

"Where is he, then?"

"I do not know."

With a step, Khama was at Molili, his thick hands tight around her throat. "Speak while you have breath!"

Molili sank to her knees, her body limp in Khama's grasp. From the watching crowd a woman called: "No more death, Khama, no more death! We have had enough. I will tell you where the Chief has gone."

Khama let Molili drop to the ground and he turned to the woman who had spoken. He glared at her, waiting.

She lifted her arm and pointed to the footpath which led northward from the village. It traveled across the flat field, then upward through the steep hills, along the edge of a sheer ravine, then onward, fringing the bush, until at last it wound its way downhill again and into the clearing which opened onto the mission of Pierre le Brun.

Khama gazed at the path, then turned his eyes to the thick growth: the short cut. Without a word he broke into a run towards the trees.

Just yards ahead of him, stumbling, falling, bleeding, ran Chief Majara, running towards the mission, the only place where he felt he might be safe from Khama. When men from Phonya's hut came and warned him that Khama had returned and was threatening to kill everyone, it was Molili who told her husband that surely the missionary would help him; he must go there. He had taken off instantly; even before he had reached the dense brush he could hear Khama at the hut, shouting his name.

He thought he could hear Khama now. He paused a moment. Yes, someone was coming, running. Majara took off again, as fast as he could, ignoring the thorned bushes that tore at him, the rocks that bruised his bones and sent him sprawling. Through the brush he saw the lights of the mission and broke out in a final rush to escape. He leapt up the steps to the porch and pounded on a window.

In a moment Pierre le Brun opened the door and beamed a flashlight in Majara's face. Before Pierre could speak, Majara pleaded: "Hide me, Moneri, hide me! Khama is coming. He is going to kill me!"

"Khama is here?" The missionary stepped back in surprise.

"He is coming to kill me. He thinks I know where Tselane is."

"But she should be with him," said Pierre. "She left here almost a month ago."

"Don't stand there, Moneri," Majara begged. "Hide me, or you will watch me die."

Pierre moved aside. "Come in," he said, and shut the door. He turned his flashlight down a short corridor and led the Chief to the end where a ladder stood against the wall, going up to the loft where the missionary stocked supplies.

"Get up there and lower the door after you," he said. He waited until Majara had done what he had ordered, then he removed the ladder and put it on the floor on its side.

There was a knock on the door. Pierre braced himself, then went slowly to the door and opened it. He was not sure how he would handle this.

Khama stood there, his chest heaving, his leg muscles quivering. "Is Chief Majara here?" he asked.

"You must be Khama," said Pierre.

"I am looking for Chief Majara. If he is not here, will you please tell me so that I can search elsewhere." Khama strained to keep respect in his voice.

"Come in, Khama. I want to talk to you."

"There are no words in me tonight for talk, Moneri. If the Chief is not here, just say so. I will believe you."

"Khama," Pierre said as firmly as he could, "I want you to come in. I want to talk to you about Tselane."

Khama's exhausted body snapped alert. "You know something about my wife?"

"Yes, Khama," said Pierre. "Come in and I will tell you. I will tell you everything."

18

THEY sat together long into the night. As Khama listened, his heart sank deeper in him. Poor Tselane. Poor little pigeon. How terrible it must have been for her. Pierre had spoken carefully, choosing his words with caution, wary of incensing Khama once again to the violence in which he had arrived at the mission.

"What is important," Pierre said, "is that she got away safely. I saw her onto the plane myself, and the pilot promised to put her on the train. I felt that under the circumstances her place was with you, and I can only hope you agree with me."

"I agree," Khama said. "You did the right thing, Moneri."

"I can't imagine what has taken her so long to arrive. Perhaps something happened to the train to hold her up; you know how often such things happen."

"It happens many times."

"And yet," said Pierre, struggling to put lightness in his voice, "she may be in Worcester right now, looking for you."

"That may be," said Khama. "I will go back to Worcester tomorrow."

"Do you have a horse with you?"

"My horse is in the village."

"Never mind; I have one for you. Why don't you spend the night here in the rondawel and I will ride with you in the morning to the plane. We can talk to the pilot together and ask about Tselane."

"If you wish it that way, Moneri."

Pierre looked across at Khama's bowed head, knowing how whipped the man must feel, and wished he could think of something to say to give him the assurance that all was well. But was it? Where in the world could the girl be? No matter what might have happened to the train, she certainly should be in Worcester by now. And if anything serious had happened, he would be greatly to blame, for it was he who had sent her on her way.

"Would you like some coffee, Khama, or a glass of water? Anything?"

"Nothing, Moneri. Thank you."

"Come, then, I'll take you to the rondawel."

They left the house and walked to the hut in silence. Pierre checked around to be sure there was everything Khama might need. He said good night and turned to leave; he stopped at the door. "Khama, I know this is an empty thing to say, but try not to worry. I'm sure you will find Tselane in safety and in health."

"Thank you, Moneri. I will be all right."

Pierre closed the door and went slowly back to the house.

There had been moments during his long talk with Khama when he forgot completely that Chief Majara was hiding in the loft overhead. So intent had he been on the young man sitting opposite him that nothing else in the world mattered. He had not even noticed when Simone discreetly left the room to leave the two men alone. Khama had listened tensely, soft moans coming from him as he learned about the diretlo and of Tselane's rush through the bush in fear, just as he this night had rushed through in hate. As Pierre talked on, softly, gently, intimately, Khama seemed to relax, resigned, his mind only on what must be done next to find Tselane. He had been submissive, almost meek, when Pierre took him to the rondawel.

Pierre stood on the porch for several minutes, waiting to be sure that Khama would try to sleep and not get up to wander restlessly in the night, then he went into the house, put the ladder in place and went up into the loft. It took a moment for his eyes to become adjusted to the darkness; he saw Majara sitting on sacks of grain.

The Chief said: "You were a long time with him."

"There was much to tell him."

"Where is he now?"

"Asleep in the rondawel."

"How will I get out of here?"

"It will be better to wait a while, to be sure that he is sleeping. Then you must get back to your village before your people think you have run away out of fear of another man."

"I do not care what the people think," Majara said sullenly.

Pierre recognized Majara's effort to recapture his pride. He asked: "What happened in the village tonight?"

"Khama turned into a wild beast, that is what happened," said the Chief. "Because he could not find Tselane or his parents he wanted to kill everyone."

"His parents?"

"They have gone away; I don't know where."

The thought occurred to Pierre that they might have become the diretlo victims. "Are you sure you don't know?"

"I said that."

It was useless to question further. Pierre said: "Come downstairs now. I think it will be all right to leave."

"What if Khama returns to the village tonight?"

"I don't think he will. Now that he knows everything his only worry is to find his wife."

"You told me you had sent her to him on the big bird."

"I did as I told you," said Pierre.

"Then why has he come back looking for her?"

"She had not reached him; he did not know she was on the way to the city. They have probably passed each other on their journeys."

Majara's voice was bitter: "Tselane has been gone a long time. Does the big bird fly slower when it carries pregnant women?"

Pierre did not answer. He preceded Majara down the stairs and put out all the lights so that they could not be seen from outside. Then they stepped out on the porch and stood quietly, listening. There were only the night sounds. Pierre led Majara around the front of the house to the path and walked with him a long way. They did not speak until they reached the place where the path fringed the deep ravine.

Pierre said: "I shall come to your village in two days. Shall I find you at home?"

Majara hesitated, then answered: "I shall be at home."

It was the nearest thing to an invitation Pierre had ever received to visit the village. He wondered if he could put hope in it. Majara walked on alone.

Pierre had only a few hours sleep when he felt Simone touch him to wake him. He dressed quickly and went to the rondawel to wake Khama. Khama was already awake and waiting. Eager to get away, he refused the breakfast Simone offered. Pierre and Khama saddled horses and left at a quick pace for Mashai, stopping only once to brush down the horses on the way. They saw the plane from a distance and went directly to it.

The pilot was supervising the loading of cargo when he noticed Pierre. "Coming along on this trip, Padre?"

"Not today, Mr. Stone, but this young man is."

Dick Stone glanced at Khama, nodded, and took out his tickets.

Pierre said: "Mr. Stone, do you remember the young woman I brought here a few weeks ago?"

"The pregnant one?"

Pierre nodded.

"I remember her. Why?"

"She is this man's wife. She has not been seen since."

Stone glanced at Khama again, then looked at Pierre. "I haven't seen her since the morning she got on the train."

"Then she did get on the train?"

"Yes. She spent the night at my house, then in the morning my servant and I drove her to the train. Anna put her in the care of an old Mosotho woman who was traveling to Bloemfontein."

"You are certain?"

"Of course I'm certain."

Pierre turned to Khama. "You understood what he said?"

"Yes, Moneri."

"Then she must be in Worcester by now, looking for you."

"That may be."

"When you find her," Pierre said, "have someone write to me. I will want to know."

"I will do that," said Khama, then he looked back to the mountains towards the village, "and if I do not find her I will be back myself."

The threat was clear. Pierre said: "Now, Khama, listen to me. You must not hate the people of your village. They are good people. I'm sure only the greatest fear of the Chief or the medicine man could have forced even one of them into taking part in the murder. When you and Tselane return, it will all be forgotten, and you must forget it, too."

"I will never bring her back here."

"Find her. That is all that matters now."

Dick Stone called the passengers to board the plane. Khama walked away. At the plane he paused and sent Pierre a brief nod, then climbed aboard. Pierre remained on the landing strip, watching the plane until it was a mere speck in the sky. Then he got on his horse and, leading the one Khama had used, rode home, wondering what he could do to help.

In the town of Beaufort West there was another man wondering how he could help Tselane. Anton Steyn leaned against the edge of a table and watched her glumly, listening to the soft sounds she made as she wept. He did not take his eyes from her as he asked the black man in the room with them: "Is she saying anything, Jim?"

"No, Mr. Steyn," said the African. "She is weeping."

"She'll have much more to weep about if she doesn't talk to us soon." Steyn ran an impatient hand through his thin brown hair. "Good God, how are we ever going to prepare a case? Jim, are you sure you speak her language?"

"Yes, Mr. Steyn," the African said, mildly offended. "I have been to her country. I know her people."

"I wonder why the devil she left them?" said Steyn. "Ask her why, Jim."

"I have done that many times, Mr. Steyn, but she will not speak to me. She will not speak to anyone."

The lawyer stood up stiffly. "I know, Jim, I know," he said in a tired voice, "but keep trying. Tell her I'm her friend, the only friend she's got right now, her counsel appointed by the court, and unless she cooperates with me there won't be a thing I can do to save her neck."

He looked at Tselane, cringing in her chair, her eyes downcast, her cheeks purple from countless tears. She felt his gaze upon her and tried to turn away but she lacked the strength to move. Once again a torrent of words had fallen without meaning on her ears. She had shut the world out from her, not knowing what was going on around her and not caring. But every day they took her from her cell and brought her into this room and the two men, the white man and the black man, beat hours of words at her, like a winter rain upon the night roof. There was nothing to tell them, nothing they would understand: Metlae had mixed his brew, rolled his bones, the damage had been done, and now she had only to wait, helplessly, hopelessly, for the end, whatever it might be. She could not stop her tears: they were the sad voice of her heavy heart, a vast desert of aloneness. Always the tears were in her eyes, even when she awoke at dawn, cold and numb. Hau, when would Metlae finish with her, when would he grant her the peace of death?

The African said: "I will try again, Mr. Steyn."

Steyn left the room and walked slowly along the corridor to the main office where Sergeant Myburgh was sitting. Myburgh asked: "Any luck, Mr. Steyn?"

"No, Sergeant. You?"

"No, sir. We can't get anything out of her either; we've stopped trying."

"Any news from the police up the line?"

"No, or from Worcester either. There've been no inquiries about a missing woman."

Steyn shook his head. "I can't understand it. You'd think somebody would be worrying about a missing woman who was obviously very much pregnant when she left home."

"Oh, well," said Myburgh, "you know these people, Mr. Steyn. They don't care much about each other."

"But she was pregnant."

"The roads are full of that kind."

"She wasn't on the roads, Sergeant, she was on a train, and somebody must have cared enough to give her money for a ticket. We know she had a ticket because the railway people said she lost it. A ticket to Worcester. She was certainly on her way to somebody."

"Or from somebody," Myburgh said. "You can't tell about these things, Mr. Steyn. We're not even sure she was married. Maybe she killed the kid because she didn't want it."

"Married or not, no Mosotho woman would kill her child without a violent reason," said Steyn. He drifted towards the door; his eyes fell upon the wall calendar. "Six weeks," he said.

"Sir?"

"Six weeks until the judge arrives for the winter session."

"Going to ask for a postponement?"

"On what grounds? Because I haven't been able to prepare my case and apparently never will? I hardly think the Crown will accept that."

"Well," said Myburgh, adjusting papers on his desk, "the docket is rather heavy already. Perhaps your case won't get posted. Then you'll have another four months to hunt around for evidence before the next court sessions."

"I won't need the four months, Sergeant," said Steyn. "The way that girl is failing I doubt that she'll even last the six weeks."

"May I put a personal question to you, Mr. Steyn?" Myburgh asked. "The girl did it; there are witnesses to that. You won't get her off, you know it. Why are you so concerned about her?"

Steyn looked at Myburgh a moment, then said quietly: "I guess I'll never rest until I discover what terrible thing drove her to it."

The two men studied each other. Steyn said: "Let me know if you hear any news." And he left.

The dearth of news gnawed at Pierre le Brun. For a fortnight he was able to control his impatience. Perhaps Khama had had trouble locating Tselane, or had found her ill and was busy nursing her back to health. But when a third week passed and a fourth and there was no news he was agonized with worry. He wished that he had made Khama promise to have a letter sent, regardless of what was going on in Worcester, and he could not escape the fear that in sending Tselane to the city he was responsible for whatever might have happened to her on the way. He was certain now that something had happened. Even if she and Khama had actually passed each other on the road, Khama had been back in Worcester long enough by now to find her, if she was there to be found.

There were two places, Pierre felt, where Tselane might have gotten into trouble. One was at Marseilles, where she would change for the train to Bloemfontein, and the other was at Bloemfontein where she would have to spend the night awaiting the train from Johannesburg that would take her on the twenty-four hour journey to Worcester. Pierre was convinced that Tselane certainly would not go looking for trouble, but she was after all a country girl, attractive, simple, naïve, and it was not impossible that someone should try to lead her astray. If this had happened and Tselane realized her predicament in time, Pierre could only hope that she would make her way to the police, if she were at all able to do so. Therefore, more than two months after he had put her on the plane for what he thought would be a happy journey to Khama, Pierre le Brun wrote the police at Marseilles and Bloemfontein and at Worcester, describing Tselane and asking if they knew anything about her.

In his concern for her Pierre could not concentrate on his mission work and because of this he found himself facing countless new problems with it. Reports he had to write for the government and the Paris missionary society which supported him were returned for corrections and improvements. Natives who assisted him at mission outposts all seemed to resign at once and he had the great chore of training new men quickly so that the work might continue uninterrupted. Medical supplies at the clinic Simone managed ran out unexpectedly and messengers had to be rushed to another station miles away to borrow medicines until new shipments could arrive. Sensing his unrest, the children in the mission school grew uncontrollable and there were constant complaints from the native teachers.

In the next two weeks, Pierre went to the village three times. Chief Majara had only one question: "Have you heard anything yet, Moneri?"

There was nothing to tell him. Pierre hoped that in view of what had happened and the protection he had given Majara the Chief would be more responsive to him. But he was not. Pierre also detected that, for reasons of his own, the Chief had not told his people of the missionary's complicity in Tselane's disappearance. Rather than risk further enmity with Majara and to avoid confounding the people further by revealing his part in the mystery, Pierre likewise remained silent. He was disturbed by the coldness the people displayed towards him, but he knew there was nothing he could do about it. Even Molili paid little attention to him. Once when he saw her in the fields she scarcely spoke to him; then he noticed that she had apparently given up her work, remaining at home, moping around the hut, sitting glumly on her haunches staring at a pot of simmering porridge.

Pierre told Simone: "I don't like the looks of her at all. She seems to have lost weight, and her eyes are like fireballs."

"Maybe I should examine her," said Simone. "Could you get her to come to the clinic?"

"I can't even get her to talk to me."

Discouraged and restless, he could not apply himself to his work but instead sat in his study and stared blankly at the papers in front of him. Simone left him alone, returning only in the late afternoon to light the oil lamps when the fading winter sun made the room dark. She was standing there, finishing her task, when they heard the sound of a racing horse. Pierre got up and went to the door, opening it just as the rider leapt from his horse.

The man called: "Moneri, you must come quickly. The Chief has sent me. His wife is dying."

"What has happened to her?" Pierre asked.

"She went to her sleeping mats when she had eaten the noon meal and now she cannot get up."

"Get my medicine bag," Pierre told Simone, then he ran to the stable to saddle a horse. In a few minutes he and the man from the village were hurrying to Majara's hut.

That he had been called to treat Molili struck Pierre as hopefully significant. Though Metlae had left the village, there was another witch doctor in the village of Majara's father, just a few miles further into the mountains; Majara could have sent for him if it were a witch doctor he really preferred. Pierre wondered if the Chief, in choosing him, had retreated a little in his opposition to the mission and all it represented. If this were so, then perhaps other doors would open, giving Pierre the opportunity to fulfill all the plans he had for the village.

The news that the Chief had sent for the missionary had spread, and there were dim lights in the huts as Pierre passed them. Fresh wood had been put on the little fires in the middle of the floors to make light while the people discussed this new tragedy in hushed voices. Everyone knew how ill Molili was; they agreed that the missionary was their only hope for her. Pierre felt many eyes upon him as he rode through the village.

At Majara's hut, Pierre did not wait for the Chief to come out and invite him to dismount. He jumped from his horse and knocked on the door. Majara opened it and Pierre went in quietly.

The flickering light threw long shadows on the wall. Molili lay with her eyes closed, and for a moment Pierre feared that he had come too late. He knelt beside her and made as thorough an examination as his limited knowledge permitted. Majara stood watching him; Pierre caught his look of uncertainty. Finished, Pierre put away his stethoscope and got up. The two men faced each other.

Pierre said: "Let us go outside and talk."

"No. I stay here. Is my wife going to die?" Majara said. "Is the witch doctor stronger than the God in whom you and my wife believe?"

Pierre was surprised. "Why do you ask such a question?"

Majara said: "When Metlae left the village he put a curse on my wife, that she would die in four days, four weeks or four months. Now it is four weeks. If Molili dies tonight, then I will know that it is because your God cannot save her and He is weaker than Metlae."

So that was it. Instead of being called to help, he had been sent for to take part in a contest. Pierre said: "The God in whom your wife believes will save her. She will not die, but she must be moved to the mission so that the doctor can come to her and my wife can nurse her."

"No," said Majara. "She stays here."

Molili made a sound and they quickly turned to her. She beckoned with a weak hand and Majara knelt down beside her. She said: "I want to go. You must let me go."

Her whisper was loud enough for Pierre to hear. He looked at Majara, waiting the Chief's decision.

Majara looked up at him, pleadingly. "Must she go now?"

"No. I'll stay here until the sun rises, and when it is warmer we will take her."

Pierre sat with Molili the whole night. He gave her medicine to bring her temperature down and a few drops of water whenever she asked for it. Towards dawn he sent a messenger to Simone with a note:

> Send a boy to the trader's store with a radiogram to Dr. Jacques Panchaud, asking him to take the morning plane from Maseru, then have someone meet him at Mashai with horses. We will need him. I shall be returning with Molili the first thing in the morning.

There was a deathly silence in the hut. Every now and again Majara put a piece of wood on the fire. Pierre sat on a low stool next to Molili. He was aware of the intent way in which Majara watched him, as if he were expecting to see a miracle, as if Pierre had only to speak to his God and Molili would be better instantly. Pierre wished that something like that could happen.

At last the long vigil came to an end. A councilor came to the hut and made coffee at the outside fireplace. Then women came and asked if they could do something to help.

"You could cook us the morning meal," Pierre said, "and send word around that I shall hold a service before we leave. Tell the people to come to the meeting place."

Ordinarily, Pierre would not have considered holding a service without the Chief's permission, but now Majara was impenetrable with worry for his wife; Pierre went ahead on his own.

The Christians came first, making a large circle around Pierre in the meeting place. The others gathered nearby, just close enough to hear. Pierre noticed that Majara stood at a distance, silently watching.

Pierre told the people to bow their heads in prayer, and the Christians did so. Then he led them in a hymn, and at last he said: "We must have faith. Only God knows what this day will bring, and we must trust that out of our love for Him He will grant joy to us. God is good and He will not forsake us. If we believe, He will give the Chief's wife her health again. And He will bring Tselane back to us. Things on earth may fail us, but God will never fail those who accept Him and believe in His power."

Pierre saw how the people looked at each other; the Christians nodded their heads in silent agreement and the others listened with deep interest. He paused a moment, then led another hymn, and then he walked slowly back to Majara's hut.

When the sun was warmer, Pierre prepared Molili for the trek to the mission. He wrapped her in blankets, and two councilors carried her in a hammock of blankets.

The whole village turned out to watch them when they left. Pierre and Majara walked on either side of Molili. Some of the councilors went with them, following behind. It was a solemn procession that passed out of the village. Women and children stood quietly by, and men took their battered hats from their heads and their pipes out of their mouths. It was as if death were already walking the footpath on the mountains, and the people were afraid.

On a knoll in the nearby foothills, Metlae, the witch doctor, stood in the morning haze and watched. On his wrinkled face was a half-smile of victory.

19

THAT afternoon the snow began to fall and by night there was a certain beauty over the land, but there were few who saw it because in many places there was a great sickness of the heart. In the mission rondawel Molili lay near death; in the village Majara sat alone in his hut, staring into the darkness. Far away in Worcester, Khama put a match to the candle in his room, then threw himself exhausted on his bed, weary from another fruitless day of searching for Tselane in the city. He had told no one the full truth, only that his wife had left the village and was on her way to him and that he feared something had happened to her because she was such a long time arriving. MaSoteli, the Mosotho woman at whose house he roomed, tried to console him, saying that perhaps the long trip had proved too great a strain on Tselane and that she may have gotten off the train somewhere along the route to rest a few days at the home of some good people she had met. This did not help Khama very much; even if it had happened, Tselane would have sent word to him somehow. So each morning he went to the railway station to watch the passengers get off the train: she was never among them. And each evening he wandered through the section where the Mosotho people had settled and asked everyone about her: they knew nothing. Stretched out on his bed, he battled the growing fear that he might never see his wife again, and he knew that if this happened he would one day return to his village with a great hate in him and he would then finish what he had begun the last night he was there.

Also stretched out on a bed in his home was Anton Steyn. His eyes studied the small fire that burned in the hearth; his mind was across town with the silent native girl in her cold cell. Never had he prepared to take a case to court with such hopelessness in him, such resignation that the case was already lost. The girl would give him no help at all, probably because she felt she had no help to give. He had defended Africans before, and always they were vociferous in their complaints of persecution and martyrdom, loudly proclaiming their innocence, demanding mercy above justice. But this girl was not like that. Evidently she knew what she had done: her continual tears indicated that. And either she did not know she could be defended in court or did not want to be. Even after weeks of visiting her regularly, Steyn had no idea whether or not she understood why he was there. She would hang; there was no question about it. And he would not be able to say a word to avoid it: she had not given him a word to say. What a terrified creature she was, and this was the thing about her that puzzled Steyn. There were times when she stared beyond him with such horror on her face that he was forced to glance over his shoulder to see who might be there. He could not bring himself to believe that she was having hallucinations; he had witnessed such displays before and would have recognized the symptoms. No. It was something else. It bore a resemblance to the expressions he had seen on his children's faces when they awoke suddenly at night from nightmares. Fear. But fear of what? Fear of the noose she perhaps foresaw in her future, or fear of whatever it was that had made a murderer of her? He would never know, and this—more even than losing the case—was what bothered Steyn. Unless some friend, some relatives, appeared with explanations, he would never know.

Tselane had given up all hope of ever again seeing a friend or relative. She was alone, completely alone, and this was her punishment for what she had done, a punishment far worse than the hanging which awaited her. She knew she would be hanged. Huddled against the wall in her cell, she pulled her blanket around her for warmth, and the memory occurred to her of the woman of her village named Josephine who had gone to work in the city for a while, and when she came back she told of the punishment white people had for anyone who murdered; she had seen it: they made you stand on a chair under a tree and they put a rope around your neck and tied the other end to a high branch, and then someone kicked the chair away, and then you swung in the air and kicked your feet and your eyes bulged and in a few minutes you were dead. The vision brought fresh tears. To die was a bad thing, but to die alone with no one you loved near, hau, this was the worst. No last looks, no last words, no last understandings, no last goodbyes. This was cruel, and it would be hers to suffer, to be sure, because Metlae had willed it and would not settle for anything less.

Metlae was not even thinking of her. His mind had room only for Chief Majara. If the medicine man was now an outcast, forced to live cold and hungry in a dark mountain cave, it was because of the Chief. Often on the bitter nights, Metlae viciously regretted that he had not thought fast enough on the day the Chief had come to him, demanding a new victim for the diretlo. Metlae had felt instinctively that it was dangerous to try again so soon after the failure; it would take time to stir the men to the point where they were ready to perform the murder: to try too quickly could have meant bungling the job, and then matters would only be worse. But the Chief had not wanted to wait; he had been angry and threatening, and so Metlae felt he must leave for his own safety. For days he had wandered through the countryside looking for another village that might take him in, but they all had their own medicine men or had become Christians and did not want any. There was no place left for him but the caves. He had not had a good meal or slept a good night for a month; his bed was cold rocks and, because it was winter and there were no herbs or fruits, he ate only the pink meat of rats dipped into hot grease. To find the rats it was necessary for him to move to new caves every few days, and as he searched he found himself moving closer and closer to the village, settling at last in a cave on a mountainside where he could look down on the man who had destroyed him. He was determined to have revenge, to do anything he must to effect the curse he had put on Majara's house. Waiting and watching, he had seen many things—the return of Khama, the excitement in the village, Molili being carried to the mission, and the way the people now left the Chief completely to himself. Metlae was certain that the time was near when he could arrange Majara's death. When it happened, the people would know that his curse had been fulfilled. Then he could return to the village and the people would fear him and obey him.

"Fear," Pierre le Brun said to Dr. Jacques Panchaud, "is at the bottom of it all." They were sitting in Pierre's study after dinner, sipping coffee. "What these people don't understand they fear, and out of fear comes the kind of troubles we're in now. I'm sure, Jacques, that none of these terrible things would have happened if only the Chief had let me talk to the people long ago."

"Where's the Chief now?" Dr. Panchaud asked.

"In the village, I suppose. I sent him home this morning after you examined Molili and said you felt she'd be all right."

Simone looked up from her sewing. "He's been back several times since. I've seen him outside the rondawel, standing there, staring at the door. This afternoon I offered him some porridge, but he refused it. He just stands there for a while, then wanders away, and in an hour or so he's back."

"What sort of person is he?" Panchaud asked.

"Unmovable," said Pierre. "Like so many pagan chiefs, he suspects that if he gives a missionary an inch it will cost him a mile."

"Does that sort of thing really happen?"

"You must remember, Jacques," Pierre said, "that a chief's best ally is his medicine man. The people believe that witch doctors have great powers, and a smart witch doctor certainly won't do anything that will endanger his position with the chief. As a result, the chief has great powers, too. Christianity removes the witch doctor; the chief fears he too will be removed. But this does not follow if he is basically a good man."

"But do witch doctors actually have these powers?"

"Not really. They have a remarkable knowledge of herbs and often their medicines are able to cure certain illnesses or stimulate certain conditions. The same way with so many of their ceremonies: they know enough about weather conditions, for instance, to realize when it might be propitious to pray for rain. And they're excellent psychologists. They understand the nature of their people so well that they can talk them into or out of anything. And my personal feeling is that it's not too farfetched to wonder if they might also get some help from the devil. After all, deep-rooted paganism keeps the people away from Christianity, and certainly that would be within the devil's design. But I wouldn't expect a scientist to go along with me on that."

"Why not?" Panchaud said. "You should know me well enough by now, Pierre, to realize that I'm not the kind of doctor who thinks science has replaced religion."

Pierre smiled. "I was teasing, Jacques. I've thanked God a thousand times already that you received my message and were able to come."

"I'm glad I could, especially now that I know the predicament you're in. But I suggest you also thank God for these wonder drugs people have been discovering lately."

Simone asked: "You're confident she'll be all right?"

"With double pneumonia, who can be sure?" Jacques said. "These people have notoriously bad lungs; you know how prevalent tuberculosis is throughout Africa. We'll have to trust to God, the drugs, and good nursing."

"Simone will provide the nursing," Pierre said.

"I know," the doctor said. "Anyway, we'll have a look at Molili tonight and again in the morning before I leave and you can keep in touch with me by radio. If everything goes well, I'll come back in a few weeks and try to find out why she hasn't been able to have children."

In his hut, Chief Majara decided that he, too, would have one more look at Molili before the long night began. True, he could only look at her through the closed door, but that was better than nothing.

Since morning, he had been unable to stay away from the mission, even though he was uncomfortable when he was there. Had Molili not asked to be taken to the mission he would never have allowed it, but her illness had shattered his pride and destroyed his powers.

All day he suffered the hungry pains of helplessness. That morning the white doctor told him that Molili must be left completely alone to rest, and the Moneri had said there was nothing he could do and might as well return to the village. But he could not stay there. The people would not come to him, to console him, as it was their duty to do, but now he did not care about their coldness. Several times he had ridden back to the mission to be as close to Molili as he was permitted. He wanted to be close once more.

He went to the kraal and saddled a horse and rode off into the falling snow. He was aware of his own position in what was happening. If Molili lived then the people would say that the Moneri had done it with the help of his God, and maybe this would be so. If it was, then more and more of the people would want to become Christians and he would be unable to prevent them. Perhaps Molili would want him to become a Christian, but this was something he would have to think about. He would need another test. He would let the white doctor come to Molili again and if later Molili would give him a son then he would not doubt any more.

From his mountain cave, Metlae saw Majara ride into the night, watched him slow his horse at the place where the path narrowed and passed along the edge of the deep ravine before it entered the scrubby bush. Suddenly he knew what he must do. When Majara was out of sight, Metlae hurried into his cave and started a small fire. He took his grease pot and put it to the flames, watching as the heat thinned the contents into a smelly liquid hot oil. Then he took the pot and hurried to the place where the path was narrow. He went into the fields and uncovered flat rocks from beneath the snow and laid them carefully along the path, and over them he poured the hot oil. Then he hid in the bushes and waited.

Majara saw the candlelight in the rondawel window and stopped his horse at the edge of the clearing. In a few minutes the Moneri came out with his wife and the white doctor and they locked the door. He heard the doctor say words. Then the Moneri spoke and his wife spoke and though Majara did not understand the words they were saying he felt no sadness in their voices and he wondered if this meant that Molili was all right.

He waited until they had all entered the big house and shut the door and put out the lamps, then he got off his horse and went to the rondawel. He tried the door, but it would not open. He said Molili's name several times softly, but she did not answer. So he stood there in the darkness a long time, until the cold night made him shiver under his blanket. At last he went to his horse and rode quickly away.

He was startled from his thoughts when his horse suddenly lost her footing in the place where the path narrowed. He reached out to pat the horse's neck to calm her, but the touch frightened the terrified horse and she reared. Her hind legs slipped from under her and she dropped to her rump. Majara tried to slide off, but immediately the horse was up again, skidding on the oiled rocks.

There was a sound in the bushes. Majara looked over his shoulder and saw Metlae approaching, clenching in his hands a dead branch he had broken off a low tree. Majara pulled the reins tight. "Help me," he said in soft fear.

The horse reared again and danced in panic. Metlae came close behind and began to beat the horse with the branch.

"Help me," Majara said again.

The horse tried to turn, but there was no room. Her hind legs slid over the edge of the cliff, her belly scraped in the dead weeds, she pawed for front footing on the greasy rocks, then she sighed heavily and let herself drop away in the ravine.

The night was suddenly quiet, with only the sound of the searching winter wind. Metlae stood at the edge of the ravine, waiting. Then he threw the branch over the side and turned and walked through the snow-covered field up into the hills to his cave.

In the morning he felt like a man who had become a father for the first time. He was content with himself. He believed that with Majara dead he had lost his last enemy. Now he was free. He could go back to the village. Surely the people would be happy to see him. In the chill of the morning he put on his full ceremonial regalia and went limping down the hill and into the village.

"Dumelang, my children." A smile lighted up his withered face but there was hardly a smile on the faces of the people staring at him. A chill more severe than the cold which had held him in agony on the mountain went through him. He had not foreseen that the people of the village would have no welcome for him.

That the Christians were cold he could well understand but not the others who had come to his hut in the middle of the night for help and for medicine. Had they forgotten the power which he had? Would they drive him back to the mountain, to the horror that he had left there? He said: "I have come to ask our Chief to take me back. The mountain is cold for an old man, the snow is not an easy blanket to lie under and food does not grow on the mountainside."

RaSobeti spoke for all of them. "Where did you rise this morning, Metlae?"

"I slept under the trees by the fields of Phofo. I have walked the whole day without food. Tonight, food and water and wood for my fire would buy the best medicine that I have." He left this tantalizing offer suspended in the air above their heads and limped to his hut. He must get away before more questions could be asked and more answers expected from him.

The old familiar smells, the warmth and dryness of his hut, a joy that he had not thought would be his again all rushed through him as he stared at the inside of the only home that he had ever known. Tears streamed down his wrinkled face. Wearily he sat down on the skins he had left there and waited for the first offers of food for his medicine.

In every hut in the village, grownups whispered their thoughts and children dared not say a word. The names of their Chief and the witch doctor who had returned were on every lip. Fear made the air heavy and tight. Strange things would come to pass, of that the people were sure.

Early in the morning, after Jacques Panchaud had left for the plane at Mashai, Pierre le Brun went to his study to work. He was surprised that Majara was not already at the mission; he would have good news for the Chief. Pierre had worked about an hour when he heard an approaching horse. It would be Majara; Pierre got up and went to the door to speak to him. He recognized, instead, the boy from the trader's store in the valley on the other side of the mountains.

The boy waved to him. "Are you alive, Moneri?"

"I am alive," Pierre returned. "What brings you here?"

"I have a message for you," the boy said, and he got off his horse and walked to Pierre and handed him a radiogram.

Pierre took the envelope. "Thank you. You have had a cold ride; go around to the kitchen and my wife will give you something warm to drink. Then I will tell you if there is an answer to this message."

"Thank you, Moneri."

Pierre stepped inside the house, closed the door and ripped open the radiogram. He read:

BEAUFORT WEST POLICE HOLDING MOSOTHO WOMAN FITTING DE-
SCRIPTION YOUR INQUIRY TO WORCESTER AUTHORITIES WOMAN
CHARGED WITH MURDERING NEWBORN INFANT ON TRAIN IF YOU
FEEL WOMAN SAME URGENTLY REQUEST IMMEDIATE ASSISTANCE
ESPECIALLY WITH MOTIVATION WITNESSES WOMAN UNCOOPER-
ATIVE AS COUNSEL I FEAR BLEAK VERDICT ANTON STEYN

Pierre stared at the words. He leaned against the wall for strength and called out to Simone: "Tselane killed her baby," he said, and he handed Simone the radiogram.

Simone read the radiogram rapidly. "Are you sure it's Tselane?"

"Positive. This explains her disappearance, her silence, why Khama hasn't located her—everything," Pierre said. "Is the boy still here?"

"Yes."

"I will send a message to the lawyer." Pierre glanced at the wall clock. "Have someone prepare our fastest horse. I must get a letter to Khama on the plane this morning."

"But a letter will take four or five days to reach him," Simone said.

"I couldn't give him this news in a radiogram," Pierre said. "Besides, that will give me time to get to Beaufort West before him."

"You are going?"

"Yes. But first I must talk to Majara."

"What can the Chief do?"

"The lawyer asks for motivation witnesses, someone who can explain what drove Tselane to do this terrible thing," Pierre said. "I must persuade Majara to go to Beaufort West with me to explain everything to the lawyer. I don't know what good it will do, but it is the only thing that can be done."

In a few minutes the boy from the trader's store was on his way with a radiogram to Steyn. Then Pierre wrote the letter to Khama, a long letter which he wrote quickly, like a man eager to escape pain. He gave the letter to a houseboy and ordered him to ride as fast as he could to Mashai to reach the plane before it left. When this was done, Pierre went to the barn and saddled a horse and began the ride to the village.

It was at the place where the path was narrow that Pierre noticed the flat rocks just ahead. He knew they had not been there before. Puzzled, he got off his horse and walked to the rocks. They looked moist; he touched them and felt the grease. He looked around and saw the footprints that Metlae had made in the snow, going off to the hills. It was when he glanced over the cliff into the ravine and saw the dead horse and the crushed body of Chief Majara that he realized what must have happened.

One thought struck him: Now who shall speak for Tselane?

He led his horse around the path where the rocks were slippery, mounted, then rode on to the village. He went directly to the hut of Khama's parents. RaKhama heard him and came outside.

Pierre asked: "Are you alive, RaKhama?" He got off his horse and handed the reins to a boy.

"I am alive, Moneri," replied the old man. "The hour is early. What brings you to us at this time of the day when the sun has not yet shown his face?"

"I have news."

RaKhama's face brightened and the words tumbled from him. "You have news to gladden our hearts? Our child is alive? We have a grandson to bring back the happiness that has gone from our hut?"

"Your child is alive," Pierre said. "She is at a place called Beaufort West in the Union of South Africa."

"MaKhama! MaKhama!" the old man cried. "Tselane is alive! We must tell the news. People must hear that we have found our child." The neighbors came running. They heard the news and sang and clapped their hands, then they gathered around Pierre.

Pierre did not know what to say. He saw the happiness all around him and he could not bring himself to crush it. He said: "She was lost. The police are holding her. They say she will not speak. They are waiting for somebody to come and tell them about Tselane."

"The Chief will go," RaKhama said. "He is not here now, but

when he returns and you tell him about Tselane, Moneri, he will go."

Pierre tried not to let his face show that the Chief could not possibly go.

Then RaSobeti said: "Metlae is back."

"Yes, Moneri. There," said RaSobeti, pointing.

"I will speak with him."

Pierre was relieved when none of the people followed him, and he judged from this that they did not want to go near the witch doctor. He went alone to the hut and he knocked on the door. No sound came from inside. Pierre knocked again, harder. Now he heard a movement inside, but still no hand touched the door.

He said: "Metlae, this is the Moneri. I come in peace. Open your door."

Metlae did not answer.

Pierre pounded on the door. He knew that the witch doctor looked upon him as an enemy because he had openly told the people that Metlae's medicines had no power, and the two men had not spoken since Pierre's first days at the village. But now he did not care about that. "Metlae," he called, "if you don't open the door I'll get the councilors to come and break it down."

Metlae said: "What does the Moneri want with an old man when the day has hardly opened his eyes?"

"I want to ask you a question."

"The door need not be open for that. It is cold; I am an old man."

Pierre seized the latch and rattled it. "I must see you. I told you I come in peace."

Moments passed before the door was opened only wide enough for Metlae's dark appraising eyes to study the missionary. He said: "It is too cold for me to come outside."

Pierre pushed the door wider and entered the hut. He threw the question bluntly: "Why was Chief Majara killed?"

Metlae's wrinkled face hardened. He turned away and stared at the small fire that burned on the floor in the middle of the dark hut. At last he said: "The white man asks me strange questions. I do not know that Chief Majara is dead."

"You are the only one in this village who would know."

"Why do you say that?" Metlae moved to the corner and sat on a rug of skins. "Could it be that the missionary who speaks against the witch doctor now wants me to throw my bones to find out why the Chief is dead?"

"You know why he is dead," said Pierre, "because you killed him."

Metlae slowly blinked his eyes absently at the fire. "You saw me do this thing? You were there when this thing happened?"

"I was not there but you were," Pierre said, "there on the mountain where the Chief's horse slipped on the rocks you greased and fell into the ravine."

Metlae lifted his head and looked scornfully at Pierre, and he said: "The missionary thinks he is speaking to a child. How are you going to prove that I was on the mountain, when this very morning the councilors themselves saw me coming on the path from the hut of Phofo. They saw me; they heard my words that I had slept in Phofo's fields."

"Can you take them to the place in the fields where you slept, where the snow shows the press of your body?" Pierre caught the sudden tension in the witch doctor's body. He went on: "I can take the councilors to the place on the path where the horse fell and I can show them your footprints in the snow, leading up to the caves where you have lived these past days."

"All men's footprints look alike in the snow," said Metlae.

"The councilors will decide that," Pierre said, "as they will decide whether you slept in Phofo's fields. Then when they realize it was you who killed the Chief they will decide what to do with you."

Metlae tried to put impatience into his voice. "If you have finished what you have come here to say, go and leave an old man to his sleep."

"I am leaving, but you are coming with me."

Metlae's shrug was heavy with derision.

Pierre said: "Tselane has been found."

The witch doctor glanced up.

Pierre said: "She is in a place called Beaufort West. The police have her. You will go with me there and speak for her."

"What can I say for Tselane? She is a bad girl. She ran away from her people. If she is in trouble with the police then she is being punished for running away. I can do nothing for her."

"Metlae, I give you a choice," said Pierre. "You will come with me or I shall go to the councilors and take them to the body of the Chief and show them what I have seen. Which do you choose? Do you want to go to Tselane or do you want to die this day at the hands of your own people?"

20

THE LETTER was on Khama's bed when he returned home from work. He stared at it for several moments, stunned by the sight of it, afraid to pick it up yet afire to know its content. He took it up gently in both hands, as if it were something precious and fragile, then ran from his small room across the garden to the house of the Mosotho family with whom he lived. Anxiety pitched his voice high as he cried: "MaSoteli! MaSoteli!"

The old woman came to the back door and watched him running towards her. "You make much noise, Khama," she said. "What mad thing have you got under your blanket now?"

"A letter," he said. "I have a letter."

"I know this thing," she said. "How do you think it got on your bed? I put it there with my own hands this morning."

He held it out to her. "Who is it from? Is it from Tselane?"

MaSoteli's frown was gentle. "How can you ask me that, my son? You know I cannot read."

"Can you tell where it is from?" he asked, putting the envelope close to her face.

She moved his hand away. "You are like a kitten who is foolish with fleas and forgets everything. I cannot tell where the letter is from any more than you can. My daughter will be home from work soon; she will read this letter for you as she has the others."

Khama stared at the envelope; it did not occur to him to open it; he was nervous, eager, suddenly hopeful. Day after day he had hunted all over the city for Tselane, returning to his room each night exhausted and greatly worried. Each morning he was at the train station, his eyes tensely on the passengers disembarking, and when at last he went on his disappointed way to work he could not keep his mind on his job and several times had been reprimanded by his boss for making mistakes. He had reached the point where he could no longer search or wait, and he had decided that if there was no news by the end of the week, he would return to the village. He had no idea what he would do when he got there: at least it was a place where he could start a new search for Tselane, covering, if need be, every inch along the route back to Worcester. Sometimes late at night he would think of what it must have been like for Tselane to realize that she had been chosen as the diretlo victim and his heart ached with pity for her. Then he would shudder with hate for Chief Majara, and he vowed, whether Tselane was found or not, that one day he would even the score with the Chief. But now all that was important was the letter he held in his hands. Surely it was about Tselane, probably from her. He was in pain to learn its news.

MaSoteli said: "There is life in your face for the first time in many days, Khama."

He tried to smile at her and to speak but there was no room in him for any feelings but his concern about the letter. He heard MaSoteli's daughter coming up the path and ran to her. "Chrissie," he called, "I have a letter," and he tried to hand it to her.

"Hau, Khama," the girl said, "you are like a wild man who has never left the mountains. Can't you see these packages in my arms? Give me time to get into the house and put them down."

"I will take your packages," he said, and he grabbed them from her, stuffed the letter in her hands, then rushed into the house and dumped the parcels on the table. When he returned to the garden, Chrissie was settling on the back steps, carefully smoothing her city dress. "Read the letter, Chrissie," he pleaded. "Where is it from?"

"The stamp is from Basutoland," she said.

"Read the letter," said MaSoteli, "before he splits open."

Chrissie tore off the end of the envelope and removed the pages. "It is written with a machine," she said.

"Read it, read the words," said Khama, and he sat down on the ground in front of her.

Haltingly, spelling each word in her mind before pronouncing it, Chrissie read the news, so absorbed in her task that she did not look at the faces of her mother and Khama until she had finished.

MaSoteli found her voice first. "Hau, Khama," she said softly. Khama sat huddled on the ground, holding his head. The missionary had used his softest words, but one thing remained: Tselane had killed their son. Khama was too dazed to realize the full portent of this. He must get to Tselane as soon as possible. He must see her and hear this thing from her own lips.

"Hau, Khama," MaSoteli said again.

It was a long time before Khama got up. He walked across the garden like a sleeping man who walks across strange fields and he took a battered suitcase from under his bed and began to pack it. He heard MaSoteli and Chrissie speaking to him but he did not understand what they were saying. He could think only that Tselane had murdered his son, and now she was in prison and soon she would go into the courtroom and face the white judge who would send her away to be hanged and then he would be without both his son and his wife. The missionary had written that he, too, would go to Beaufort West to do what he could for Tselane. Hau, what could be done?

When he was ready, Khama took his suitcase and the pot of food MaSoteli had prepared for him and he left the house. MaSoteli and Chrissie stood in the doorway watching him as he walked down the street, and big tears rolled down MaSoteli's face. She called after him: "Go well, Khama, go well, my son. May the white judge have mercy and give you back your wife."

The train trip to Beaufort West would take twenty hours: all that night and into the next day the train rushed to the north and west but to Khama it seemed to be standing still. He did not sleep, he did not eat, he did not leave his compartment, nor did he speak to the two men who shared it with him. He was devoid of all thought, all feeling, aware only of what Tselane had done and what she must suffer because of it. He had no idea what he would do when he arrived at Beaufort West and he could not bring himself to plan. He sensed only that the train was taking him where he was needed, but so slowly, so slowly. At each station where the train stopped he fretted because the people did not get off and on fast enough, and at one station he waited so long that he finally realized something must be wrong. The two men with him got out and returned in a few moments.

Khama asked: "Why are we not going?"

"There's been an accident up the line and we must wait," one said.

Khama groaned. He left the train and went to the window where natives bought their tickets and he asked the white man: "Is it true that we have to wait here?"

"Yes, and what about it?"

"How long will we have to wait?"

"Until the train moves again."

"I know, but how many hours will that be?"

"How should I know? Do I look like a fortune teller to you?" And the man turned away.

Tense with anger, Khama went back to his compartment and sat down. The two men there were grinning, knowing he had been told what they had been told and they were ready to make fun of it because they thought the white man had joked with them, but when they saw the look on Khama's face they felt he wanted to fight about something so they left him alone and did not speak to him.

It was evening before the train moved; the day was lost, and not until ten o'clock the next morning did Khama arrive at Beaufort West. He jumped from the train before it stopped and asked a porter the way to the court. The man pointed down the street and Khama set off at a quick pace.

It was the third day of the trial; for the third time Tselane had been taken from her cell and brought into the courtroom that was crowded with people. Three days they had spoken; the men from the train, the women who had traveled with her; the Judge in his high chair asked questions and every time he had spoken, fear had taken all thought from her. Her heart had turned to stone, all feeling inside her was cold, like the winds that blew from the snow on the mountain in winter.

Tselane lifted her head. The Judge and the men with him were talking among themselves. The black man who sat next to her and who had to tell her in her own language every word that was said in the courtroom turned slightly towards her and whispered under his breath: "Why don't you speak up and tell them about yourself? They are saying those words which will hang you. Speak and plead with the Judge."

Many times in the past three days he had whispered these words to her. Dazed, weary and hopeless, she had not listened to him. From time to time the words he interpreted for her broke through to her but they meant nothing. She wished only that it was all over, that they would stop talking, talking. If they were going to put her on the chair under the tree, why all this talking?

Wearily Tselane looked at the other black people in the last rows at the back of the court. Not a face that she had seen before, nobody to return to the mountain and tell them in her village what had happened to her. She buried her face in the coarseness of the ugly gray prison blanket they had given her.

The white men were talking and the black one next to her droned the words in her direction. Suddenly Tselane thought she heard a familiar name. She turned to look in the direction of Anton Steyn. In the quiet of the court, tension had become sharper and people waited eagerly. Disbelief shone in her large troubled eyes as Tselane turned her head towards the interpreter. Could she have heard amiss? Was it the truth they were saying? The Moneri from the mountain? For the first time since she had been brought into the court there was an interest in her eyes for what was being said.

The Judge looked displeased when he answered Steyn: "I don't see any reason why this man should sit with you at counsel's table."

Anton Steyn's quick reply brought a stir among those listening to him.

"With your permission, my lord, I would like to move outside the usual court procedures and request that a person intimately associated with the crime be permitted to sit at counsel's table. I intend to use Mr. le Brun, the missionary from the area, who has an intimate knowledge of witchcraft, to assist me in the examination of the witness."

"Precisely who is the person you wish to call as a witness?"

"The witch doctor from the village where the accused lived."

Nervous chatter broke out in court as people stirred in their seats and eagerly discussed this new turn of events. The witch doctor! Could it be possible that an advocate with the status of Anton Steyn could hope to achieve something by calling as witness one whose very existence made a mockery of civilization and everything that the court stood for? Would the Judge permit such an unusual procedure to waste time in a case where the outcome of it all had been clear from the very beginning? The accused had murdered her child and for that there could be only one punishment.

"Order in the court!" The loud rasping voice of the court orderly brought immediate quiet.

In the deadly silence that followed, the Judge asked his next question: "What connection has the witch doctor got with the crime?"

Steyn answered calmly: "He caused it."

The Crown's attorney got to his feet. "My lord, I must object to that observation. The Crown fails to comprehend how the witch doctor could have caused a murder on a train hundreds of miles away."

Steyn turned to the Judge. "My lord, may I reply to that question in the presence of the witch doctor?"

Immediately the prosecuting attorney said: "The Crown finds all this most unorthodox, my lord, I must say."

"I agree. Mr. Steyn, what is it that you are trying to establish?" The Judge set the question and waited for Steyn to reply. A few seconds passed before Anton Steyn made his answer. "A motive, my lord. I concede that the Crown's representative has the right to demand punishment for crimes committed in his region, but I am sure that he is equally interested in justice. Unless the motive for this crime is established, my lord, I assure you that justice will not appear to have been done in this court."

"That is not a very prudent observation." There was clearly an expression of displeasure on the face of the Judge. "You have worked in this room often enough, Mr. Steyn, to understand that justice is the reason for the court's existence."

Eagerly all eyes followed the young constable who left the court-room, and in a moment he returned leading Pierre. With a nod, Steyn motioned Pierre to a chair next to his own. The constable left the room again.

This was the moment in which Anton Steyn had invested all his hopes. Twelve hours earlier he had met Pierre for the first time when the missionary had arrived at his home with Metlae. Then it was that he learned all the things that had happened in the moun-tains, and when he added them to what he had heard in the court-room from the Crown's witnesses he began to understand why Tselane had acted as she did.

"May I see her?" Pierre had asked.

"No," Steyn said. "I don't think you should. You say her husband is on the way here?"

"I wrote him; I imagine he is."

"Well, keep him away from her, too." He studied Metlae.

"Terrifying, isn't he?"

"Yes," Steyn said appraisingly. "Now let me tell you what I want to do. Both of you stay here tonight; I don't want any word to reach Tselane that anybody from her village is here. We can lock this fellow up in the servants' quarters to keep him safe. In the morning, give me a half hour's start, then bring this chap around to the witnesses' room. I'll think of some pretext to get you down front in the courtroom; then when we get the witch doctor on the stand I want you to sit there and stare at him so that he doesn't forget how much you know about him."

"And then?" asked Pierre.

"Then God help us."

Now the moment had come. Pierre took his seat next to Steyn. He looked over at Tselane and was startled. How thin she seemed, how small, how beaten. Her face was hidden in her blanket; she had not seen him. Pierre turned around and sent a quick search over the crowd. There, in the back, leaning against the wall, looking bewildered and afraid, was Khama. Pierre lifted a hand, almost in blessing, but Khama was watching Tselane.

The door of the witnesses' room opened again. Metlae entered, dressed in his full ceremonial outfit. In the crowded room where everyone but Tselane wore Western clothes, he looked unreal, like a bad dream, half remembered. The monkey-tail necklace around his neck swayed from side to side, the skins around his waist made a rustling noise, the blown-up bladders on the string tied to his right arm gleamed yellow in the dim light of the courtroom. In his long woolly hair the porcupine quills quivered at a rakish angle. On his face was arrogance, defiance, self-assurance and hate. For a few seconds everyone in the courtroom stared. Then an agonized shriek shattered the stunned hush.

Tselane was on her feet. She tried to climb out of the dock. Strong arms held her, but she fought with all the strength left in her thin body. She screamed again and again as she tried to escape the evil that had entered the room.

The court orderly hammered his gavel to still the noisy confusion. Tselane, exhausted by this terror which had followed her, gave way to the force of two matrons who led her from the dock and out of the court. The court heard the orderly's "Silence in the court" and responded with a tense silence.

Displeasure edged the Judge's voice, "The court will adjourn until two o'clock."

The benches were cleared. Anton Steyn wiped the sweat from his brow. The first part of their fantastic plan had succeeded. There was not a person in the court who could have mistaken the insane fear that came over Tselane when she had seen the witch doctor.

Khama, weary and dazed, waited in the passage. Pierre saw him as he left the courtroom. Silently they gripped each other's hands. Khama's voice sounded old and without expression when he said: "Will they let me see her?"

"I am afraid not. You will have to wait until afterwards to speak to Tselane." Pierre said these words with great compassion for Khama. "Until afterwards" . . . they were ordinary words, but what would they bring? Would Khama have to face his wife declared a murderer by the court and sentenced to death? Would there be mercy and understanding for Tselane?

When they returned to the courtroom at two o'clock the room was already filled. Pierre explained to a policeman: "This is the husband. Is there a place where he can sit?" The policeman went to the front row of seats and spoke softly to the people there. They looked over their shoulders at Khama and they made room for him. Pierre went to the table and took his chair near Anton Steyn. Before they could speak, the Judge came in and the orderly rapped for attention. Then Tselane was brought in. Her face was wan and her eyes were empty and she did not look at anyone. Then the door of the witnesses' room opened and Metlae was led in. He was dressed now in an old shabby suit that was too big for his small frame. He shuffled uneasily, a woeful figure. For the first time in his life he had shoes on his feet, and he walked awkwardly like a man in deep mud. He was taken to the witness box, and there in a trembling voice he repeated the oath the court interpreter asked of him to tell the truth.

The contest was about to begin. Pierre le Brun, the missionary from the mountains who for years had striven to break a power that was crippling a people, against Metlae the witch doctor, who represented that power. In the few seconds before Anton Steyn spoke, the sly hooded eyes in the wrinkled face of the witch doctor rested on Pierre. Calmly, with no fear in the depths of his clear brown eyes, Pierre met the challenge. Anton Steyn's voice rang across the court.

"I apologize, my lord, for what happened this morning, but I firmly believe that it will support what is about to be said in this court."

Steyn turned to Pierre. He, the advocate, became only the instrument through which Pierre by means of the court interpreter set the questions to Metlae. Quietly, methodically, and with deadly logic Pierre drew from Metlae answers which could leave no doubt about matters from the evidence presented.

"What is your name?"

"Metlae."

"What is your work?"

"I am a medicine man."

"In the village of Tselane?"

"The Moneri knows that."

Metlae explained that he had always been a medicine man, as had his father before him. Because of his heritage he could communicate with the spirits of the ancestors of those who lived in the village. Through his bones and his shells the spirits gave him messages and through his rituals he could obtain favors from the spirits.

"Can you make the sun shine?" Pierre asked.

"Yes, I can make the sun shine."

"Can you make it rain?"

"I can bring rain."

"Can you make plants grow?"

"I can make plants grow."

"Can you make a sick man well?"

"Yes."

"Can you make a well man sick?"

"If the spirits wish it."

"Can you make a man die?"

"If the spirits wish it."

"Did your Chief have children?"

"You know he did not."

"Did this make him unhappy?"

"Yes."

"Did he ask you to help him?"

"Yes."

"In what way?"

"He wanted me to make a medicine for his wife."

"How?"

"From the parts of a pregnant woman."

"What would happen then?"

"If the Chief's wife took the medicine, she would become pregnant."

"Do you have the power to make such a medicine?"

Metlae said sharply: "I do!"

"Which woman was chosen?"

Metlae looked from Pierre to Steyn, then to the Judge. He sent his eyes to the people and then pointed to Tselane. Before the court there unfolded the picture of pagan belief in the power of the spirits of their ancestors, the sincerity of primitive minds who believed in diretlo.

"It was wrong to take a woman from our own village, a woman

so young; but the Chief wanted Tselane for his diretlo. I warned her, I warned Tselane," Metlae cunningly fixed the responsibility on Chief Majara. "I knew her from the time that she was still sitting on her mother's back. How could I do this thing?

"Her body got away from the mountains. But the spirits of our ancestors who are ever with us went on the wind with her. They were in the train. They took her child away from her. Her child had been chosen for the diretlo of a chief. He could not escape." Metlae was excited, and afraid.

"Your questions are like gnats on a hot afternoon by the river." These clever white men with their many words must think that he, Metlae, was a child who could not see where things were leading. "I have no more to say to the one who is speaking. I want to speak to the great Judge himself."

Anton Steyn turned to the Judge. The Judge was sitting forward, completely absorbed in this phenomenon. The Judge nodded and Steyn returned to his seat after the interpreter asked Metlae to proceed.

The pathetic old figure, wrinkled with age in clothes that were too big for him, had a somber kind of dignity. The sniggering of some of the whites and the Africans who were in court had ceased. They listened with quiet attention to a man who obviously once had power and authority and in whose presence people trembled. Metlae looked directly at the Judge. His bright little eyes glittered, but there was the ring of sincere conviction in his voice.

"You white men," he said at last to the Judge, "you speak in a loud voice, but your words are like wind in a winter tree: you only make the cold snow fall on the hearts of my people. My people will not listen to you; I do not listen to you. We listen to our ancestors, who speak to us softly and give us wisdom. Your ways are not our ways, and we do not want them. But you take away our lands, and you take away our young men and put them to work in your mines and in your factories. Now we have lost our lands, and we are losing our young men. When our men come back to us they are different because of what you have done to them. They do not obey their fathers any more, they do not respect their chiefs and they have no fear of their medicine men. We who stay in the mountains where we belong hate you for this. You are taking the meaning out of our lives and making us weak. Now you are trying to make me weak. You have taken my things from me and made me a stranger to myself. In these clothes that you have put on my body, the spirits that speak to me are afraid to come near me. Now that I have seen with my own eyes the things that the white man has, I weep for my people. You will make us strangers to ourselves as you have done to me this day. You want to take the medicine that I make away from my people. A sad day will dawn over the mountains when the ways of the white man come to sleep in the huts of those who live there. You saw this morning what happened to Tselane when she saw me. Now she sits there trembling, but she does not scream. Her fear has left her and she sees me as a stranger. Now she does not flee from the spirits who took her child, but weeps for herself and the son who was taken from her. She knows she cannot escape the spirits. She will know it again when her ancestors turn their backs on her as now she turns her back on me."

There was silence after these words were translated. The Judge turned to the prosecuting attorney: "Does the Crown have any questions or objections?"

The prosecuting attorney did not look up from his papers. "Neither, my lord."

"Mr. Steyn?"

Steyn came forward slowly, his mind searching for words. "My lord," he said, "I do not feel it necessary to make any remarks pertaining to what we have just heard. But I should like us all to keep the witch doctor's words in mind for the remainder of this case. The Crown will remember, I am sure, that in my cross-examination of its witnesses I was able to establish that while traveling on the train the accused exposed herself for what she was: a simple country girl away from her people and her village for the first time in her life. She was a country girl not only in her naïveté but also in her fears.

"The ticket examiner admits to this court that she was distraught when she lost her ticket, though he assures us that he did nothing to terrify her and we can accept that to mean that he was no more annoyed than he would be with anyone who caused him the same inconvenience during this busy hour of his work. But I point out to you that the loss of a ticket to a girl like this would be the same to any one of us as a loss of our passport in a strange country. To her, her entire safety was threatened.

"Let us consider now the conduct of her fellow passengers after the train left Bloemfontein, again men and women brought here by the Crown. They are Africans like the accused but better traveled and better acquainted, they think, with the world of the white man. They discovered that the accused was pregnant and they tell us they warned her that she would be in serious trouble if she gave birth to her baby on the train. Would this be enough to terrify a woman into killing her baby when this unfortunate prediction takes place? It might, at least to this kind of woman. Now that her baby's safety as well as her own is threatened.

"But there was another threat, far greater than the temper of the ticket examiner on the train. In revealing it, I must confess to the court that I have received little cooperation from the accused in preparing her defense. She told me nothing about herself; she scarcely spoke during the weeks I tried to prepare my case for her. I did not learn about the great threat upon her life until yesterday, when Pierre le Brun arrived in Beaufort West.

"Now that we have heard the witch doctor and have seen the reaction of the accused when brought face to face with him, there could be no doubt in our minds about the seriousness of this other threat. I am sure the court is familiar with tribal rituals and the reasons for which ritual murder seem legitimate to them. In this case the reason was provided by the Chief: his wife had not given him a son and he was convinced that a brew concocted from the dismembered parts of a pregnant woman would supply the power to make his wife conceive. The chosen victim was the accused. One look at this woman should assure the court of the terror she carried within her from the moment she discovered her fate.

"Discovering it, she hurried in the night to the only place she felt she could find help—the nearest mission station. When she revealed her terrible news, Mr. le Brun decided it would be best for her to travel to Worcester where her husband was working in a canning factory. She never arrived there, and we now know why.

"But what we do not know is the immense fear that followed this young woman every mile of the journey. My lord, we as Christians believe that we can never escape the eye of God; wherever we go, we believe, God knows about it. In the same vein, and after hearing the witch doctor, could this girl, born and raised under the shroud of pagan fears, expect that she could ever escape the decision of death made upon her and therefore upon her unborn child?

"I put it to the court that she could not. All that happened during her journey—and we may never know the full extent of her misadventures—was nothing compared to the terror which haunted her every step. I put it to the court that her deed upon the train was committed out of the reason of the greatest fear and that she herself, being in a terror-stricken frame of mind, was without any form of reason whatsoever.

"What happened in the court this morning when she saw the man who had stirred the fear initially needs no words of further explanation. Fear of the medicine man, which was instilled in her from the time that she was a very small child, took on proportions undreamt of when he became the instrument by which she had to die. Men away from their villages speak in whispers of the power of the medicine man. How much more is the fear of a woman, alone, destitute, in pain and terrified by what was happening to her."

Anton Steyn paused. No sound broke the intense quiet that lay heavy on the cold atmosphere of the courtroom.

"My lord, fear is the murderer in this case. If there is any guilt attached to what was done in the train, then it is the guilt which must be shared by every man in this room today who has done nothing to overcome the cause of that fear.

"My lord, I put it to the court that this woman, Tselane, who stands accused of murder of her child, has not been in her right mind since she left the village. That out of immeasurable fear she lost all responsibility for her actions and that in the circumstances there can be no basis of true guilt for what she did."

The Judge looked at Steyn with an expression of patient interest, then he turned to the prosecuting attorney. "Does the Crown wish to reply to Mr. Steyn's remarks?"

"No, my lord."

The Judge let one brow rise, then gave his attention to the papers before him. Everyone waited. Pierre glanced over his shoulder at

Khama. Khama studied Tselane with pain in his eyes. Tselane's face was hidden. Steyn, standing where he had finished his remarks, watched the Judge. The prosecuting attorney was preoccupied with the tip of his pencil. No one in the room moved.

At last the Judge said: "In view of the extenuating circumstances, the court is willing to entertain a motion to change the indictment from murder to manslaughter."

Steyn moved forward quickly. "My lord, extenuating circumstances still indicate an area of guilt, and I wonder if anyone who was present in this court this morning can believe that there was the slightest shred of guilt involved in the incident before us."

The Judge turned to the prosecutor. "What has the Crown to say?"

"The Crown has nothing to say, my lord."

The Judge stood up. "The court will adjourn for half an hour so that we may consider the verdict."

No one made a move to go. A half hour was not long to wait, and no one wanted to lose his place in the room. After the Judge left, everyone sat down and watched the clock on the wall.

And they were thinking.

Anton Steyn was very tired. For weeks he had carried the heavy weight of trying to help a terrified girl who would not speak to him. The only sounds he had heard from her were her meaningless mutterings, until the screams this morning. Those screams. Steyn had not imagined that anyone could be so frightened. And of what? A ridiculous old man in feathers and smelly skins. How did the old devil ever get such a grip on the girl, on all his people? What a horrible atmosphere for people to exist in. Yet millions did. That was the stumbling block in this racial business, at least here in Africa. How were you going to civilize the poor blacks when their whole lives were ruled by fears of old men in feathers and smelly skins? But who was there to change things?

Pierre le Brun was praying. He begged God to free Tselane, not only for herself but for himself and all he wanted to do. He felt abjectly helpless. He looked back over his missionary years and could not name one moment when he might have been concretely successful with the Africans. He wondered if he really understood them. Had he treated them too much like children? Had he convinced even one of them of the true worth of Christianity? Had he brought one of them, if just a child, to God? He pledged that whether or not Tselane was freed, things would be different now. He would spend more time in the village, all his time. He would learn more about the paganism that engulfed so many of the people, and with love and patience and understanding he would try to draw them away from it so that, if nothing else, they would escape the fear, the awful fear. Without the fear, the path to their hearts would be open; without the fear they would become human beings. Then there might be a chance for him. If he could die knowing he had brought one, just one of them, to God, then everything else—the hardships, the heartaches, the discomforts and disappointments, even this—would have been worth it.

Khama thought of his dead son, then put the thought out of his mind. There would be other sons. He would never leave Tselane again. He would stay with her in the mountains, protect her, hunt and work for her, love her, and he would never leave her. Little pigeon. How she must hurt inside. If the white man freed her, Khama would see to it that she never hurt again. If only she would stop trembling there, her face behind her blanket. If only she would look up and see him and know that she was safe. Now she would always be safe. He would never again let anything frighten her. Never again would any medicine man put such fear in her that she would do such a terrible thing. He would see to it that Metlae did not return to the village, even if he had to fight every man in the village to keep the witch doctor out. And if a new witch doctor came, neither he or Tselane would speak to the man, nor would their children. That was the root of it: the medicine man. If there had been no Metlae they would not all be here today in this courtroom. He saw that now; he would make his friends in the village see it. There must be a way to prevent that in the future. He would talk to the Moneri about it.

Tselane had no thoughts. She perceived that the courtroom was silent, but she did not know why.

The half hour passed. The Judge came in and took his place; all the people stood up for a moment, then sat down, and Steyn and the prosecuting attorney went to the Judge and stood in front of him, waiting.

The Judge said: "It is the court's conclusion that the accused did not have the intention and the will to kill, but that she committed the deed at a time when her mind was deranged by fear, by superstition and complete panic. She was therefore not responsible for her actions at the time. The court finds the accused not guilty."

There was a heavy sigh in the room, and even before the Judge left his high table the people were in the aisle, going home, little smiles of relief on their faces. She would not die. The woman would not die. The Judge understood about the witch doctor. The woman would not die for something the witch doctor had caused. The people were relieved.

Pierre shook hands with Steyn, then signaled Khama to join him. Steyn went across to talk to the prosecuting attorney and they talked like two friends who had lost the reason for being angry with each other. Khama was at Pierre's heels when the missionary reached Tselane. He said to the interpreter: "We will take her now."

Tselane felt the new hands about her and when she turned and saw Pierre fresh tears flooded her cheeks. "Moneri, my baby—" Then she saw Khama and she weakened in Pierre's arms.

Pierre said: "Take her, Khama. I will arrange for our trip home."

Tselane felt herself being moved into Khama's familiar embrace. "My husband," she said, "I have killed your son."

"You must not say it," consoled Khama.

"I was afraid of Metlae and I—"

"You must put it out of your heart," said Khama. "We will go home to the mountains now, little wife, and you will put it out of your heart."

He looked around. The courtroom was almost empty. A policeman stood nearby, watching. Khama tried to lead Tselane away but she was heavy against him, her sobs pounding upon his chest. He wanted to hold her tightly and kiss away her fears but he could not bring himself to do it in front of the white man.

"Can we go now?" Khama asked.

"Yes," said the policeman. "She is free. You can go as soon as the matron brings her bag."

The two men studied each other. Tselane's sobs sent deep tremors through her and she clung to Khama desperately.

Khama asked: "Is there somewhere we can be alone? My wife has lost her heart."

The policeman led them away to a quiet room.